SCRIBNER PAPERBACK FICTION

PUBLISHED BY SIMON & SCHUSTER

MARC LAIDLAW

THE THIRD FORCE

A NOVEL OF GADGET

SCRIBNER PAPERBACK FICTION
Simon & Schuster Inc.
Rockefeller Center
1230 Avenue of the Americas
New York, NY 10020

SCRIBNER PAPERBACK FICTION and design are trademarks of Simon & Schuster Inc.

Designed by Songhee Kim

Set in Adobe Aldus and Futura

Manufactured in the United States of America

1   3   5   7   9   10   8   6   4   2

Library of Congress Cataloging-in-Publication Data
Laidlaw, Marc.
The third force : a novel of Gadget / Marc Laidlaw.
p.   cm.
I. Title.
PS3562.A333T48   1996
813'.54—dc20   96-22578
CIP

ISBN 0-684-82245-8

For Yoshio Kobayashi
Yoshitoshi, Miyazaki, and the
Yamanote line

ACKNOWLEDGMENTS

My grateful thanks to the Gadget team at Synergy, Inc., in Tokyo—Masanori Awata, Haruhiko Shono, Hirokazu Nabekura, Eri Osada, and David—for making me a member of the team, and especially for welcoming me to Japan. To Shigeru Chigusa at Synergy Interactive in San Francisco for his kindness and enthusiasm. To my editor and champion, Sydny Miner. To my agent, Matt Bialer, for making this happen. To my wife, Geraldine, for her patience and support. To Wren for making it easy. And to Rowan for waiting till I was finished.

ONE

ELENA HAUSMANN ARRIVED IN GRAND CENTRAL
Station at precisely 9:37 P.M., September 3, in the Eighth Year of
the Empire. Disembarking from an Alpha-type train, her father's
design and no less efficient for its having been outmoded by Beta
and Sigma locomotives, she found herself alone on the polished tile
walkway at an hour when she would have expected the station to
be bustling with citizens.

The nature of her errand had already put her in a state of
extreme paranoia, but the desertion of the ordinarily busy station
was enough to set off every alarm her barely suppressed dread had
not already triggered.

At 9:39, as she watched the Alpha resume its journey, she
allowed herself a moment's panic. There was no one to wonder at
the mild-looking woman in the long gray hooded coat who covered
her ears and silently howled as the train hissed and clanked and
thundered past, surging into the tunnel toward East End.

Before the clangor faded, she had mastered herself. Smoothing
her coat and her long red hair, faintly streaked with ash, she began
to stride along the platform toward the stairs as if it were perfectly
natural to find herself alone in the station.

The next return train toward West End did not pass through Grand Central until 10:13. She intended to catch it, but this depended on Diaghilev's punctuality. He had set an inconvenient rendezvous; the least he could do was appear on time. In order to test her, he might well cause her to wait until the last possible moment. He seemed to enjoy making her anxious.

The old man refused to ride the trains; on this point he was most insistent. They represented everything he despised about the Empire, and were the motive behind his founding of the Third Force—the resistance movement in which she, despite their mutual hatred of the Emperor, was still a mere courier after years of service. She must come to him, always to him, as if her work were of no importance. She had to endure a great deal to prove herself worthy of Diaghilev's trust—more than many other members, thanks to her background, her family name. And endure she would, if it meant she could play a role in Lord Orlovsky's downfall. Still, the old man must have seen her sincerity at last, since he had seen fit to entrust her with his latest set of instructions to Krystoff Moholy.

Diaghilev was full of bitterness, full of pride. He was fond of reminding her that in his first campaigns, his glory days of war against the nation that had preceded the New Empire, she had not yet been born. It was no use to remind him that the New Empire was younger than any of them, that all rebels had been born anew on the day Lord Orlovsky made his speech of ascension and declared Day One of his reign in West End Square.

What had he railed against in his prime? Her memories of the old days were not so bad. True, those days were enveloped in the magical glow of childhood, and hers had been a youth full of privilege and plenty. But even so, even for Diaghilev, things could not have been as bad as they were now. What had he battled against before Orlovsky?

Unfortunately, none of his early writings were available to answer her questions conclusively. She had searched for his name in the classified catalogues of the Imperial Library as far as she dared. Even the privileges that came with her post as chief librarian did not convey the liberty to pursue every document in the archives. All searches were automatically recorded, collated, and reported to the Department of Records Analysis. Requests for particular items were instantly flagged and brought to the attention of the Head Analyst, who brought them in turn to the attention of some higher authority whose name and position Elena never had been able to determine. She supposed that the swiftest way to learn that figure's identity would be to conduct a thorough search for all pamphlets, tracts, and manifestos authored by Bernhard Diaghilev.

If only all the books had been burned, she found herself wishing. Or stored away somewhere completely inaccessible. Or even marked *Forbidden!* so there would be no question of accidentally opening them. But Orlovsky had found it far more effective to allow free access to the volumes to which he most objected, and in this way winnow out those who sought information concerning the past, those whose criminal thoughts and research led them inevitably in the direction of criminal acts.

After eight years of Empire, there were few fools left to order such books. And those who remained were understandably reluctant to look at any book at all, unless it bore Lord Orlovsky's signature.

The echoing silence of the station had begun to remind her of the vast archives where she spent her life. The Imperial Library was like a train station without commuters.

It occurred to her that the train from Downtown Station had also been deserted. She had spent most of the ride alone in a private car, pretending to pore over her ragged gold-letter edition of Orlovsky's *Mentations and Excursions,* but she could recall encountering no one else in the corridors, apart from the conductor who had let her on and off again, collecting her ticket, giving her a familiar nod in lieu of more formal greetings, as if they had known each other for years. For some reason she had thought nothing of it at the time. But now the thought of the deserted train unnerved her.

The cavernous lobby of the station was as empty as the platforms. The rows of untenanted benches reminded her of pews in an abandoned cathedral. All the stations of the Grand Central Line had a gloomy air of sanctity about them, as if down here technology and progress had achieved the status of a ritual. A silent, muffling hand seemed to press down on her; worse, she was almost certain she knew whose hand it was. The massive lines of girders and cold pale polished stone offered a chilling glimpse into the architect's hard and mirrored soul. She wished no further insight into that soul. She had seen enough of it already.

She listened for any sound other than that of her footsteps, half convinced that the Imperial Guard or the Army had cordoned off the station. There must be a crowd outside, held back by force of arms, angry and unruly at being shut out; but as she listened, she heard nothing beyond the galleries.

Surely they were watching her, waiting for her to betray herself. She glanced at her watch and wondered if she should simply return to the track and board the westbound train, her errand unfinished. Diaghilev was canny and suspicious; he would understand the instinct that made her flee. He would never have come this far into such an obvious trap.

It was this thought which led her across the broad lobby, along the aisle of benches. For if Diaghilev *were* inside the station, that would tend to prove all was well. If she did not catch sight of him, that would suggest he had been detained. No one would blame her for returning empty-handed.

She moved close to the wall of a ticket office, rounding it slowly, searching the benches across the way for the seat he had described. The second seat was occupied, and at the sight she sighed with indescribable relief.

But her relief was fleeting. Someone else had come in Diaghilev's stead. The figure spied her and straightened, beckoning her forward.

In spite of her shock, she found herself moving closer. The benches were surmounted by the large circular emblem of the Grand Central Railway, enclosing the winged unicorn that was Orlovsky's personal herald and which he had made the symbol of the New Empire. The tall, thin man who waited sat with his head perfectly encircled by the emblem, as if it were a halo. He wore a perpetual sour half-scowl, a faint sheen of fluorescence upon his pale and bulging forehead. The same dead light filled the dark lenses of his spectacles, in which she now saw herself emerging like a ghost out of blackness. She wondered, not for the first time, what manner of cold thoughts passed to and fro beyond those smoked panes.

She sank onto the bench beside him.

"Theodore," she said. "This is a surprise."

He inclined his head very slightly. "Elena. My very dear Elena."

His voice was like something cold and slimy spilled along the edges of her mind, seeping in. With it came memories of long-ago conversations when, in company with Orlovsky, he had paid so many visits to the house of Count Otto Hausmann.

Now, as then, she found it impossible to look away from him. She focused on his suit, made of some material so black and slick that it gleamed like wet ink. He had worn such suits in the days before his rise at Orlovsky's side. Infinitely familiar, infinitely horrible, were the glossy black outfits, always paired with a matching black shiny tie against a crisp white shirt. His lank brown hair, always thin and receding, now more than ever resembled a shrunken skullcap made from the pelt of a diseased rodent.

The naive girl who had once welcomed such monsters into her home—unaware of the scheming that whirled all around her—was long dead, crushed in the crucible of the Revolution. That there remained any gentleness in her at all was a source of constant surprise to Elena. It survived only because she kept it carefully hidden, where the likes of Emperor Paulo Orlovsky and Supreme Commander Theodore Slowslop could never, ever get at it again.

"I missed my station," she said, slowly regaining her composure, wondering what she would do if Diaghilev appeared. Surely Diaghilev, stumbling upon this particular tableau, would know to run away. Although Slowslop controlled the railroads, and had overseen the renaissance and remodeling of the stations and laid many miles of public and private track throughout the Empire, he was not the sort to be seen in Grand Central Station. He rode in private limousines and had never been known to board a train.

"Missed your station," Slowslop repeated. "How inconvenient."

"I—I was reading," she said.

"Something engrossing, I trust."

She held up the *Mentations and Excursions*. Slowslop made a slight stifled noise; she could not imagine that it was a laugh. He took the book from her hands; she had to restrain herself from clutching at it, betraying her nervousness.

"The words of our lord," he said, in a tone of distant mockery. "And in gilt letters, too."

He riffled the edges, so that the smattering of gold characters flashed beneath the station lights. She prayed he would not examine the volume too closely, for he might detect its extraordinary character. In all gold-lettered editions, Lord Orlovsky's compressed "mentations" were printed in gold ink; while his meandering, incomprehensible "excursions," which took the mentations as their starting points, were an ordinary black. Even the excursions were occasionally punctuated in gold, where Orlovsky considered his thought processes had achieved some peak of brilliance or concision. But Elena's edition was rather more liberally splashed with gold, according to a code which had been in use for some time by the Third Force. A code which, to this day, no Imperial agent to their knowledge had cracked or even appeared to be aware of.

As intended, the book provided its own camouflage. Slowslop handled it with something like disdain, setting it down on the bench between them.

"This could never have held your interest, Elena," he said, very solemn now. "What really brings you here?"

She felt her cheeks grow warm, but even this she could use to her advantage. She forced an embarrassed smile.

"Well . . . no . . . I admit, trying to read it, I fell asleep."

He straightened slightly, tapped the book. "Is that why you lie to me? You think I hold Paulo in that sort of reverence?"

"I know you are very loyal and faithful to him."

Slowslop stared at her—or so she supposed. With his eyes utterly hidden behind the black ovals, and his face otherwise quite blank, it was impossible to be completely certain of his expression.

"You have a ticket," he said quietly.

"Yes, I—I mean, I'd better see about getting one. That's why I came up here. I must catch the next train back to the museum district. I'm involved in an inventory, and I'm already running late."

"You have a ticket," he said again.

"Well, but I've missed my stop. The conductors are not always understanding."

"Elena. You must not miss my meaning. You already have your

return ticket. Use it. Return to the westbound track. If you hear anything unusual, any sounds from other parts of the station, I advise you to ignore them. You will wait until your train arrives, and then you will board it. Ride back to the museum district, Downtown, West End . . . wherever you wish. But do not remain in this station tonight. And do not expect business as usual."

She found herself rising, but she was not at all sure if it was of her own accord, or if he had somehow released her. "Business as . . . What do you mean?"

"Go," he said, handing the book back to her.

"Theodore, I—"

"Go."

Elena stepped back. The station was still deserted, with no sign of Diaghilev.

Diaghilev missing, and Slowslop in his place.

Why does he spare me? she wondered.

As she turned and hurried back toward the tracks, she felt cut off from everyone and everything that had meaning for her. How could she mention this meeting to Krystoff without making herself seem suspect? She could not bear to think of betraying his trust, yet what else would come of telling him that Slowslop had spared her for reasons unknown?

She had struggled to prove herself worthy of the Third Force. It was agony to consider lying to them now—withholding vital information from her comrades which might mean their own lives in the end.

As she reached the track for the westbound train, she felt almost grateful that there was no way of resolving the matter right away. In minutes the train would arrive, and then there would be a long ride back to the museum district. During that ride she need make no decision; and in any event, there was no safe way to inform Krystoff before tomorrow that Diaghilev had missed the rendezvous. But she already knew there would be no mention of her meeting with Slowslop when she gave her report.

In the meantime, she stood on the track with her shoulders hunched, waiting for an explosion, for screams or the shrilling of whistles—something worthy of Slowslop's ominous warning.

She listened to the station's usual symphony of random noises, none of them evoking anything but emptiness. There was nothing unusual, nothing at all, until she sensed the faintest humming in the tracks at her feet, a far-off clatter and distant roar which presaged little more ominous than the approaching train.

At 10:10 precisely, another Alpha thundered into the station.

At that very instant, she thought she heard a scream echo through the reaches of marble and steel—a scream of flesh and blood, nothing like the gleaming grind and wail of the engine, the silver squeal of the brakes, or the throb of the slowing pistons. The sound was lost in the riot of other noises. As the train sat hissing, puffing, waiting for passengers, she listened for a sequel to the *human* scream. Finally the conductor signaled for her to board or be left behind. She clambered aboard, having heard nothing she could be sure of.

As Grand Central Station fell away behind her, the events of her detour, transpiring between 9:37 and 10:13 in the evening, began to take on the aspects of a dream.

T W O

IN DIAGHILEV'S NIGHTMARE, INFINITY HAD BEEN compressed to the dimensions of a railway station.

Under his feet, tiles green as weathered copper, black as polished onyx, lay in a pattern apparently modeled on the intricate yet random schemes of corrosion. Enormous girders, black iron beams, marched in all directions as far as he could see, bracing up a ceiling that might have been the heavens. One single set of tracks crossed the limitless terminal, two parallel silver slashes passing directly under his feet.

The train approached with a fuming roar like that of an acetylene torch. There was no clanking of rods and pistons; no keening of wheel rims on the metal tracks; only a chill that moved through the rails and stabbed up into his bones.

The headlight limned the pylons in gold and green, suffused with misty orange and blue. The lamp set the twin tracks on fire with the same electric colors. He shaded his eyes against the glare, trying to see the train that bore this blinding eye, but beyond was a fathomless darkness betraying nothing, a void that swallowed light and heat and even thought.

It is nothing more than a symbol of my imprisonment, he realized.

And at this thought, so lucid, so rational, the dream shattered, revealing its essential unreality. He awoke to the true darkness of which the dream was only a shadow.

Such uninspired symbolism, he remarked to himself. *The mind struggles and fails to find adequate symbols to describe the simplest facts. Nothing in the dream has half the resonance of horror and hopelessness which I feel in one waking moment in this cell. In fact, it demonstrates the weakness of the psyche, with its continual pathetic attempts to avoid reality by indulging in fantasy. Thus the mind—even my mind—openly invites disaster by ignoring its environment!*

Only the strange light still resisted logical explanation. He had never imagined its like. The fantastic colors seemed more extraordinary than remembered sunlight.

It was almost . . . beautiful.

But how meaningless, he thought, *compared to the burning in my guts, the smell of bleach and excrement, the worsening throb of broken ribs and infected sores.*

And dreams of light offered small consolation when he heard the door opening at some distance down the corridor. He had heard the sound a thousand times but it never failed to raise in him the warring emotions of hope and dread. As hinges wailed and the door slammed shut, he found himself sliding down from the cold, bare wooden shelf that served as his pallet. He limped to the door of his cell. The bruised soles of his feet objected at every step, but he disdained such minor complaints. With his ear to the metal, he tracked the advance of footsteps—more than one pair this time, he felt certain, and unaccompanied by the usual squeak of the meal cart's wheels.

The footsteps slowed. One belonged to a guard of the Grand Central Penitentiary; he knew those bootsteps well enough. But the other wore softer shoes. He listened closely, detecting no conversation, which might mean the two had known each other for some time, or were total strangers with nothing to say and no desire for small talk. He had no time to wonder at their destination; they stopped before his door.

"Is this it?" asked a voice he could not place. A young man's voice, firm and clear.

The voice that responded was familiar enough. It had taunted him, withheld food, and expressed joy at leaving him to fester in his own filth when the brutalities of other inquisitors had borne no fruit.

"Diaghilev," said that well-hated voice.

"He's the last one then," said the other. "Bring him out."

He straightened, agony in all of his joints, and moved back from the door, shading his eyes against the sudden painful flood of dim yellow light. The guard thrust his heavy head into the cell; he was pockmarked and thick-jowled, with ears that stood out from his head. He looked surprised to find his prisoner standing.

"You," he said. "Turn around."

Diaghilev turned, waiting to be manacled, but not before he had caught a glimpse of the stranger, a trim blond man in the neat black uniform of the Imperial Army. When the heavy clasps were in place on his wrists, the guard caught him by the chains and dragged him backward into the corridor.

"Gently," the other man said, as if to the abuser of a prized dog. Diaghilev looked up, grateful in spite of the condescension in the man's voice. The soldier's eyes were deep blue, clear and unwavering; his features handsome, boyish, unblemished. An ideal Army recruit on a physical basis alone. He was everything Slowslop idealized; everything the Supreme Commander was not.

"Mr. Diaghilev," said the soldier, clicking his heels smartly, making a slight bow. His formality had an odd effect on Diaghilev, who found himself attempting to return the courtesy.

"I'm afraid you have me at a disadvantage," he said weakly. How long had it been since he had used his voice? How long had he lain in the dark?

"This is Lieutenant Hausmann," said the guard. "You're being released into his custody."

Hausmann? Diaghilev thought. Was *this* Elena Hausmann's brother?

Hausmann said, "I'm afraid I cannot authorize your complete and immediate release . . . but it may come to that eventually, if you cooperate."

"How so?" Diaghilev asked, astonished that it was even a possibility.

The guard looked as if he too wished to hear the question answered, but Hausmann merely smiled and shook his head. "Come, we have a bit of a journey."

"Not a . . . a journey by train?" he said hopelessly, in a quickening panic.

The lieutenant straightened, regarding him curiously, as if he were joking. "How else?"

Diaghilev felt again the cold that went before the nightmare train. It was all he could recall of the dream right now, but it was strong enough to resuscitate older memories. The dream had deep roots.

He found himself shaking uncontrollably. The few steps he'd taken outside the cell were more than he had walked in weeks. The lieutenant must have seen a tremor, for he put an arm around Diaghilev and clapped him firmly on the arm.

"Can you walk?"

"I can walk," he gasped, "but I will not ride."

"We don't have to tolerate this," the guard snapped, glaring at Diaghilev.

"He's an elderly man," said Hausmann. "It's nothing."

"No older than Lord Orlovsky," said the guard. "His years should have brought him the wisdom to keep his mouth shut."

"Age also brings eccentricity," Hausmann said. "Now, come along, sir. Or shall we send for a chair?"

"There are no *chairs* here," the guard said scathingly, and he strode ahead with obvious scorn to open the door at the end of the hall. Hausmann led him haltingly forward.

"Now, we will give you a good meal and some new clothes. You'll have time to gather your strength for the ride. It will not be a long one, I assure you. And there will be others to converse with, like-minded fellows."

"Like-minded?"

"You were imprisoned for crimes against the Empire, weren't you?"

"Not crimes," he gasped. "Thoughts!"

"That's right. The twelve of you will have plenty to talk about, I imagine. Thought-criminals, all of you."

Twelve of us, Diaghilev thought desperately. *Can it be true that they would put twelve like-minded men together? Why would Slowslop allow such a dangerous combination?*

He found himself laughing. He was a frail old man, beaten and malnourished; he would never trust anyone this Hausmann threw him in with. Even if the other eleven were true criminals, by Orlovsky's definition, why would they be any more trusting or less suspicious than he? Twelve prisoners, broken in body if not in spirit. What sort of uprising could they possibly muster?

So Diaghilev laughed.

Then he remembered the train once more, and his thoughts grew clouded and dark.

■ ■ ■

Once aboard the train, he found a strange relief. Thirty years of dread slid away, leaving him feeling liberated, even in the confines of the prisoners' car.

The car lacked seats, and the prisoners stood stiffly without looking at each other, full of mistrust. Like something used to transport cattle, the car was windowless, but made of metal slats. Peering out he saw the gray stone walls of a tunnel. They were moving slowly through dimness, underneath infrequent bulbs. He rocked on his feet, fitting his fingers into the slats to hold himself upright; weak as he was, he dared not reveal his vulnerability to these other men. Besides, they looked as miserable as he.

If he had not deliberately maintained his fear, he would have realized long ago that the swiftest way to end his horror of trains would be to ride them once again. There had never been another accident like the one that took his wife and child; never a rail disaster of such magnitude. Most people rode the trains every day of their lives without mishap. It was random chance, never to be repeated, that he had booked passage aboard a doomed train. Chance, also, that had spared him.

He steadied his breath. Here he was, riding a train again, at last. And indeed, what did he have to lose? Let another disaster strike him. He nearly laughed at the thought.

Diaghilev's spirits rose in adversity. He lifted his head and tried to study those around him. They passed out of the tunnel into the open air, and the stagnant chill gave way to a bitter wind that had movement and life of its own. At least it was fresh and clean. Light burned through the slats into the car.

The man nearest to Diaghilev, who had receding brows and a dark widow's peak, caught his eye for an instant, then nervously looked away. But this opening was all Diaghilev needed.

"You," he whispered. "How long were you in?"

The other's expression, already pinched and wild, contorted with fury. "Shut up! You'll have them down on us again!"

Diaghilev recoiled. The man went back to his former position, breathing heavily and hunching his shoulders against the air as if daring anyone to speak another word. But then a greeting was whispered in Diaghilev's left ear, and he turned to see a taller man with a gentle face regarding him with a smile.

"How can any of us say how long it's been? There's no telling the date."

"I know," said another man across the car, his face fixed in melancholy.

"You know?" came another voice. All of them were stirring now, flickers of hope beginning to turn them into human beings again, instead of manikins to be hauled from one depot to another. In spite of himself, Diaghilev found himself wanting to trust them.

"I asked him," said the mournful man. "The lieutenant, Hausmann. He said it was November fourth."

"You think that's the truth?"

"Why lie about such a thing?"

"November fourth!" The quickening continued. They muttered, sighed, counting quietly to themselves.

"I've been inside four months!"

"Eight months!"

"Nearly a year."

Diaghilev could not conceive of a year under such conditions. And yet they must count themselves the lucky ones, for now they were out. From what he heard, he was luckiest of all, for he had endured almost exactly two months in custody. A mere two months. Peering through the slats, he could see that they were riding away from the rising sun, through a rugged landscape of low brown hills like hardened dunes eroded by wind but rarely by water.

The barrens.

Suddenly the floor seemed to lurch beneath his feet. He was falling, the sunlight reaching through the slats, raking his face as the whole car began to tilt.

■ ■ ■

"Are you all right?"

He came back to consciousness slowly, blinking up at the man who had first spoken to him.

"Just lie there. You're weak. We all are."

"I'm old," Diaghilev corrected him. "None of you so old as I."

"Nonsense."

"Old and . . . and I was not prepared to see this place again."

"Which place do you mean?"

Diaghilev shook his head. The other man helped him sit against the side of the car. Hausmann had provided him with a heavy coat, but he could feel the wind all the same, and the metal walls were even colder than that. He glanced through the slats once again, and confirmed that the same brown hills still waited for him.

"Tell me," he said, "have we crossed the bridge yet?"

"Not yet," the other said. "It's just ahead, I think."

Diaghilev shut his eyes and put his head back.

"I have avoided this stretch of track for over thirty years," Diaghilev said. "The *span* in particular . . ."

"You are Bernhard Diaghilev," the other said abruptly, and then looked up to make sure no one else had heard. A few of the other men were talking among themselves, but none so much as glanced in their direction. Not that it would matter if they knew his identity; he had already been imprisoned for being who he was. But he knew the habit that forced the other man's caution.

"Pardon me," the other said, lowering his voice. "My name is Gregor Stillson. It means nothing to you, I know, but . . . I am a great admirer."

"And you know me . . . how?"

"Well, Hausmann said we were all imprisoned for similar crimes. And now you mention the bridge. If I am not too presumptuous, and not completely mistaken, you were involved in the *Phaeton* tragedy."

Diaghilev bowed his head. "You are not mistaken. And do you, Mr. Stillson, know any of these other gentlemen?"

"Not on sight, sir. And I doubt any of them have a reputation for thought-crimes to match yours."

"Reputation," Diaghilev repeated, suddenly aware of a hollowness, a changed tone, in the clatter of the wheels. The wind seemed to cut into the car from below.

Stillson placed his hands firmly on Diaghilev's shoulders. "Yes," he said. "Yes, we're there. I beg you, close your eyes and try to think of nothing. It will soon be over."

Diaghilev tried to speak, but he could not. Stillson nodded urgently. "Please, sir."

Diaghilev shut his eyes.

The wind was wrong. It came from all sides, pulling him away again, shrieking through the slats, screaming with many voices, but especially the voices of his wife and child. They were all falling, including himself.

But Stillson did not let go of him. The other man held him bodily in the present. And somewhere along the span, as he finally released his burden of grief and broke down weeping, he felt the other man's arms around his shoulders.

Stillson whispered: "I am with the Third Force, too."

And then earth was beneath them again, absorbing the shock of the train's passage. He had survived the crossing.

He opened his eyes, knowing he could face whatever lay ahead. Why fear anything ever again? Why fear the Empire? What could Orlovsky or Slowslop or any of their minions possibly do to him now?

■ ■ ■

They halted in a train yard near West End Station. The young blond lieutenant entered the car. The prisoners had sunk to the floor during the journey, but now they rose again, standing at attention like listless recruits in Hausmann's army. There had been much talk during the trip of what might lie behind the lieutenant's easy smile; the nearest thing to a consensus was that one so friendly could only be delivering them to the most terrible kind of fate.

"We will board a van shortly," he said. "If you could be patient a few moments longer."

Someone barked a laugh which the lieutenant, oblivious to irony, seemed not to notice. Diaghilev again noted what a perfect soldier he made. Utterly trustworthy, no doubt, in whoever's employ he labored. Of course, he might have been a spy for the Socialist Republic, owing his ultimate loyalty to Ernst Onegin, awaiting only the proper time to betray Slowslop and Orlovsky. He struck Diaghilev as the most dangerous sort of soldier: naive, and an idealist.

The lieutenant aimed a strange gadget at the men. At first, in the dimness, Diaghilev thought it was a weapon; but as Hausmann put it to his face and the older man caught the glimmer of light in six lenses, he realized it was a motion picture camera, with the lenses mounted in groups of three on two revolving disks.

"What's this?" said one of the prisoners. "Home movies?"

"A record," Hausmann said pleasantly.

"For posterity?"

"I wouldn't put it that way, as it implies you might not be around to see it."

"How considerate."

"Would you like us to dance? Tell stories? Perform in any way for the amusement of posterity?" said a man with an enormous moustache.

"Just stand still, Mr. Perplies, if you don't mind," Hausmann said, perfectly serious. "The light is rather poor."

Suddenly there was a sharp rap on the door behind Hausmann. The lieutenant turned as another officer entered behind him, balding and coarse of feature, with wide flat cheeks and heavy brows. He was apparently Hausmann's superior, although there was a look of something like envy in his eyes when he addressed the lieutenant.

"Are they ready?"

"Yes, sir." Hausmann turned to the prisoners. "Gentlemen, this is Captain Gondarev. He will escort you to your final destination. This way, if you please."

Gondarev had already backed out of the car. The prisoners trooped past Hausmann, not into the open air as Diaghilev had expected, but into a passenger car, empty except for Gondarev and a train conductor in uniform. The men moved in single file; Stillson kept an arm around Diaghilev, who was having difficulty walking. The soles of his feet, beaten and possibly broken during his interrogation, made every step an agony. Slowslop's trains were marvels of comfort and efficiency. How he would have loved to sink down on one of the padded seats, soft and well upholstered. Yet the captain hurried them along, and the conductor waited stonily, holding the far door open for them as they passed out of the car and off the train.

Rows of tracks curved away to either side; the air was dense with oily smoke that gave the sky a sepia tinge. It smelled of iron filings. He could see nothing more, for most of the tracks were taken up with locomotives. Looking toward the rear of the prison train, he saw soldiers urging them toward a covered truck. To his chagrin, one of the soldiers had to help Stillson get him into the bed of the truck. When they were all aboard, two soldiers climbed in and another dropped the canvas flap and lashed it to the gate. Then the truck began to move.

There was no sign of Hausmann or Gondarev. Diaghilev clutched his seat desperately as the truck bounded over tracks and rough ground. When at last they glided onto a smooth road, he almost dozed; but no sooner had he closed his eyes than Stillson was tugging him to his feet. He realized that the motor was silent, the truck had stopped, the canvas flap had been pulled aside.

This time there was no sunlight, no trace of sky. They were in a large garage, dark and echoing with the sound of the truck's gate clanking down. Diaghilev lowered himself painfully to the cement. The guards led them toward a lighted landing. Just beyond that, an elevator waited.

The soldier in the elevator was uniformed in red, gleaming with double rows of polished brass buttons. Gold piping ran around his collar and the brim of his red cap.

Diaghilev could not remember where he had seen such a uniform before. He took a place in the farthest corner and studied the red outfit, so out of place here that it took him a good minute to recognize it.

He's no soldier, Diaghilev realized. *He's a bellhop!*

The young man, as blank and earnest as Lieutenant Hausmann, held the door for all twelve prisoners. Then Hausmann and Gondarev entered as well. It was a somewhat shabby service elevator, hung with quilted cloths. The few visible spots of bare metal showed dents and scratches, and the laminated floor, of black and white checks, was gouged and peeling.

"Is that all, sir?" the bellhop asked Captain Gondarev.

The captain nodded. As the doors shut, Diaghilev saw the other guards returning to the truck.

He exchanged a glance with Stillson, twitching his eyes toward the bellhop, but the other man was plainly as puzzled as he.

Diaghilev could make no sense of the bellhop's appearance here, but something else puzzled him as well. As they moved up through the elevator shaft, he felt a growing sense of alarm.

When the car eased to a stop and the doors slid open, the memories came instantly. They made no sense at all.

Between the heads and shoulders of his fellow prisoners, Diaghilev stared out into the dim and quiet corridor of the West End Hotel.

Once, he had known these corridors well. Years ago, he had spent some of the happiest days of his life here, with his bride, on their honeymoon. Their son had been conceived here.

As they shuffled forward onto the plush carpet, Diaghilev hung back. The last thing he saw as he left the elevator, lifting his eyes to the row of lights above the door, was the illumined number 3.

The very floor, he realized with a pang of dread.

It was close to blasphemy, an attack on the symbols of happiness he had always prized. This place, so dear to him—this very floor, where he had always been able to remember his dear wife in memories of sacred purity—was now contaminated. It was as if the Empire had somehow reached into his soul and stolen his inmost treasure.

———

He looked around wildly, aware that he was about to panic, but not caring if it led him to any rash act. To one side he saw a plush rope, barring access down an adjoining corridor. He had to restrain himself from running, from leaping the cordon . . . not that he could have done more than hobble a few yards before they dragged him back.

It was with great difficulty that he held on to his dignity.

Looking up, he found Hausmann filming them again. The prisoners marched forward, more or less in unison, as the lieutenant walked backward with the camera at his face. Diaghilev looked sidelong at the doors on the left side of the corridor, counting them under his breath, praying that one room in particular would go unvisited.

312, 310, 308 . . .

Hausmann halted. Gondarev hurried to the front of the group and suddenly ducked sideways into Room 306, squeezing through the door so that Diaghilev had only a glimpse of the wallpaper inside, the yellow glow of a lamp, a stifled mutter of voices as the door slammed shut.

No! he shrieked inwardly. It was the room of his greatest happiness!

He jumped as someone touched him in the small of his back, on the opposite side from Stillson. It was the bellhop. Diaghilev looked at him in numb dismay.

"This way, sir," the boy said, plucking at his elbow.

Diaghilev caught Stillson's eyes, but the other man was as helpless and puzzled as he. The bellhop tugged a bit harder.

"Your room, sir. This way."

The boy took him toward the main guest elevators, just ahead. He led Diaghilev to Room 301 and opened the door with a master key. Diaghilev was still thinking of Room 306, but at least he was not to have his memories entirely destroyed. Surely he would never be invited into Captain Gondarev's quarters.

He came to himself at the sound of the door closing behind him. He tested the knob, but of course the door was locked from the outside. He turned to face a room of unaccustomed luxury—so different from the cell in which he had awakened that dark morning. And yet, so familiar.

It seemed unchanged in every aspect from the room in his memory. The wallpaper, the carpeting, the bedcovers; the furniture, lamps, and curtains. Only the pictures on the wall might have been different, showing scenes of the Empire under Orlovsky. And he doubted the old hotel had included the huge propaganda photograph of the Command Tower of Onegin's Socialist Republic, which hung above the small writing desk. As he took a hesitant step forward, he cast around and saw a map of stations along the Grand Central Railway. This also was new, marked with the Imperial unicorn emblem.

He went to the bed and sank down onto it, disbelieving its softness. If this were only another cell, at least he would be able to sleep in comfort. There was a covered silver tray on the writing desk; beside the desk was a large radio cabinet. Time later to see if there were pen and paper in the drawers, or if he could pick up any broadcast.

He went to the desk and lifted the tray, releasing a cloud of fragrant steam that nearly overwhelmed him. Lamb chops, still warm; chopped turnips and carrots; a bit of baklava; a glass of milk and a cup of black coffee.

Hausmann had seen to it that they were fed before boarding the train. But this . . . !

For a moment he forgot he was confined in a nightmare.

He drained the milk first, to ease his burning gut, and then cut into the chops, seared on the outside, rare within, crusted with coarse pepper. He ate standing up, without bothering to pull out the chair. Then, what seemed like seconds later, he staggered back to the bed and stretched out upon it. He had never tasted such a meal. He could still taste pepper and butter and the satisfying bitterness of coffee cutting through the richness of other flavors.

When he opened his eyes, it was to the sound of a gentle knocking. Disoriented from his nap, he lurched from the bed and staggered toward the door, as if they needed his help or his permission to enter.

"Come in!" he croaked, but the door was already opening.

It was Hausmann, with the bellhop. The lieutenant stepped inside, while the other held the door open for him.

"Mr. Diaghilev, I wonder if you'd come with me."

Diaghilev was already on his way. He tried to shake off the blurriness of sleep, but he seemed enmeshed in strangeness.

He let Hausmann lead him into the hall, empty now. The other prisoners, he imagined, were being similarly kept in the other rooms of this floor.

"I hope you had time to eat," Hausmann said. "And to get some rest."

"Yes," Diaghilev said warily.

"The hotel has an excellent chef," said the lieutenant cheerfully. "I wish I had occasion to take more meals here myself, but usually my post is elsewhere. Confidentially, Captain Gondarev has been putting on a bit of weight."

This last was delivered with a chuckle as they came to a stop before Room 306. Diaghilev found himself almost numb at the thought of entering it.

Hausmann rapped on the door.

The plump captain opened the door and Hausmann urged him in.

The room of his wedding night was almost identical to Room 301, with one critical difference. The thing he had most feared to see—the bed where he and Nora had first lain together and conceived their son—was gone, replaced by a large piece of equipment whose function he could not imagine. He felt almost grateful to it, for this thing was too foreign, too inexplicable, to pose any threat to those hidden thoughts, those memories of intimacy, which were all he had managed to retain of his past happiness, those days of innocence and youth.

There was one other man in the room, sitting in a chair on the far side of the device, a silver-haired fellow with the look of a frightened mouse. His skin was pale, his face drawn, his eyes both wild and timid. When he saw Diaghilev he stood up abruptly, his mouth working silently, his hands tensing at his sides. Gondarev noticed the man's behavior and wheeled on him.

"What's wrong, Reif?"

"Nothing," the other man said, the terror plain in his voice. "Nothing, I—he's the first, and I—I'm still uncertain . . ."

"You were certain enough until you saw him."

"Well, it—it's different. I mean, here he is. It's real now, isn't it?" Reif started to sit again, then straightened and backed toward one of the windows. The heavy red drapes were pulled tight, but he glanced at them as if seeking reassurance from something beyond.

"What did you think? This was a game we'd been playing for your benefit?"

"No, of—of course not. I'm fine. Everything's fine. I just—I just—"

"This is a big day for Charles," Hausmann said, crossing the room to clap the silver-haired man on the shoulder. He brought him around again, back to the center of the room. "But I'm sure he's up to it. Right, Charles?"

"Yes," Reif said. "Yes, I'm—ready."

Reif, Diaghilev thought. Charles Reif. Formerly of the Academy of Science, an associate of George Tessera. In recent years, keeping a low profile—some curatorial position in the Imperial Museum, far fallen from his days of pure research, when science was conducted for its own sake and not merely for the glory of Orlovsky. But everyone with any sense kept a low profile these days. What had brought him to the notice of the Army? What service had they called upon him to perform?

"So begin," said Gondarev.

Reif adopted an apologetic expression, and Diaghilev realized that he was also a prisoner here. He came forward slowly and put his hand on a chair positioned at the end of the strange device, facing into what looked like an enormous multifaceted lens or translucent dome. Diaghilev did not think much of the chair until he noticed the padded brace mounted on the back of it, at the end of a segmented arm, clearly intended to hold the head of its occupant steady. It might have been a barber's chair, or a dentist's.

Reif swiveled the chair to face Diaghilev. "Please, Mr. . . ."

"No names," Gondarev said abruptly, and Reif flinched at his voice, going paler.

"Would you please sit?" he said more faintly.

"Can I ask . . . ?" Diaghilev started.

"No," Gondarev snapped. "Get in the chair."

Pitying the scientist, wishing to spare him further humiliation,

Diaghilev seated himself without another word. He tried to meet Reif's eyes, but the man avoided every attempt at contact. Once Reif had swiveled the chair back to its starting position, Diaghilev found himself transfixed by the device before him.

It looked something like the engine of a skeletal locomotive, although on a smaller scale. Heavy coils and tubes of gray metal enclosed a central cavity where mirrors and lenses hung suspended; silvered panels lined this space, each of them a densely textured pane of circuitry and micalike crystalline projections. It was finely engineered, streamlined like one of Slowslop's demonic trains, with every piece of polished metal, every black arc and rivet, machined for efficiency as well as a cold beauty. At the near end of the device, spaced around the segmented dome, were five lenses in rotating mounts, each capable of independent motion. Staring into the dark glass hemisphere, he could see his own distorted features, as well as the occupants of the room behind him. Hausmann and Gondarev stretched until they seemed to merge with the dull wallpaper; nearer, Charles Reif's face seemed to scream silently as it slid and drooled across the polished surface.

"Are you comfortable?" Reif asked, almost whispering in his ear.

"Quite," Diaghilev said, unable to take his eyes from the dome, although at that moment he had noticed something beneath it, near his feet. He glanced down to see what looked like a small glass lantern, a capsule of some sort, containing a dense clot of glimmering matter.

The color . . .

He had a momentary memory of that morning's dream—the headlamp of the hurtling train.

"Please forgive me," Reif whispered, startling Diaghilev into looking up again, into the dome or lens as it began to glow.

Blue fire was born in the heart of the machine. A deep radiance edging on indigo, tinged with luminous darkness, like the glow of a methane flame, but deeper, steadier, unwavering. As it brightened, the mirrored panes inside the hollow core began to give off their own light, violet and green, running like plasma down the center of the cavity. Tiny red flickerings like the carapaces of iridescent insects sat clustered farther back in the depths. So many colors merged and separated, colors without name, without precedent. The machine crackled with an electric sound, then began to give off a deeper hum as servos went into action, as gears began to mesh and turn.

The five surrounding lenses began to revolve around the central dome. Each mirror began to spin in its own mount.

The first flicker of light now blossomed in the heart of the dome, extinguishing the reflection of the hotel room, casting it from the glass. He could no longer see his own face in there now, hard as he stared. The light thickened, amber, green, brightening into gold that never lost the qualities of all the other colors.

The five mirrors spun faster, catching light from the central dome, throwing it from one to the other, weaving intricate patterns across his eyes. The central glow shifted, deepened, as if someone had banked the fires at the core of the device; and once more he sensed a shift in power.

Every hair on his body twitched. Fire ran along his nerves, trailing from his limbs. He realized that his jaw was clenched, his rotten teeth were grinding together, yet he could feel nothing so gross as that. Every nerve was individually etched in something like pain but subtler. An itch, an agony so deep that he could find no source and no end to it. The light lanced into his eyes, blinding him; he had no lids to shut against it. His body would not obey him. The fire poured over and through him, as if he stood in the doorway of a blast furnace.

And now he heard a shriek that might have been his voice, though it sounded too high and metallic for that. He thought it was the whistle of a train. And here was the headlamp of the beast itself, bearing down on him, thundering and throbbing as it coursed straight toward him, that strange light flaring across the tracks, bridging the incalculable distance between this moment in the West End Hotel and the dream from which he had woken that morning in the Grand Central Penitentiary.

The train whistle screamed again, and this time the sound filled him with pleasure.

There was nothing like a train ride. Nothing like it!

The pleasure of standing outside, between the cars, with a pipe in one's teeth, the air so brisk you could actually taste it. It made the tobacco itself taste better, the rich cherry-cured smoke like an accent on the streaming air. Nora did not appreciate the smell, or his smoking, which she complained merely deadened his palate and burnt innumerable tiny holes in his clothes. He smiled indulgently, taking secret pleasure in her dislike of his habit; for much as he loved her, he was a man who appreciated solitude, and in moments like these the pipe provided a rare opportunity for peace and the majestic unfurling of philosophical thoughts. He could always, when he wished to find a moment to himself, announce he was going to have a smoke. She would hardly tolerate it in her house, begrudging him the privilege in his own study, but she certainly would not allow it in the confines of the private railroad car. And especially not with young Alexander there, immersed in his puzzles and picture books. She blamed tobacco for all ills, everything from asthma and emphysema to tuberculosis and the gout. For children in particular she considered it unhealthy. Which was all to Bernhard's advantage, in this instance, as it allowed him to escape for a moment and put the responsibilities of family somewhere behind him—although they were in reality just ahead of him, on the *Phaeton*.

He stood and watched the dunes roll past, absorbed in contemplation, the evening sky across the barrens echoing something in his mind—a sense of the depths of space, the blue-tinted reaches of infinity out beyond the atmosphere where even now the first stars had come twinkling. A man might think anything, believe anything, but always infinity was there to challenge him with its cold permanence, like the kernel of truth at the heart of an axiom. This was reality; this was fact. And what pleasure it gave to a man like himself, who could ponder it objectively, pipe in hand! He savored the moment.

The Great Span lay just ahead, the engineering marvel of the decade. This was the true motive for his excursion. He leaned against the *Phaeton*'s rail, putting his head out to look forward along the length of the train. The track here took a slight curve, and not far off he could see the bridge itself, an intricate geometry of girders that even as he watched began to glow with orange light, catching the rays of the setting sun. He wished he could see the span more clearly, and at that moment he felt for the first time, or perhaps remembered, the binoculars that weighed down the deep pocket of his overcoat. He fished them out, wondering where he had acquired them, for they were a finer pair than any he could recall owning. Perhaps they were an anniversary gift from Nora, smuggled into his pocket, a surprise for the journey—if so, he was grateful for them now.

They were a completely unfamiliar model. Between the twin barrels that held the chief lenses was a complex smaller chamber set with several tiny lenses. From these came a strange light, green and gold and orange all at once; a familiar light, though he could not recall now where he had seen it. The binoculars seemed to glow in his hands, as if powered by the twilight through which the *Phaeton* carried him.

The bridge was getting closer. He put the barrels to his eyes and felt for a dial to adjust the image, but found the lenses shifting focus automatically, probing for the sunlit span and finding it there in the middle of the plain, as if reading the intent of his eyes. The image held steady despite the rocking and jolting of the train. He had never seen such a crisp picture. He marveled at the design of the bridge, brought so close by the lenses that he could practically count the rivets.

Tobacco be damned, he must fetch Nora and Alexander and bring them out here to share the marvel—

But at that moment, the bridge disappeared in a gout of flame and smoke.

Unable to move, even to lower the binoculars, he waited in terror for the smoke to clear. The bridge was just ahead of them—the train was thundering straight into the conflagration. Yet he heard no squeal of brakes, no train whistle crying in alarm to echo his own. How could they not see the hellish cloud ahead? The train raced on, and as a gust of wind from the depths of the abyss pushed up and parted the veils of smoke, he saw the near end of the span sagging raggedly into the gulf. Raw and twisted ends of metal, the tracks curled and splintered, huge pieces of the bridge dangling, swinging, giving way and plunging into the smoke. Any instant now the *Phaeton* too must follow them.

Finally the whistle shrieked, drowning out his own cries. The abyss was almost underfoot. Bernhard screamed and leaped over the rail—leaped for the safety of the barrens before the earth could disappear beneath his feet.

He landed tumbling, rolling. He felt as if every bone had been bruised, yet he forced himself upright to see what must become of the train as it thrust into the cloud of flame and destruction. Thinking only then of his wife and child, aboard the very car from which he had leaped without warning them . . .

But the *Phaeton*, inexplicably, rolled on peacefully toward the bridge, still some distance ahead of the engine car. There was no cloud of smoke, no flames except the reflected light of the sun which revealed every unbroken line of the gleaming bridge.

Bernhard sat dumbfounded where he had landed, thinking—I am insane. Insane!

The binoculars lay in the sand beside him. The weird greenish glow seemed brighter now, streaming up from the small lenses of the central chamber like twin shafts of luminous vapor. He dug them from the sand, raised them to his eyes, and peered at the bridge again.

—Black fumes . . .

—Dangling metal he could almost hear screeching as it swung and tore free . . .

—And the rear cars of the *Phaeton*, following the engine and all the forward cars into the gulf.

It struck him now that he had not *heard* the explosion; had witnessed it only in the binoculars, imagining the sound because the images had been so vivid.

But they were only images, illusions, somehow prerecorded and now played back in this deceitful instrument that resembled a pair of ordinary binoculars.

He lowered the binoculars and studied the bridge again. Yes, it was intact. His wife and child were safe. Only *he* had been injured, in his foolish leap.

He felt himself for broken bones, but he was such a mass of sprains and bruises that it was impossible to distinguish one pain from another. He got to his knees, and then to his feet, wondering when or whether they would notice his absence. Halfheartedly, knowing it was futile, he raised a hand and waved wearily at the receding train.

At that instant, the bridge exploded.

Smoke. Flame. Flying sparks of shattered metal. Everything he had seen moments ago in the binoculars, but this time accompanied by the horror of sound.

This time, it was really happening.

He screamed as the train screamed. Oh, yes, this time they had seen the explosion. How could they not? The brakes wailed. Bernhard ran, forgetting his trivial pains—ran as if he could catch the train and hold it back, keep it from plunging into the abyss. Ran as if he could at least save one car, one particular car.

But even the engineers of the *Phaeton* could not slow it in time. The engine ran headlong into the cloud of flame just as a gust of wind thinned the smoke so that Bernhard could see there was nothing left of a track to carry it across the chasm. The train rushed on into emptiness and the smoke closed in again. The sound of the whistle, which the prophetic binoculars had spared him, soared loudly once as the train took flight, and then sank away into the depths. He imagined he heard other voices in that scream, but they were drowned out by the thunderous crashes and secondary explosions that came repeatedly, randomly, for what seemed an infinite length of time, as car after car vanished into the smoke, and into the gulf, and as pieces of the bridge fell after them.

Silence eventually came, along with darkness. Bernhard stood at the edge of the gulf, and never knew quite what kept him from throwing himself after them. There were stars above, and nothing at all below. No sound, no screams, not the faintest sign of light or life all through that long, moonless night.

Just before sunrise a lone aircraft flew out of the west, gliding parallel to the track. It circled several times and dipped into the canyon, then rose and droned on toward the rising sun.

He sat at the edge of the gulf and waited as daylight slowly gave shape to the chaos below. When he thought there was light enough, he took the binoculars from his pocket and trained them on the depths.

The early morning sky lay captured and shattered in the broken windows of the fallen cars. There was no movement there. He scanned the lengths of the sleeping trains, searching for bodies.

At last he found one window intact. The sky had begun to brighten in the glass, the deep dawn blue turning to gold as sunlight spread above the canyon. The binoculars, as if sensing his interest in this one window, homed in on it, and the image sharpened further. The window seemed to grow, its glossy surface crawling with color. Was that something, someone, moving just beyond it? Yes, a heavy red curtain was being pulled back, away from the glass, allowing the binoculars to cast their light into a darkened room. He saw a bored and irritable man glaring out at him, balding, with thick features, and wearing a military uniform. Beyond him were others: an aging, mousy silver-haired fellow and a blond man in a soldier's uniform.

But the binoculars took a particular interest in the room's fourth occupant. Very old, very gray, features slack with exhaustion and despair. He sat upright in a complicated chair, his hands clenched on the armrests, his head vibrating rapidly from side to side. His eyes were fixed wide open. Bernhard could not see what the old man was looking at, but it must have been painful, for his cheeks were wet and his eyes were full of tears.

Then the balding man released the curtain, and as it fell, everything was obscured.

THREE

ON A DARK SUNDAY AFTERNOON IN EARLY DECEMBER,
Elena had the Imperial Library practically to herself. Rain swept
the streets and pavilions outside, making her office seem snug and
comfortable, making Elena herself feel almost content. On the desk
before her were the guts of a retrieval instrument, its lenses and
pulleys arrayed in careful order so that she would not confuse
them when she began to reassemble the device. Her brushes and
micro-tipped screwdrivers, pliers, and tweezers were arranged in
order of descending size, in the pockets of a soft unrolled chamois.
Her toolbox sat open on the floor beside her, full of larger and
more complicated tools she could not imagine needing ever again.
Neither could she imagine giving them away. Most she had not
touched since her days as a graduate student, but she still held on
to them, and took them out from time to time, dreaming of what
she might have achieved with them had things gone differently.

She carefully extracted a gray clot of oily dust and fibers from
the inner workings of the device. It had been sluggish for weeks,
and yesterday it had finally come to a complete stop, giving off an
odor of singed lint and ozone. She fit a thin tapered nozzle onto the
end of a small bellows, fit the tube down into a tiny clogged aper-

ture, and squeezed the bellows several times. When she removed the tube, light could be seen through the hole. She threaded a fine reddish fiber, hardly thicker than a strand of her hair, through the opening, and then wrapped it around several microscopic flywheels. As she fastened the thread into a loop with a link so small she needed tweezers to handle it, she thought she heard voices echoing in the lobby.

She rose slightly, peering from the window of her office across the broad marble counter where the librarians received patrons. Beyond was a cavernous foyer, three steps leading down to a wide walkway of gray marble softened only slightly by a soiled red carpet. The stone columns to either side of the tall glass doors had once been etched with the names of great authors, poets, and philosophers, but they were blank now, the carved names filled with stone amalgam and polished over, waiting to be re-incised with the names of those intellects Orlovsky approved.

Apparently, the Emperor still had not finalized his list. Apart from installing a torso of himself just inside the doors, he had left no mark on the lobby. The statue was posed, pen in hand, over a heavy stone volume opened to several unfinished lines of the *Mentations*. The torso was of alabaster, but it managed to look hurried and sloppy—characteristics she had never before seen in a monument. Orlovsky had been in a great rush to memorialize his achievements back in Year One, in case they might be erased forever before Year Two.

None of us thought it could last, she thought. *But here we are with Year Nine nearly upon us. How have we endured this long?*

The sound came again. A muttered voice. Was it in conversation with another, or speaking to itself? She laid the bellows aside and stepped out of the office. Resting her hands on the cold countertop, she peered down at the doors.

Outside, through the rain, she could see the lamps in the pavilion. They had come alight early, twin rows of luminous globes that seemed to float in the gloom, distorted and fragmented by the tiny lenses of raindrops. Directly opposite the library, on the far side of the pavilion, she could just make out the entrance of the Imperial Museum.

She never saw that grand entryway, an imposing portal to an even more imposing institution, without a pang of regret at the thought of all the instruments gathering dust inside the museum, relics of bygone days of actual research, invention, and progress. The regret, of course, had deeper roots than she cared to revive too often; it had to do with a part of herself which had also grown dusty with misuse. This part still took what pleasure it could in the maintenance of the humblest piece of the archives' automated retrieval system. But still, whenever she opened her toolkit, she had to fight down a terrible resentment and a frustration that never seemed to die, no matter how much time had passed.

The voice came again, and this time she saw movement in the alcove between two pillars. She went around the counter, down the steps, and over the damp red carpet to investigate.

As she drew near, she smelled damp wool and rancid sweat, a human fetor that promised to ripen into something worse with the application of heat. Another mendicant, she thought, seeking shelter in the library. She had always allowed them access, never turned away a single patron. Since the library was immense and mostly untenanted, there was no one they could bother; and most of those who came were attracted not merely because it offered shelter, but because it was a library. They could feed their minds, or at least occupy their eyes, while they passed the hours. Sometimes they disappeared into the depths of the archives and reappeared only after the passage of days.

But it would not do to leave one in the foyer. The pavilion guards were wont to check the entrance at intervals. For all she knew, they had already rousted him from some other spot outside, and he had sought sanctuary here, as if the library were a church of sorts.

"Excuse me, sir," she said patiently, "but you can't stay here. You'll have to come into the main building. We don't want anyone tripping over you. You'll only bring yourself harm, you see?"

The face tipped toward her, swathed in ragged wool, deep-sunk in a collar blackened and crusted and foul. The eyes were empty; they roved here and there, into the echoing heights of the library, across her face, toward the rain-spattered doors, as if all these things were of equal importance or lacked any meaning whatsoever. She thought he was very old, although it was difficult to assess age with these unfortunates; every cold and sleepless night seemed to rob them of a month of life. His face, especially around the eyes, was a webwork of burst capillaries, yet she smelled no alcohol on him. Too poor to afford it, no doubt.

"I beg your pardon," she said again, "I know it's a great deal to ask, but—"

"In the abyss, in the abyss, I saw it spinning. I saw it spinning, do you understand?"

"I'm not sure I do," she said gently. "But if you can just get to your feet . . ." She was reluctant to assist him. She thought of her office, her project still unfinished. If she were another sort of person, she would have called the sentries and let them deal with him. Perhaps placing him in confinement would be doing him a favor. He might receive some treatment, or at least dry clothes and nourishment.

"Onrushing . . . and then the burning, the terrible burning. I had no chance to warn them. No chance!"

"Please." His voice was building in volume, echoing through the library. Someone would come to investigate soon, unless she quieted him.

Suddenly he sprang to his feet, seizing her arm, putting his face close to hers, and growled, "It was the Third Force! And they will pay!"

Elena went cold and still. Staring into the madman's eyes, she finally recognized him.

Under the mask of burst blood vessels, he was hardly the man she remembered. When last she'd seen him, he'd worn a thick beard that hid the lower half of his face. That beard had been shorn away and now only stubble remained.

"Mr. Diaghilev?" she whispered.

He looked up at the name, his eyes striving to focus. Something familiar passed through them for a moment. He gathered himself to his full height, clenching her arm, and spat the phrase again, as if it were a password: "The Third Force! It was *them!*"

She caught hold of his elbow and led him slowly up the stairs, toward the main counter.

"Ele . . . Ele . . . Ele . . ."

He was whispering her name, or trying to.

"Shh," she whispered as they rounded the counter.

"Elena—I—I must know."

She guided him into her office, and pushed a stack of books from a chair. "Here, sit down."

He sat blinking, disoriented, but he had recognized her, if only for a moment. She knelt in front of him, patting his hands, which were cold and damp. "I'll get you some tea, would you like that? Some hot tea?"

He leaned forward and gripped her fingers in a panic. "The light was spinning, spinning down there. Down there!" He pointed at the floor. "And then the ship came, do you remember? Just there!" He pointed at the ceiling. "I looked and I—I—my eyes!" He raised his hands to his eyes, fingers curled into tubes, like a child pretending to look through a pair of imaginary binoculars. "Will you see it?"

"Mr. Diaghilev," she said urgently, trying to bring him back, "do you know where you are? You started to say my name. I am Elena Hausmann. Do you remember me?"

He bit his lower lip and sat silently for a moment, contemplating. An interval of peace and lucidity. "The . . . this is the library," he said suddenly.

"Yes, that's right. The library."

"My—my books, they're all here. I need to remember them. I need to see them now. For the truth."

"Your books," she repeated, and then it came to her. Here was an opportunity that might never come again. Diaghilev, with no fixed address, a man who had seemingly dropped out of existence, could order a search for his own books with impunity. His request could never be traced back to him. And what if it were? Had he not already been seized by the Empire? Hadn't that been the meaning of Slowslop's warning to her in Grand Central Station that night three months ago?

If the old man dared to access his books, then he was beyond caring and beyond censure.

"Can you walk?" she asked.

He lowered his head and sighed. She put her arm under his

elbow and got him to his feet again, then led him haltingly out of the office. The huge hood of the retrieval terminal waited as it had waited all day, vainly, for a single request.

"I'll need your hand for a thumbprint," she said. He offered no protest. She set his thumb on the print-reader and a blue light flared beneath it. After a moment, an access code in luminous liquid characters appeared on the narrow gray screen.

An authorization code! So Diaghilev was still considered a citizen; he had not been deleted.

Next to the print-reader was a converted typewriter, its clumsy black casing of grain-textured iron now pierced with thick rubber cables that linked it to the cabinet of the retrieval system. The library made do with antiquated equipment. She typed the authorization code onto the big round keys, followed by her request:

Diaghilev, B.
All Titles

After a moment, the typewriter began to tremble. She pulled her hands away. The keys began to hammer on the roller, covering the waiting paper roll with several lines of text. While the final row of X's was still being typed, she tore the sheet from the typewriter.

There were no titles on the paper, nothing but codes and coordinates. There was no telling if they were works authored by Diaghilev, or works about him. No way of telling, aside from retrieving the books themselves. In all, there were a dozen books represented, and they were scattered all over the library. She pressed a switch beneath the countertop, throwing the electric latch on the front doors. It was nearly closing time, after all; and she did not want to rely completely on the automated retrieval units for this particular task.

"The very bed," Diaghilev was saying, oblivious to her efforts. "And in that room. Three-oh-six, remember it? How could you have forgotten. Our own room! Dear Nora . . ." Suddenly he rose and took her arm. "I couldn't have saved my wife and child," he said. "I had no warning! The things I saw . . ."

"That's fine, sir. If you'll give me just a moment, I'm tracing your books. Hold on just a moment."

She left him there and went into her office, keeping a close eye on Diaghilev through the glass. She picked up the phone and punched in Krystoff's number.

He answered with his usual surly "Yes?"

"Mr. Moholy, this is Miss Hausmann at the Imperial Library."

"And?" Speaking as if to a stranger.

"A volume has turned up—something you requested three months ago. A work of philosophy by Stone."

"Stone?" he repeated. "Are you certain?"

"I have it right here, waiting for you. Please ring when you arrive and I will let you in."

"I'll be there right away."

The phone went dead.

Since the fictitious name "Stone" did not appear on the forbidden list, it would trigger no alert in whatever section of Imperial Intelligence monitored her telephone conversations.

She went back out to Diaghilev. He was the philosopher, whose code name Stone referred to the philosopher's stone, that mythic agent of alchemical transmutation. Now the philosopher himself had been transmuted, but by an evil alchemy: Gold had turned to lead. His eyes shone brightly, but it was the glib brightness of idiocy. He began to smile as she helped him once more to his feet.

"This way," she said.

"You remind me of Nora," he said, as she led him down the steps into one of the corridors that branched off from the lobby, deeper into the library. "Nora was my wife, you know. We were very happy. Very happy. And our son—such a clever boy. I blamed myself for their death, made myself *miserable*, you know, until recently I came to understand the truth. I even blamed it on the Empire, yes, but that was wrong. Do you know the Third Force?"

Elena shook her head vigorously. "No, and you should not talk about such things."

"The Third Force. A network of spies, reactionaries, enemies of humanity! Devils! They are the ones who dynamited the bridge."

To hear these words from the founder of the resistance movement was terrifying, but no doubt he had good reason, Elena reassured herself. This prospect was even more nightmarish.

"They are agents of the Republic, you know," he said confidentially. "Yes! Working for Onegin, to bring about our downfall! They killed my wife and child! They were responsible!"

"That's dreadful." Elena tried to keep her voice neutral.

"Yes! And they live in the whirling light, in the colors, where I still see them. Down in the chasm. I shouldn't have opened that window, my dear—shouldn't even have looked inside. Did you leap? Or will you leap as I leaped? Can we signal the aircraft? Circling low, circling low. I tried to get down in there, but it was the very same room! Oh no . . . no . . ." He wept and snuffled. She was glad to have gotten far away from the doors, into the vast deserted interior of the library.

"Three-oh-six," he mumbled. "Three-oh-six."

She glanced down at the sheet in her hand, reminding herself of the archive coordinates she sought. They were getting close to one of the books. Without the identifiers, she wouldn't have had a chance of finding his books; and without entering his authorization code, there was no way of getting the identifiers. And even now that she had the numbers, there was no certainty that she could ever find them again, for one function of the automatic retrieval units was to continually reshelve and rearrange the volumes so that no book's location could be memorized.

Even now, the units went about their ceaseless work, purring along on suspended tracks high overhead, sliding back and forth along the shelves. As they glided past each volume, they scanned the small reflective code on the otherwise unmarked, identical spines. Every book stored in the Imperial Library had been rebound in black buckram, so that apart from size, there was no way of distinguishing them. Every aisle was walled with black-spined books; and everywhere, the little humming boxes glided, plucking volumes from the shelves and carrying them away to new locations, forever scrambling and reordering. Once she reshelved Diaghilev's books, their location would immediately be altered, along with their identifiers.

She stopped at a librarian's kiosk in the general area of the nearest book and typed in her direct order. One unit was freed from its shelving function and dispatched to locate the requested title. She had given it a point-only instruction. After several seconds, she heard a loud signal from an adjacent aisle.

Diaghilev had retreated into silence, rocking on his heels, his hands at work deep in the pockets of his coat. He tagged along as she followed the sound to where the assigned retriever rested with its pointer on the spine of one volume indistinguishable from so many others. As she touched the book, the machine broke away, reaching a track intersection at the edge of the shelf and then shooting swiftly toward the ceiling, where it fell in among the other constantly shuttling units.

The book opened in her hand to a picture of a young man, thoughtful and serious, gazing in partial profile from an open window. There was a pipe in his hand, trailing a wisp of smoke. On the opposite page was the book's title:

My Life Underground
by Bernhard Diaghilev

A Personal History of
the Third Force

It was exactly the kind of book the Empire waited for someone to request, dangerous as a baited trap. She wondered if even Diaghilev could examine it with impunity. What if he had only just escaped? They might be looking for him, and now her actions would have alerted them to his whereabouts. Why hadn't she thought of this before?

Diaghilev snatched the book from her hand, studying the picture as if it were someone he dimly recognized. He began to flip through pages rapidly, coming across more photographs, and sketches done in his own hand. There were photographs of the Great Span and newspaper images of the *Phaeton* disaster, scenes of the catastrophe that she knew had shattered Diaghilev's comfortable, staid life of the mind, turning him from a philosopher into an activist, driving him underground. She had never understood exactly how the accident had catalyzed such a change; he had been a passenger aboard the train, that much she knew, and the lone survivor of the wreck. But how had this translated into political action? She was eager, now, to see the book herself, to study it for clues to the old man's motives. But he did not look as if he would soon let go of it. He was studying the photographs of the shattered bridge, inspecting an image of the wreckage as if he might enter it and search for survivors.

At that moment, she heard the distant buzz of the night bell. Krystoff had come more quickly than she thought possible.

"Wait here, just one moment," she said. "I'll be right back."

Diaghilev had sunk to the floor, the book spread open before him. He didn't seem to hear her.

She ran back down the aisles and along the corridor to the lobby. She slowed as she came in sight of the doors, suddenly apprehensive that it might not be Krystoff at all, but Intelligence agents. But that was absurd—they would not have bothered with the bell.

She could see one figure outside in the rain, and she did not have to get much closer to recognize Krystoff Moholy, tall and thin and agitated, pacing and smoking as he waited. He was about to turn and stab the buzzer again when he saw her through the glass. He threw down his cigarette. She hardly had a chance to open the door before he had squeezed through and lunged in, rounding on her.

"Where is he?" he said, his eyes wide, his face incredibly pale. He had been sick with a fever for days. Rain had plastered his long dark hair to his scalp and cheeks. It was dangerous to bring him here, but far less dangerous than trying to bring Diaghilev to him.

"This way," she said.

He kept turning and turning as they walked, looking up at the ceiling, darting glances down the corridors.

"It's damn weird," he said.

"I know—"

"Not this. Stillson's turned up, too."

"Stillson?" She stopped and faced him.

"Yes. This morning. Marnham saw him downtown, walking in the middle of the street. Nearly struck by a guard car, till someone pulled him out of the way. Marnham said he was raving. He tried to make arrangements, get him to a safe house, but he slipped away. It—it's no coincidence, both of them reappearing like this, at the same time."

"I suppose not," she said. "But where were they?"

"We're working on that," he said. "Maybe Diaghilev can tell us."

"I'm afraid he's not exactly lucid."

"What do you mean?"

"Maybe he's just very ill. He looks terrible." She was whispering now, because they were approaching the place where she had left him. "He keeps talking about his wife and child, and saying things that make no sense about . . . about us."

"What do you mean, his wife and child?"

She stepped around the end of the aisle, but there was no sign of Diaghilev. Could she have the wrong aisle? She went to the next row, knowing she'd been right the first time.

"What is it? Where is he?"

"He was right . . . here." She retraced her steps to the exact spot where she had left him, and confirmed the fact by locating the gap in the shelf where his autobiography had been stored. Even as she watched, one of the retrieval units slipped down with a book of the same dimensions and fit it into the slot. Then it whirred away.

Elena took out the reshelved book, to make sure.

The Topiary Garden:
Function and Philosophy

She replaced it, then hurried down the aisle to the far end. Krystoff was right behind her.

"Could he have gotten out?"

"If he went all the way around, or passed us going down another aisle. But he seemed so . . . so disoriented. I wouldn't think he'd be able to find his way around that quickly."

"Maybe he's lost."

"Yes." She began to hurry deeper into the archives, calling, "Mr. Diaghilev!" Krystoff cut off along a perpendicular aisle, and then kept pace with her, so they might catch the philosopher between

MARC LAIDLAW

them. They ended up back at the lobby, with still no trace of the old man.

Elena stood at the doors, testing them. They were unlocked, but she could not remember if she had bolted them after admitting Krystoff. Diaghilev could easily have slipped out—but why would he?

"He seemed so helpless," she said. "Where would he go?"

His eyes drifted past her, narrowing with curiosity. "What's that?"

She turned to see the alabaster torso of Orlovsky, now embellished with something she had failed to notice earlier in the evening. She felt certain Diaghilev must have left it there, as a sort of sign or token, on his way out. She remembered him fidgeting with something in his pocket. Was this it?

Krystoff was the first to the statue, first to lift the object from the stone pages of the *Mentations.*

"Binoculars," he said. "Are they yours?"

She remembered Diaghilev's strange pantomime of peering through his curled fingers.

"No, I . . . they must be his."

"Is he trying to tell us something?" Krystoff started to raise them to his eyes.

"I can't imagine what," she said. "I told you, he was speaking such nonsense . . ."

"Yes, you mentioned. His wife and child." He put the binoculars the rest of the way to his eyes, and stared straight at her. Through the lenses, she thought she could see his pupils quite clearly, miniaturized but luminous, with an inner golden light.

"Why is that nonsense?" she asked, taking a step back, assuming she would only be a blur to him until she moved farther away. But he seemed to be peering at her intently, as if he had focused on her quite clearly. His mouth gaped, and then he said faintly, as if his mind were on something else now, "Because he doesn't have a wife. He never married. Certainly never had children."

"What a strange delusion," she said. "Are you quite sure?"

"Positive." He swung the binoculars away, as if following some movement invisible to her.

"He was so . . . insistent."

"People in the movement . . . some have known him all his life. No family. Never anyone. Student. Loner. Philosopher. No place for a wife or children."

"How sad," she said, as the binoculars drifted back in her direction. "As if he's created them now, to console himself. Created them, and then convinced himself he lost them in that crash."

Krystoff dropped the binoculars abruptly. "I need to take these with me," he said, without looking at her. "It's not a good idea, me coming here. We'll meet again tomorrow."

She nodded, wanting to say more, but knowing he was right. It was foolish to take any greater risks. Krystoff hid the binoculars under his coat, and waited for her to open the door for him. He started to slip through, again too impatient to wait for her to open it all the way; but this time, in the instant before he vanished, he turned and gave her a worried smile, and reached out for her face. Lightly, his hand brushed her jaw. She started to lean toward him for a kiss, but he was already gone.

She locked the door and turned off the foyer lights. Stood behind the glass, staring out at the pavilion and its rows of floating spheres like glowing pearls. She wondered if anyone might be looking across at her from inside the Imperial Museum. One of the men she had worked with under George Tessera in her student days, perhaps. She had seen them in and around the museum at various times. Charles Reif had managed the collection for a while, although she had not seen him recently.

Agitated by more things than she could identify, she turned and went back to her office. The sight of the disassembled retrieval unit, a pleasant challenge to her an hour ago, now filled her with despair. She rolled up the chamois that held her precious tools and threw it into the box.

FOUR

"BY THE WAY, HOW IS YOUR SISTER?"
Louis Hausmann hesitated, lowered the three-dimensional scanner from his eyes, and regarded the Supreme Commander of the Army with surprise. "Elena?"

Slowslop's eyes, behind the smoked ovals of his spectacles, betrayed nothing; but a very faint smile had found its way to his lips. It was such an incongruous expression, one so out of place on Slowslop's features, that Louis found himself staring at the Supreme Commander's mouth until he felt he must be making a fool of himself.

"Yes. She found a position in the Imperial Library, I understand. I hope her talents aren't being wasted there. A very capable woman, Elena."

"Yes, she and I . . . well, we don't see much of each other these days."

"No? That's a shame."

"We move in very different circles. Very different."

Slowslop stubbed out a cigarette in the ashtray on the small red-draped table beside him. The glare of the lamp slid in liquid bars and spots of light along his glossy sleeve. "Do you think she would respond to an invitation to dine with us? If it came from you, I mean? Lord Orlovsky mentioned that he has been curious about her lately. He always took an interest in her future, as you may recall."

"We both owe the Emperor greater debts than we can ever hope to repay," Louis said. "I will be sure to extend your offer whenever I see her next. Or, if you like, I could try to reach her sooner."

"That's not necessary. He just wishes to know if she is well, and if she would allow us to entertain her for an evening. Personally, I regret she hasn't taken a greater interest in serving the Empire. There would be plenty of work for her now. The barriers she encountered in the National Academy simply don't exist in the Empire. I only wish I could have interceded on her behalf at the time . . ." Slowslop's voice grew increasingly faint, then came back to full volume as he watched Louis heft the scanner. "That gadget, for instance, would probably have interested her immensely in the old days."

The old days, Louis thought. Slowslop's words had an odd ring, considering that he had taken it upon himself to carry out Lord Orlovsky's command to eradicate all mention of the past—to obliterate memory itself, if necessary. Hausmann knew better than practically anyone how far Orlovsky was willing to go to achieve this end; yet Slowslop spoke of the past without the slightest tremor. Not that anyone would ever accuse the Supreme Commander of flirting with treason. After so many years as Orlovsky's right-hand man, and chief engineer of the Revolution, he was probably comfortable in making such comments directly to Orlovsky—although never in anyone else's presence.

"I think she's happy enough where she is," Louis said. "Elena never took any interest in politics."

"The failing of many a scientist," Slowslop said, and rose from his chair. "Which is fortunate for us." He took the scanner from Louis's fingers. "They make their little toys without worrying about how they might be used. Like children, with no thought to the future. They're simply happy to have laboratories and funding and staff to carry out their research. It doesn't matter to them whether the Academy of Sciences is a National or an Imperial institution. The main thing is the investigation. Science blinds them. The pure investigators do not even bother to consider applications . . . or wouldn't, without someone like Horselover Frost stirring them up."

At the mention of Frost, Louis became anxious to change the subject. The name was a source of constant embarrassment, an emblem of the continuing failure of the manhunt which Louis himself had initiated more than three years ago. Yet Slowslop had never openly chastised him for his failure; it was almost as if he didn't expect Horselover ever to be found, but had merely set Louis the task as one more test of his diligence.

"Is there a manual for that?" he asked his superior. "One I could study before I have to use it?"

"It hasn't been written yet, but that won't be necessary. I've calibrated the scanner. You merely aim the condensing screen, here, at the boy, and press this red recording button. I've set the switches, so be sure not to change them. When the scan is complete, the screen should show an even red light. If you see anything less than that, broken lines or sparks, you're not finished yet. Do not switch off the device until you have taken a complete scan. Then bring it back to me immediately. Simple enough?" Slowslop handed the scanner back to him.

"Yes. Quite." Louis set the scanner carefully into its padded case, lowered the lid, and clicked the snaps. "Will they be expecting me?"

Slowslop's smile was gone now, and it was hard to imagine it had ever existed. "Not at all. They are keeping him a secret, or so they think."

"They must know Intelligence has informers among the hospital staff," Louis said.

"If they thought about it, they would realize that the men who brought him in were also required to file a report. But you know Constantine. He thinks he can keep secrets even now, even from me, after everything he's endured. Well, you know how his mind works."

Louis allowed himself a smile. "I remember."

"I hope it won't be necessary to threaten him again. Last year's interrogation should have made a strong impression. I imagine when he sees you, he will resign himself to the inevitable."

"Very good, sir. Is that all?"

"That is all, Lieutenant."

"Thank you, sir."

Louis Hausmann saluted and let himself into the hall. Slowslop's office and adjacent private quarters were situated in the basement of Intelligence Headquarters, deep beneath the West End Hotel. The corridor was furnished much like those above, with wall lamps like goblets of frosted glass. Only Orlovsky's suite, on a still lower level, would be any safer in the event of an attack by the Socialist Republic. Orlovsky, obsessed with the possibility of aerial bombardment, had deepened the hotel's basement to provide shelters for the Imperial Command Center, despite the fact that Intelligence reports from within the Republic had confirmed Louis's long-held belief that the Empire had little reason to fear the enemy's inferior aerial armaments. In addition to its spy satellites, which kept constant watch on the Republic's key strategic centers, the Empire possessed a missile interception system more than adequate to the job of dispatching Onegin's clumsy gray cones. Ernst Onegin, leader of the Socialist Republic, was also a man obsessed; but in his case he had sunk his country's wealth into the construction of an immense and purposeless "Command Tower," a grandiose spire in the middle of a man-made lake. It was a marvel of engineering, but apparently little more than that. Onegin had quarters in the peak of the thing, and had never ventured to the earth's surface since the tower's completion. It was as if he, too, awaited some manner of apocalypse. In Onegin's case, it was death from *below* he seemed to fear.

As Hausmann padded down the corridor, a figure in the uniform of the hotel staff appeared at the end of the hall. Small, wizened, with a smooth and liver-spotted pate, he looked like an old bellhop kept on out of pity by some manager who could not bring himself to discharge an ancient but loyal employee. He moved along at a cramped pace, slightly hunched and muttering to himself. Hausmann stood very still, waiting until the old man was several feet in front of him, then cleared his throat abruptly and pretended that he had just noticed they were about to collide. As the old man looked up, startled, Hausmann bowed very deeply. When he straightened again, he saw the eyes in the soft face had grown narrow and cunning. Louis reminded himself that the appearance of senility was deceptive. Those eyes were as alive and as intimidating as they had been in Louis's boyhood. They had both frightened and drawn him when he was a child. They still had the same effect; he supposed that a part of him had never completely grown up.

"My lord," he said, with all possible formality.

"Hello, Louis." Lord Orlovsky held out his withered hands and Louis stooped to kiss the Emperor's molybdenum unicorn ring. "You've been in with Theodore?"

"Yes, my lord."

"He asked after your sister, I trust?"

"Yes, my lord."

"Good. Good. You will bring her in, won't you? See that you do."

"As soon as I can, my lord."

Lord Orlovsky nodded and retracted his hand, in which the bones felt brittle as tinder. Then he shuffled past Louis without another word, going on toward Slowslop's door. As he passed in and out of the light surrounding the bracketed lamps, he seemed to waver in and out of existence.

Two requests for Elena's presence. Slowslop's had been polite, almost hesitant, although Louis had never doubted for an instant that it was actually a command. But Orlovsky's request was on the order of an imperial decree. If Slowslop had not already given him other instructions, he would have proceeded to the library immediately, in search of his sister.

But first, there was the matter of the recalcitrant doctors to be dealt with.

■ ■ ■

The driver of the silver staff car slowed at the Army Hospital checkpoint, and an Imperial Guard stepped up to take a look at Louis's identification. Seeing his name, and the sigil of Army Intelligence, the guard immediately motioned for the gate to be opened. The small red flag of the Empire, hanging limp above the hood while the car idled, slowly lifted as they passed through the gates and down the long drive. The proud little banner, featuring a red star encircled by a geared wheel, always reminded Louis of his own role in the Empire. They were all cogs in Orlovsky's beautiful machine, well oiled, running in perfect harmony with every other piece of political machinery.

Ahead, like a brick monolith, the Army Hospital appeared above the stooped forms of sickly, untended willows. The grass had gone wild, overrunning its borders; rodent holes and mounds of bare earth pocked the lawns. A large herb clock, planted for the pleasure of convalescing patients, was now completely unreadable; an overgrown clump of rosemary at the center of the wheel had rendered one hour indistinguishable from another. Since its conversion from a civilian facility, the Army Hospital went largely unused. One of its wings had been turned over to military biomedical research; another had simply been abandoned. It pained Louis to see any part of the Empire's military infrastructure in such sad condition, but he supposed it was a positive sign that Orlovsky had kept his promise of peace. A bustling military hospital would have been more ominous, and Louis was not the heartless sort of soldier who wished for war merely to keep in practice.

The staff car pulled up in the semicircular courtyard, settling in the shadow of the brick building. For a moment, stepping out of the car, he felt as if he were making another trip to the Grand Central Penitentiary, collecting another batch of prisoners to ferry back to Room 306. The Army Hospital and the Grand Central Penitentiary had shared the same architect. Both resembled fortresses; both had been designed to keep an unhappy population in confinement. And while the hospital discharged its function with greater comfort for its inhabitants, it was no less secure than the prison. It kept a full complement of Imperial Guards, Intelligence agents, and lesser security personnel. No one had escaped the Army Hospital in the nine years since the Revolution. In that regard it had a better record than the penitentiary.

The foyer smelled of dust. An Army nurse moved in the distance, gliding like a shadow in her gray uniform, gone. The overhead lights were as dim as the remnants of December sky that managed to seep in through thick windows of milky glass embedded with wire mesh. The nurse at the reception station rose to attention as he approached.

"Lieutenant Hausmann," he said to her. "I have come to see Dr. Wallace."

"I'm not sure if he's available. He—"

"I believe he is restricted to the grounds by military order."

The nurse hesitated, looking panicked. "Yes, but—"

"Then while you summon him, please direct me to the boy who was admitted on the second of this month."

"The . . . the boy?"

"Yes. The fellow apprehended in the Restricted Zone."

"I—I'm sorry, but—but there aren't any children being treated here."

"He is a patient of Dr. Wallace's."

Now her look was simply blank. Either she was adept at bluffing, or the boy's presence had been kept secret from her. As he pondered his next move, he heard his name being uttered with displeasure. He turned to see Constantine Wallace moving toward him with a faltering step, as if the doctor had checked himself in midstride.

"Constantine!" Louis said warmly. "How long has it been? More than a year, hasn't it?"

"What are you doing here?"

"Visiting a patient. You might know him."

"I wasn't aware—"

"A young man. A boy."

Wallace's thin lips pressed so tightly together that they all but vanished. His eyes were dark and mistrustful, taken by surprise; but Louis could see him already rallying, preparing a defense. Which meant he had something to defend.

"Slowslop sent you?" Wallace asked.

"He's not the only one who takes an interest in your work."

"I thought you'd gone away convinced there was no 'work.' Not of the sort you were looking for."

"I know you have nothing to hide, Dr. Wallace."

"Then why are you here?"

"Merely as a concerned visitor. Will you take me to him?"

Constantine Wallace pinched the bridge of his nose vigorously between thumb and forefinger, then pulled his fingers slowly down the length as if drawing it into a sharper, narrower beak than it already was. It was a nervous habit Louis had witnessed hundreds of times over the course of several days, and it vividly recalled Wallace's interrogation. Constantine must have realized he had no alternative. He finally turned without a word and walked away, leaving Hausmann to follow down a corridor cluttered with trays and carts.

"How is Dr. MacNaughton these days? Are you both still busy with your electromagnetic research?"

"John spent all night with the boy. I told him to get some sleep. You don't have to bother him."

"So the boy *is* here."

"I don't believe he should be receiving visitors. His condition is very unstable."

"Is it?"

"You obviously know something about him. From your spies on my staff, I presume."

"That doesn't mean I wouldn't value your professional assessment of his condition."

They reached the doors of an elevator. Constantine pushed the button to summon the car, then stood silent for a moment, considering, before going on.

"He appears to be aphasic. I suspect some sort of psychic trauma. Physically, he's unharmed. When we admitted him, we thought he was suffering from hypothermia. But everything was normal at first. It wasn't until the next morning that his temperature began to drop, for no apparent reason. He's been comatose for several days now."

"Comatose?"

"You can see why I think visitors are at best irrelevant, and might possibly cause his condition to deteriorate."

"May I ask why you neglected to file a report about his admission?"

"I assumed that was done by those who brought him here. He was found in the Restricted Zone, after all. That's your territory."

"A medical report would have been welcome."

"I didn't think it was important—certainly not important enough to bring you here. He's just a boy. Probably broke into your operations just to prove he could do it and then—well, who knows? I thought I would take some time to question him myself, but he never spoke while he was conscious. Perhaps if I had employed the sort of techniques you Intelligence agents specialize in . . ."

"Constantine, *really*. Did I ever hurt you?"

The doctor simply stared at him. The elevator doors opened, and he gestured for Louis to enter first. The doors closed and the car began to rise.

"He carried no identity papers?"

"He was naked."

"Naked?"

"The men who found him dressed him in an old Army uniform—something they scrounged up at the site." The elevator started to slow. Constantine took a key from the pocket of his gray lab coat and inserted it into one of the buttons; the elevator continued its ascent. "At first I thought the Army was taking its cannon fodder younger than usual."

Louis ignored the jibe. The elevator doors were opening.

They stepped out into a dark corridor at the top of the building. The locked ward. Lightbulbs dangled from ancient, thick, black cloth-wrapped cords. The hall had the air of a corridor far underground.

"You should feel at home here," Wallace said.

This was the floor where Slowslop had ordered the interrogation of Constantine Wallace and John MacNaughton. Louis and Gondarev had taken turns with each of the men in separate rooms, comparing stories, testing them on the most trivial points. Pain had not been a necessary part of those sessions, but the possibility of torture had never for a moment been in doubt. It had presided over the meetings like an invisible yet menacing third party; like Slowslop himself, who sat quietly in a darkened room at the end of the hall, awaiting their reports.

Louis would have used violence if ordered to do so, but logic, and a precisely planned series of questions, had served equally well to satisfy Slowslop. Louis had found that his honesty, and perhaps something less definable in his nature, usually persuaded people to tell him what he needed to know. He had treated both Wallace and MacNaughton with respect, and felt they should have returned the courtesy; but unfortunately, Gondarev had conducted himself like a brute, nearly undoing everything Hausmann strove to accomplish, and in the end the captain had turned the scientists against all of them. Now Constantine Wallace blindly hated the uniform and anyone who wore it, without discrimination. This prejudice was most unfair, but Hausmann understood its origin.

At the end of the hall, the doctor hesitated. Hausmann felt his skin prickling, as if a cobweb had been draped across his neck. To the left was Slowslop's former room. The Supreme Commander's presence seemed to fill it even now, sitting in the darkened chamber, one small spot of light from a reading lamp falling across his hands, his face in shadow. *"By the way, how is your sister?"*

It was the door to the right, however, that Constantine opened.

There were two windows, on either side of the bed, and each of them gave out on a view of yellowing willows, with the wire perimeter of the hospital grounds in the distance. The glass was old and full of ripples that made the willows seem to squirm as Louis stepped forward. He went to the foot of the bed and stared down at the boy, who was covered up to his shoulders.

Incongruously, the boy was still dressed in the brown dress-shirt of a private, with its single gleaming collar button. The shirt was the least puzzling element of the scene, however, for above the boy's head, between the bed and the wall, floated an array of curved vacuum tubes like the coils of a neon sign, leading to a large flask which contained a pair of immense coils that might have been electrodes or the filaments of an enormous lightbulb. Several large and fragile-looking tubes and bulbs were connected in series, the electronic equivalent of an alchemist's distillery. The entire assembly was apparently controlled by a large wooden cabinet to the left of the bed. At the sight of all the dials and switches Louis felt his mind go blank.

"What—what is all this?"

"Be very careful around it. Everything is finely tuned. I'm afraid to have too many people in here at once, for fear of distorting the field."

"But what are you doing?"

"We've been working with biomagnetics, trying to stabilize the boy's vital field—his . . . aura, for lack of a better word."

The apparatus looked suspiciously like something forbidden—research that should have been conducted only with Slowslop's approval, yet Slowslop had not mentioned it. Louis quickly checked the bulbs and tubes for some indication of a power source, but his electrical knowledge was not what it should have been. For all he knew, one of the restricted-type batteries could have been hidden inside the cabinet. But Constantine did not seem overly nervous about Louis observing the device, which suggested that it did not in fact utilize the power source developed by Charles Reif and George Tessera. The fact that something about the apparatus reminded him of the Sensorama in Room 306 could easily have been attributed to the fact that Constantine Wallace and John MacNaughton had been part of Tessera's original research team at the then-National Academy of Sciences, and had been involved in developing the early prototype of that very device.

There was a chair on the far side of the bed. Louis sat down and set the scanner case on the floor. He leaned toward the boy and searched his face, but there was nothing much to see. The features were the epitome of blankness. Because he lacked eyelashes, his eyelids appeared seamless, like those of a fetus. Pointed chin. Dark, close-cropped hair. Louis looked up and saw Constantine watching not him, but the dials of his machine.

"What would happen if you shut it off?" Louis asked.

The doctor looked horrified. "For all I know, this is the only thing keeping him stable. To shut it down now—"

"I'm not suggesting you turn it off. I was only asking. But I would like you to leave me alone with the boy."

"Alone?" Constantine's apprehension deepened. "Why?"

"I'm under no obligation to explain my orders to you," Hausmann said.

"Your orders? This boy is in my care."

"And you are in mine."

"What is Slowslop's interest in this?"

Good question, Louis thought; but he merely stared at the doctor until the man's panic flared. Finally Wallace managed to stammer, "You—you will not tamper with the apparatus."

"Of course not. I only wish a few moments to observe him. I am supposed to report on his condition, since you failed to."

"I—I'll be glad to prepare a report. If you can give me a few minutes—"

"Take all the time you need while I'm in here. But I've come all this way. I might as well see him for myself."

"There—there's really nothing else to see. This is it."

"Constantine. Please."

Louis stood up, and it was as if Gondarev were suddenly standing beside him again. The threat of imminent violence pervaded the room, and Constantine clearly had no stomach for it. Very pale now, he retreated toward the door. "I will be . . . across the hall."

"You might want to prepare the report you mentioned."

"Yes. Yes, I'll do that."

The door was too long in closing, so Hausmann crossed the room and snapped it shut, then threw the lock. He could hear Wallace's hesitant steps backing away across the hall. The other door opened but never shut. He imagined the doctor hovering, listening.

Louis stared for a moment at the hideous old wallpaper, like the cratered surface of something that had hung in space for eternities. If you stared at it long enough, faces began to grin at you, insects started to crawl. He pulled his eyes back to the boy and set the scanner on the chair.

He had never seen the scanner before today, but it was clearly more of the meteorite-powered technology to which the Army, and Orlovsky personally, claimed total priority. There was apparently no end to the applications George Tessera had found for the extraterrestrial energy source. The Sensorama was the most potent and important of Tessera's devices so far, but even the lesser gadgets were quite fascinating.

The scanner comprised two units locked together into one. The segment that fit in his left hand was squat and rectangular, with a rounded screen like a polished opal mounted on the upper surface; it bore six buttons, two black, three white, and one red. The red one was his only concern. Slowslop had already set the switches at the front of the box to the appropriate positions. This component of the scanner also contained a large round dial on the side; and, at the rear, a fifteen-pin cable connector and two coaxial jacks, apparently for transferring whatever the scanner recorded.

The right-side unit was half the size of the other, and rounded to fit comfortably in his hand. There were two silver buttons under his fingers, but Slowslop had said he need not worry about them. The device was set for automatic operation. A short rectangular tube jutted from the rear of this segment, and set in the end of it was the indicator screen. As he switched on the scanner, this screen filled with greenish blue light mixed with golden orange, in which colors beyond them seemed always at the edge of visibility. Unfamiliar combinations, unnamed hues: the telltale spectrum of the meteorite.

Louis rose and stood over the bed. The boy's face was pale and flattened, almost froglike; the eyes did not so much as flutter beneath the seamless lids.

The right-hand chamber of the scanner began to grow warm. A slight tingling sensation spread through the case, prickling the nerves of his fingers, shooting down his wrist and into his right forearm. He hesitated to put the indicator screen to his eye, but there was no other way to aim the thing. The shapes of the room were gradually becoming visible in the viewfinder. He tilted it until he could see the boy below him in the bed. He found the boy's face in the screen. Then he pressed the red recording button.

The image in the screen darkened, seeming to condense around the head of the boy. For an instant he thought he could see the boy's skull glowing beneath the flesh, as if it were formed of the same shimmering gold and green radiance that powered the scanner. Brilliant eyes glared up at him, burning from the screen, searing straight along his optic nerves and burying themselves like thin golden knives in the back of his brain.

He lowered the scanner, but the boy's eyes were still shut. He had not moved.

Calming himself, Louis began methodically to move the scanner down the boy's body, holding it away from his face while keeping his fingers locked on the buttons. There was no reason to think the scanner was anything like the Sensorama; no reason to think that merely looking into the light would harm him. Surely Slowslop would not have risked his most trusted Intelligence agent in such a manner. Just because he hadn't shared the workings or nature of the scanner with Louis did not necessarily mean that Slowslop himself did not completely understand the device.

Louis was used to receiving only exactly as much information as he needed to perform his duties. This was business as usual.

He passed the scanner slowly over the boy's throat, chest, and abdomen, peering into the viewer at arm's length, just to make sure he had it properly aimed.

A shiver passed through the boy, rattling the bed, and jarring the glassware perched above it.

Louis hesitated, holding the scanner in place, holding his breath. Had he imagined it?

The boy twitched again. Leaped so the bedsprings squealed. His mouth was gaping, audibly sucking air. His eyelids began to tremble, opening to narrow slits of blackness and moisture.

At that moment, the sinuous tubes above the bed began to glow. The large bulb above the bed gave off a crackling sound as tiny arcs of violet light leaped between the electrodes' poles.

The scanner began to hum in resonance with Constantine's apparatus, as if both had locked into the same frequency. The hum, inaudible a second ago, was already as loud as the buzzing of a fly, and growing louder as it rose in pitch.

Hausmann pressed the off switch, but the scanner seemed to be running itself. He was fearful of bringing it any closer to his body; it was burning his right hand badly. He snatched that hand out of the grip, and frantically jabbed at the buttons.

The boy's tremors continued to increase. The glass tube circuitry sparked and sizzled. The largest of the vacuum tubes was already full of black smoke that flared with sudden explosions of violet fire, like lightning striking through dense storm clouds.

"What's going on in there?" Constantine pounded on the door.

"Just a minute!" Louis struck the scanner with the side of his hand, finally triggering the power switch. The instant its whine began to subside, he thrust the scanner into its case and locked the lid. But the tubes of Constantine's therapeutic device were blackened with carbon, and the stormy reek of ozone filled the room.

Louis leaned over the boy and put a hand on his brow. His eyelids suddenly leaped open, flaring with golden light. Louis reeled backward into the chair and almost tumbled over onto his back.

An illusion, an afterimage from the scanner, he told himself. Nonetheless he covered his eyes until the glare had faded from his retinas.

When he looked again, the boy was gone.

He blinked.

No . . . not gone. There was something wrong with his eyes even now.

The boy was transparent, but fading into view; the longer he stared, the more clearly he saw him.

The apparatus against the wall continued to flicker and spark. That certainly contributed to his misperception that the boy was slipping in and out of sight.

Louis rose and bent over the bed. He couldn't possibly be vanishing. He was there in the bed—yes, quite clear. Quite clear. It was the coarse texture of his skin Louis saw, not the texture of the sheets beneath his head. Perhaps the greenish meteoritic glare had affected his eyes somehow.

The boy was solid. He was exactly as he had been.

Constantine's equipment, however, was another matter.

Louis finally unlocked the door and let the doctor enter.

"You'd better come in," he said. "Your equipment seems to be acting up."

Constantine went to the bed first, and checked the boy's condition, taking his pulse. Only when he saw that his patient was unharmed did he turn his attention to the equipment.

"My God . . ."

"It looked like an electrical fire," Louis said. "I didn't see an extinguisher."

Wallace turned furious eyes on him. "Get out of here!"

"I understand your—"

"Get away from my patient!"

Louis could have pressed his authority, but in truth he was glad to leave. He took a last look at the boy, to reassure himself that he was still completely substantial, then went into the hall and found the elevator. As he pressed the button and stood waiting for the car to arrive, he remembered that he could not leave the locked ward without an escort—without Dr. Wallace's keys.

He stood frozen in a moment of panic, until the doors opened suddenly. Dr. John MacNaughton, gaunt and grim, his eyes ringed in dark circles, started to step from the car. Dismay and disbelief rapidly overtook his expression of utter exhaustion when he saw Hausmann blocking his way.

"You . . . " he muttered.

"Hello, John. I don't wish to presume, but could you give me a ride to the ground?"

MacNaughton, clenching his jaw, stepped back into the car. They dropped quickly and in silence, the scientist eyeing him covertly but making no attempt to open a conversation. When the doors opened, Louis managed a smile, then strode out without another word.

The staff car was waiting for him. As he slipped into the luxury and security of the dark, richly appointed car, he found himself remembering the face of the boy. Whenever he blinked, he could see the afterimage of those burning golden green eyes.

What manner of illusion left an afterimage?

"West End Hotel," he told the driver when he had caught his breath. Once the car began to move he set the scanner's case on his lap and flipped open the lid.

The device was quiet now; it had cooled quite a bit. But the indicator screen was alive and flickering with meaningless patterns, tiny red flecks, sliding trails of ruby light that came and went. The irregular shapes of failure. He had not completed the scan.

Louis let the case fall shut, staring numbly out the window at the dying willow trees.

FIVE

KRYSTOFF MOHOLY WAS THE LAST TO ARRIVE. Elena could always identify him by the grating sound his cello case made as he dragged it unceremoniously along the floorboards of the hall, allowing it to bump up every single stair until he reached the landing opposite her flat. By then she was waiting for him, she and the others, with the door open.

"Mr. Moholy!" she said into the hall, loud enough for those neighbors who might be listening, although by now they had grown accustomed to the sounds of the twice-weekly rehearsals. She shut the door when he was inside, whispering, "You make an unconvincing musician."

"Damn heavy instrument I chose."

Krystoff shed his coat and went to the radiator, warming his hands directly on the pipes since they hardly gave off any heat at all. The only time the flat ever felt warm in the winter months was when the group had gathered to warm it. And then it was almost cheerful and lively—or would have been, if not for the grim nature of their meetings.

There were seven besides herself. She had to open the curtain of her sleeping alcove so that all could have a place to sit. There were four chairs pushed in around the table, and a sofa barely big enough for two. Her flat consisted of one room, with a sink and a small stove. Even so, on nights when she was alone, it seemed a vast cave. An ice cave.

Her visitors had put their instrument cases against the walls, on the bed, in the kitchen. For appearance's sake, and because one never knew when they might be interrupted, they kept the instruments out and near to hand; but music was hardly their agenda. Instead, after they had engaged in a reasonable amount of casual socializing, Elena would put on a recording, turn up the volume, and underneath the noise they would discuss their plans.

Tonight, as soon as she switched on the music, mounting a continuous tape reel on the cabinet in the corner, Krystoff pulled out Diaghilev's binoculars and set them in the middle of the table.

"Does anyone recognize these?" he asked.

A medley of traditional folk dances, approved by Orlovsky, swirled through the flat as the cell members studied the binoculars. Krystoff picked up the binoculars and activated a switch she hadn't previously noticed. Between the two lens barrels was a third, somewhat smaller and set with a cluster of lenses that gave off a strange golden green light.

Marnham, leaning over the table, hissed between his teeth, "It's more of the same."

"Yes."

Elena didn't understand, and she could see confusion among the others as well. "The same what?" she asked, reaching for the binoculars.

Krystoff gave them all a sterner look than usual. "These binoculars are powered by Slowslop's new energy source."

She nearly dropped the binoculars. She felt they should have been somehow shielded.

"Can you turn them off?" she asked.

Krystoff clicked a switch and the lights blinking from the central barrel faded.

"The meteoritic ore, you mean," she said.

"Exactly."

"I didn't realize they had gotten this far along," said Felix Milanova.

"What it demonstrates," said Krystoff, "is how little we know of the Empire's actual plans. All we know is that they've somehow reduced some of our best people to babbling idiots."

"Yes," said Ada Gauss, rising animatedly. "Have you seen Diaghilev?"

"I've seen him," Elena said wearily.

"He's writing outrageous things on scraps of newspaper, dried leaves, bits of fabric. He's not afraid of anything now."

"Because he's too much of a lunatic to pose a threat," Krystoff said bitterly. "Somehow they've destroyed his mind."

"He came up to me in Downtown Station yesterday," said Felix. "He didn't seem to recognize me, but he gave me this."

Felix pulled out a train schedule, crumpled to tissue softness, gouged repeatedly by a pen-point. Around the margins of the schedule, and in every available bit of blank space, Diaghilev had penned a rant without beginning or end, a discursion on what might have been the nature of the timetables themselves: "... *the arrival inevitable unforeseen the flaming wanderer through the black tunnel hurtling hurling shields stones and schedules through the eyes hid in smokepools swamped stations scattered in rust and sunken shining ...*"

"And Stillson sits in the park and stares and laughs."

Marnham said, "According to new sources in the penitentiary, they were both transferred from confinement on the same day, then taken to Intelligence Headquarters."

"And what happened there?" Elena asked.

Krystoff scowled, and she regretted asking the question. It was a source of perpetual frustration that they had not managed to infiltrate the West End Hotel. The Third Force had not a single agent close to Slowslop, let alone Lord Orlovsky.

There had been great hopes for Gregor Stillson. He'd been a promising candidate for infiltration, with political ties that eventually might have brought him to Orlovsky's side. But he had been picked up for thought-crimes unrelated to his underground activities. While patronizing a shop whose proprietor was notoriously critical of the Emperor, Stillson had muttered some word of agreement with the shopkeeper's diatribes. That evening he had opened the door to find the shopkeeper pointing him out to a contingent of Imperial Guards. Such traps awaited even the most innocent of citizens.

Before anyone spoke, there was a rap on the door. The musicians instantly grabbed their instruments and took up the poses of interrupted players. Elena switched off the tape, which cut off perhaps too abruptly, without the usual squawks and lingering chords a real band would have made. As she checked to make sure everyone was ready, she saw the binoculars still sitting in the middle of the table. She gestured frantically at Krystoff to remove them.

She put her eye to the spyhole and stifled a cry.

The man in the hall wore the uniform of an Imperial soldier. His face was hidden; he appeared to be leaning to put his ear against the door. When he drew back, revealing his features, her terror eased only slightly.

"Who is it?" Krystoff hissed. He had concealed the binoculars under his coat.

Elena swallowed. "My brother."

"Elena?" Louis called, pounding on the door now.

"Well?" she whispered.

"Open it!" said Krystoff.

The others tried to hide their consternation. She opened the door and there he stood, in full uniform, smiling but nervous. He started to open his arms for an embrace, but then his eyes went past her to the crowd of "musicians." His hands fell to his sides.

"Oh, I'm sorry."

"Come in, Louis," she said, catching one of his hands.

"I'm interrupting. I should have called ahead. I didn't realize you'd have—"

"No, it's all right, come in. You're very welcome."

Still Louis hesitated; the faces of her friends were not exactly inviting. Only Krystoff managed a smile. He came forward to take Louis's hand and greet him warmly.

"Lieutenant Hausmann!" he said. "How fine to see you!"

"Yes. Moholy, isn't it?"

"Krystoff, please. Come in, come in, we were just finishing, really."

"Oh, please," Louis said, "there's no need—not on my account. Elena, I only came by to extend an invitation. I won't take up your time."

"It's all *right*, Louis," she said emphatically. "They were just going."

"But . . . well, you mustn't rush off," Louis said, addressing all of them. "You sounded wonderful from the hall. If you wish to rehearse, I'll just wait till you're done. I love those old tunes!"

"We were just finishing up," she said. "I usually make tea for all of us about now. Would you like some?"

Louis stood nervously, stared at, trying to keep a smile on his face. How strange he looked in his uniform; after all these years, no matter how well it fit him, she could not quite believe the path her brother had taken. How could he have forgotten or grown blind to the things that seemed so obvious in their youth? How could he have put himself in the service of the decrepit Paulo Orlovsky and his sinister accomplice?

After filling the kettle, she turned to find the others quietly packing their instruments and taking their leave. She tried not to show her relief. Indeed, she supposed she should be grateful for the time alone with Louis. They hardly ever saw each other these days.

"I feel terrible," he said, as she set cups on the cleared table.

"You shouldn't," she said.

There was no lemon, which Louis had always liked in his tea, but she found a few prized lumps of sugar in the cupboard. It occurred to her that he probably had access to all the sugar he wanted; the items she scrounged and saved and fought for in the markets were probably deposited on his table as if by divine intervention. She felt suddenly embarrassed by her dingy, cluttered apartment. The tablecloth was full of holes; the chairs creaked whenever one sat.

"So how is the Empire these days, Lieutenant?"

Elena spun around, startled to find Krystoff still present. She had seen him slip out the door, whispering to Marnham, but now he was back, taking a seat at the table.

"Call me Louis, please. I can't speak of the whole Empire, but my little corner of it is well enough."

She reached for a third cup, wondering what Krystoff intended. There was an odd, mocking look on his face, as if he intended to toy with her brother, but such a game seemed too dangerous even for him.

"And what corner might that be?" Krystoff asked. "Are you stationed at the base, ordnance depot, or somewhere else?"

"My duties take me all over the Empire."

"East End? West End?"

"From one to the other." Louis smiled and glanced at Elena, apologetic. "I can't be more specific, you understand."

Krystoff shrugged, spreading his hands. "Of course. One can't compromise state secrets. Who knows who might be listening in; there are spies everywhere."

"Krystoff, please," Elena said. This was a dangerous tack to be taking.

"What? Oh, I meant *Onegin*'s spies, of course." He looked from her to Louis and began to laugh. "You didn't think . . . oh no! Not Imperial spies—what a ludicrous concept!" His laughter carried him from the chair. He paced the apartment and went to the window, and pulled aside the curtain very slightly. "Spies . . ."

Louis cleared his throat. "Lord Orlovsky has asked about you, Elena."

She could see Krystoff, from the corner of her eye, stiffen and slowly turn to stare at her, unnoticed by her brother. His eyes burned into her, but she dared not look up at him.

"Really?" she said, suppressing any reaction at all. Krystoff deliberately turned away, as if intent on the street and oblivious to their conversation. "I'm surprised. I can't imagine why."

"You were always a favorite of his. It's only natural that he ask about you every now and then. He wonders how you are. In fact, he asked me to extend an invitation, if you'd be willing."

"An invitation?"

"Yes, to dine. With, well, the three of us, I suppose."

"Three?" And then she realized who the third must be. "Oh, you mean Theodore?"

"Of course. Would you like that?"

"I had hoped you'd come here to see me for your own reasons," she said stiffly, unable to hide her disappointment even in Krystoff's presence.

Louis tried to deflect her anger with a laugh. "Elena! It's not as though I were under orders to invite you. I—"

Fortunately, at that moment the kettle shrilled and she went to silence it. When she had filled the pot, she turned to discover Louis standing again, his hat on his head.

"I'm sorry, Elena," he said, his eyes downcast. "I'll come another time. When there's nothing else. I'm sorry."

He started to pull away, even as she reached for his arm to hold him there. But Krystoff was suddenly between them, brushing her aside, taking Louis's elbow.

"Really, Lieutenant, are you off now? Because I was just leaving myself."

"Yes, I think I'd better go."

"Louis . . ."

"Goodbye, Elena." He kissed her quickly on the cheek, and then he was at the door.

Krystoff opened it for him. "I'll be right down, Lieutenant."

As Louis started down the stairs, Krystoff closed the door and whirled on Elena. His face was transparent; she could read every thought, could see how he believed every scheme of his would come to fruition now, through her.

"Don't say a thing," she said.

"Elena, you must—"

"You cannot tell me what to do, Krystoff. We're equals in this, and I make my own decisions."

"But I already know what you will decide. You will do what is best for everyone!"

"Everyone except myself," she whispered. "You don't know these people."

"How can you say that? I've devoted my life to their overthrow, as have you. How can I not know them?"

"Be glad you can never know them as I have—as I do. Just go, Krystoff. Say no more to me tonight."

He smiled a mad smile, seized her jaw, and kissed her on the mouth. It was shocking to her that his passion surfaced only in such moments. She saw clearly how the lack of such moments, and the slow erosion of their plans for resistance, had led to the decline of their relationship since Diaghilev's abduction. But as long as there was hope, as long as Krystoff saw the imminence of victory, he was demonstrative with his affection; he was carried away in his dreams of revolution, and to the extent that she was a part of those dreams, he desired her.

But he had other things to do right now. "Hold my cello for me," he said. "And you'd better take these. It wouldn't do to be caught carrying them around tonight." Reaching under his coat, he pulled out the binoculars and handed them to her. "By the way, I think Louis may have been followed. There's someone down below, watching your flat. He arrived with your brother."

He kissed her again, more fleetingly, then pulled the door shut behind him. His last comment had unnerved her.

She went to the window and pulled aside the curtain. There was someone out there, alone in the pool of light below a streetlamp at the corner. She strained to see the figure, but at such a distance she could make out little.

Louis and Krystoff appeared on the street below, heading away from the watcher. The figure made no move to follow them. She had the distinct impression that he was looking directly at her window.

She dropped the curtains and lowered the lights so as not to cast a shadow. Then, peering out once more, she raised the binoculars to her eyes.

At first she saw nothing. It was not merely the darkness, for no matter how she scanned the Downtown skyline, not a speck or streak of light appeared.

She fumbled with various small mechanisms on the barrel of the binoculars until a small switch moved beneath her finger and the bluish orange glow sprang from the tiny lenses. As she raised the binoculars to her face, some of this light shone straight back into her eyes, and for a moment that was all she saw. Then she saw rooftops, lit windows, a woman caught in a sheet of broken mirror, washing under her arms with a cloth dipped in a cracked enamel basin. She lowered the lenses and trained them on the street, where the cobbles were so distinct that she could almost see what lay between them. The picture was astonishingly bright.

Suddenly she saw a pair of shoes and gray kneesocks, the lower legs of the watcher.

Yes, it was he. Wearing short pants in freezing weather. Why, it looked like a boy!

A boy, very serious, his face almost like a manikin's in its blankness. The Empire certainly had not set a boy on her brother's trail, but someone might have paid a street urchin to watch her flat. She couldn't tell, despite the brightness of the lenses, if he was actually looking up at her. The flickering of golden green that seemed to dance in his eyes was no doubt an effect of the binoculars, with their odd power source.

Now someone was approaching along the avenue, walking right up to the boy as if she would speak to him. A woman, judging from the long, gray hooded cloak she wore. Elena had one just like it. The woman went straight up to the boy and appeared to speak to him. The boy turned abruptly, slipping around the lamppost, moving rapidly down the street. As soon as he left the lamplight, Elena lost sight of him. He reappeared, passing beneath a window a quarter block away, moving so swiftly that he seemed to glide. Then he was gone into the next stretch of darkness, and this time she did not see him again.

Elena turned the binoculars back to the lamppost.

The woman stood looking after the boy. Then, very slowly, she turned. She looked toward Elena's building, and in a gesture that might have been frustration, though it seemed like revelation, she threw back the hood of her cape.

Long red hair spilled out. In the lamplight she could see it was streaked very faintly with gray. The woman stared straight at Elena now, squinting toward her window with an intensely curious and fearful expression.

Elena lowered the binoculars and moved back from the window, but before the curtains fell she had a clear view of the street.

The boy remained at the lamppost, as if he had never moved. But the woman was gone—or had never been there.

It made sense, in a way, for the woman she had seen in the binoculars, with the ash-streaked red hair, was herself.

Trembling, Elena set the binoculars on the windowsill, knowing—but not understanding—what she must do. Reaching for her hooded gray cloak, she headed for the door.

Outside, the air was dry and cold, and a wind tasting of ice threaded through the street; her lungs ached at every breath.

The boy was still there. She started toward him, then hesitated. The woman she'd seen in the binoculars had crossed the street with her head covered.

Despite the cold, Elena drew back her hood. The wind bit into her ears, burnishing her cheeks. Feeling somewhat more in control, she headed toward him.

She had no reason to fear a boy, she told herself. There must be some innocent explanation for his presence; but if he had followed Louis, why did he linger to watch her?

As she drew closer, she found her hands fingering the edge of her hood. She fought the urge to cover her head. It was so cold! She tried to take a different route than the woman she had seen, stepping onto the opposite sidewalk and then heading past the lamps toward the boy.

Finally, to further assert her free will, she looked back at her window, fearful of seeing the curtains slightly parted and herself looking out.

But in the unlit window it was impossible to see if anyone waited behind the curtain.

Looking ahead, she found the boy had moved. He was no longer at the corner lamppost but instead waited at the one beyond that, across the street. She did not see how he could have moved so quickly.

As she passed the corner lamppost herself, she felt a peculiar sense of relief, as if now she had definitely broken whatever spell had drawn her down here. Still she kept on, intrigued by the boy. As she stepped off the curb, she glanced down to make sure she was not stepping into a storm grating. When she looked up again, the boy had once more receded into the distance, watching and waiting under a farther lamp.

She hurried across the street, keeping her eyes fixed on him even when she stepped up to the other curb. She would not let him out of her sight.

Now he was close—close enough that his features were as clear as they had been in the binoculars. There were no more lampposts between them, and she would not so much as blink until she could touch him.

A moment before she reached the boy, he slowly began to turn away.

"Wait!" she cried. Her voice sounded flat, as if she were standing in a small, shut room instead of the open street.

He continued to turn, and then, without a sound, he fled. It was exactly as she had seen him do from above. He vanished into the dark and then reappeared briefly under the next lamppost, and then the one beyond that, and the one beyond that, flickering more frequently as he dwindled in the distance.

She watched the darkness for a long time. The street was impossibly still. Again she had the feeling that she was standing in a small enclosed space, as if the receding avenue were an illusion painted on a flattened surface. Where were the other people? Even with the restrictions on automobiles, some traffic should have been in evidence—at the very least, an Imperial patrol van. But as far as she could tell, she was alone, peering into the dark for any last sign of the boy.

Then, far out there, she saw a spark. It came again, closer and brighter. Closer, brighter. Closer—and now burning steadily. Growing. It was not the boy returning, but something mechanical. She could feel the pulse of engines, the churning storm of pistons, steam, and steel. Impossible, but here it came. An engine, a monstrous train thundering down on her. Tearing up the avenue, roaring between the tenements, as if it had veered from its track and careened out of control through the city.

Elena could not move. She watched it come on, the headlamp rising, carving a green tunnel into the night air. Around the train itself, a flaring corona of dark fire, flames edged with ultraviolet and infrared. The sound of engines merged into a steady roar like the sound of a furnace. It filled the sky, a blazing star, pushing a wall of intense heat ahead of it, forcing her to shield her eyes.

She turned, then, and ran. Her cloak in flames, her hair sizzling, her skin blistering, she ran for shelter and found the door of her building.

Slamming it behind her, she sank to the ground, her face in her hands, sobbing.

When she pulled her hands away from her face, she was amazed to find her flesh unsinged. Her hair hung down, still long. Her cloak was whole.

What did it mean?

The boy, the train, the fiery onrushing star?

What did they mean?

The boy had come with Louis tonight, trailing in his wake. And the binoculars had appeared after Diaghilev's stint in the West End Hotel.

Intelligence Headquarters. Orlovsky and Slowslop. The strange meteoritic ore.

All the mysteries came together in one place:

The West End Hotel.

She knew she could not long ignore the Emperor's invitation.

SIX

"ELENA! ELENA!"

Her mother was calling. Elena pulled the pillow over her head, trying to drown out the sound; but she had already heard too much. The sun was up; she could no longer ignore the day, even though her shades were drawn and the room itself was as black as she could make it. The house was full of noise already, with cars coming and going on the cobbled drive below the house, and the voices of the servants in the hall outside her room.

Suddenly someone began pounding on her door. "Elena, get up! It's nearly eleven! Lord Orlovsky and Mr. Slowslop will be here any time!"

It was her brother, Louis, calling from the hall. She heard him try the knob, but she had locked the door before retiring. Nearly eleven o'clock, Sunday morning . . . and the last time she'd looked at the clock it had been nearly five. When had she last gotten a full night's sleep? She could feel the weight of open books spread face-down on her bed, lying on her ankles like sleeping cats. When she shifted, moaning, several of them slid and then thumped to the floor.

"I know you're in there," Louis said, and suddenly she heard the lock click open. As she pulled the pillow away from her head, Louis came into the room.

"What do you—how did you *do* that?" she said, sitting up in the gloom.

Her brother grinned, holding up a curved bit of wire. "I figured out this old lock months ago," he said. "I've been saving the trick till I needed it." He sat on the foot of her bed. "Come on, Elena, you've got to get up. Mother is frantic."

She fell back, pulling the covers over her head. Another book slid to the floor. Bedsprings squealed as he bent to retrieve it.

"Translanthanide compounds, telluric screws," he said. "What have you been reading?"

"Go away."

"You're not still dreaming of joining the Academy, are you? You're lucky even to be in the university, Elena; although what you'll do when you're out, I can't imagine. What man would want to marry a woman who's always got her nose in books and beakers?"

"I thought I told you to go away."

"Well, how do you think you'll get in?"

"Dr. Tessera intends to sponsor me."

"Old George, eh?" Louis laughed. "Why does he bother with you, I wonder? Unless . . . could it be . . . he feels a certain *affection?*"

She grabbed the heaviest thing that came to hand, in this case a textbook of physical chemistry, and flung it. Louis ducked it easily, and as she reached for another, he slipped out of the room, laughing.

"You'd better get up," he called as he ran away down the stairs.

She sighed, looking down at the book in her hands. Ironically, it was a collection of George Tessera's lectures on optics and electromagnetics. She smiled at the ridiculous thought that her professor, stern and pedantic, might feel anything but the respect any mentor feels for a promising student. At extravagant moments she thought of herself as his protégée, but always quelled the thought as egotistic. Still, he had promised his sponsorship if she applied for graduate studies in the Academy, and she had hopes of eventually becoming an integral member of his research team instead of merely a technician. Lacking acceptance in the Academy's graduate program, armed with nothing but a university degree, she might still pursue a "career" in the sciences; but this would amount to little more than replacing vacuum tubes, keeping logs, and other menial work assisting the *real* scientists. Elena intended to be one of the moving forces in science, like her idols—George Tessera, Charles Reif, John MacNaughton, Thomas Reich, Wilhelm Draun, and Constantine Wallace. To see the way they worked together, intense and dedicated, filled her with desire and stoked her ambition. She knew it was possible that she would one day make herself a place at the cutting edge of knowledge. Given the opportunity, she would make great discoveries, and prove herself worthy of joining the nation's finest team of scientists. By virtue of her intellect and abilities, by steady application and perseverance, she would make a great contribution to humanity.

These were the concerns of scientists. To think anything less of Dr. Tessera was absurd. Besides, he was at least thirty years older than she.

She looked wistfully at her strewn books when she finally dragged herself out of bed. Gathering them and stacking them neatly on her desk, she regretted that she couldn't spend the rest of the day in study—or, better, at the laboratory. What did she care for society, for formal visits by creaking old ladies and lords like Orlovsky?

In truth, she loathed the old man, his vague yet unwavering smile, his spotted skull which always looked freshly varnished, and the way he continually tried to trap her hands between his. But she could not very well avoid him. He had been a great comfort to her mother the Countess, and a very generous benefactor to the Hausmann family, since the death of her father, Count Otto. It would have been disrespectful to flee his presence, as she always wished she could do. He made her squeamish, yet Paulo Orlovsky had assisted the Hausmanns in every way, even providing some of the funds for her education; and he spoke of finding Louis a position in the Army or in industry, as the boy preferred.

"I feel as if Otto's children are my own," she had once heard him tell her mother. "I can deny them nothing, Countess. Nothing. Especially since I will always feel some responsibility for Otto's death."

"Nonsense," the Countess had said. "An accident. An accident, Paulo! Don't torture yourself."

"Even so—"

Even so, Elena thought. And wondered why he felt responsible. She went into her bath chamber and washed at the basin. Her hair was a tangled mess. As she struggled with a comb, she noted more of the premature gray streaks that were her mother's legacy. The Countess dyed her hair, but Elena thought the gray gave her a sort of dignity, and she was glad in a way to see the bands thickening.

Her mother was calling again, urging her to hurry. Elena restrained herself from screaming back, abandoning an attempt to pin up her hair. She swept it severely from her face and snapped a band around it, then reached for the blouse she had tossed aside the night before and the same thick blue skirt she had worn yesterday. What did she care for appearances? She was a student, a scientist; she was pleased to make herself unsuitable for formal company.

She pulled on high stockings and laced up heavy black heel-less shoes, then stomped heavily from the room and down the stairs with the chemistry textbook under her arm. Her mother, waiting at the bottom of the stairs, heard her steps and turned to greet her. Elena felt a thrill of satisfaction when she saw her mother's dismay.

"Elena! What do you mean by this?"

"By what?" she said calmly, still descending. The front door was open; a breeze wafted up the stairs as a guest entered from the foyer. The Countess was torn between greeting him and hurrying Elena back up to her room; torn between graciousness and rage.

"Get back up there and change into something appropriate!"

"What's wrong with this?"

"I think it's perfectly lovely," said a voice from the entry. The Countess faltered, turning away from Elena.

"Oh, Theodore." She hurried to take Slowslop's hands, leading him toward the stairs. He tipped his head back to gaze up at Elena; his eyes were hidden as always behind the smoked spectacles he wore indoors and out. "She's being obstinate."

"As we expect of Miss Elena." He bowed slightly. "Good afternoon—or should I say, good morning?"

"How late *were* you up last night?" the Countess asked. "It's ridiculous, how these studies of yours are ruining your complexion."

"Mother . . ."

"And where is Lord Orlovsky? Not with you, Theo?"

"Slightly delayed. He asked me to come ahead."

The Countess took Slowslop by the arm and led him around the stairs; as she went, she cast a stinging glance at Elena, who was long since immune to such looks.

Elena went straight to the kitchen. It had been a good eighteen hours since her last meal, and she was ravenous. She picked at the luncheon platters until the chef prepared her one of her own; then she went into the small kitchen greenhouse. It was always humid and quiet, smelling of herbs and orchids. There she ate, staring at the high stone walls of the rear garden, gray and gloomy, full of frost-stricken plants and tangled bare branches, hanging planters from which colorless fronds and dried stalks dangled.

As she ate, she heard footsteps behind her; a tall reflection shimmered on the glass.

"Might I join you?" said Theodore Slowslop.

She turned with her mouth full, and nodded. Theo unnerved her, although not as much as Lord Orlovsky. Slowslop at least seemed to have all his faculties. He had devoted his intellect to civil engineering, the orchestration of large projects. His latest project, in the service of Orlovsky, was the new Grand Central Railway. The Grand Central had been her father's dream, too; one line uniting the nation, instead of a cluster of small local lines, the *Phaeton's* and *Courier's*, whose schedules were rarely coordinated. Old track was a disaster waiting to happen, as were the old trains, charming but inefficient, many of them still steam-driven despite the advances in engine technology. Her father had designed and built the first Alpha-type locomotive; but he had never seen it glide along its first mile of gleaming new track. Otto Hausmann had, she believed, always respected Slowslop, and so she accorded him respect as well.

Toward Orlovsky, her father the Count had been less charitable.

She wondered what he would have thought of Slowslop now that Theo had devoted himself to Orlovsky, wasting his brilliance on the old man's grandiose schemes.

Slowslop dragged a wrought-iron chair across the flagstones edged with bright, damp dichondra. He settled there, not looking at Elena, but gazing at the garden as if seeking whatever might have caught her interest.

"How are your studies?"

"Going very well, thanks," she said, since his interest seemed genuine. "I'm doing better than I had hoped."

"Is it true what Louis tells me? That you're hoping to enter the Academy?"

"Well . . ." She felt herself grow flushed. "Not immediately, of course. I'm only taking the first step, by applying for graduate work under Professor Tessera."

"I applaud you," Slowslop said. "You can't be ignorant of the resistance to females in that area."

Now she grew even warmer. "Of course not. It's infuriating, but I think I can succeed."

"Where others have failed." Slowslop nodded. "I'm sure you can. Your father would be very proud of you, Elena."

She felt a smile, involuntary, and a glimmer of pride in herself. "You think so?"

"I know it. He was a fine engineer. I believe he hoped you would find your way into a similar field. Something progressive."

"Me?" she said, faintly surprised. "Didn't he hope it for Louis, instead?"

"Not 'instead,' no," Slowslop said with a trace of amusement. "I think Otto suspected Louis had somewhat different interests."

They both laughed together. She was surprised to see Theo smiling; it was the most at ease she had ever seen him. And yet, almost immediately, as if the pressure of her direct gaze had caused him to retract into himself, his mouth grew very thin and strict again, and he settled his glasses more firmly on his nose.

"Elena . . ."

The mood had decidedly changed.

"You are very important to Lord Orlovsky, as you know."

She waited for him to say something more. After a long interval, she nodded. "Yes, I know."

He seemed uncertain how to proceed. She had never seen him uncertain of anything before; silent, yes, but always in deliberation. Now he seemed at a loss.

"You and Louis are like his own children, since Otto's death."

"I know he feels that way."

"But—but even more than that. He wants the best of everything for your family, but most particularly for you. He is very fond of you, Elena."

"Well, and I'm fond of him, of course," she said, trying to hide her discomfort. Lying did not come easily to her, but she did not want to insult Paulo or offend Theodore. "I can never hope to repay what he's given me personally. I know I certainly could never have afforded the expense of the university."

"Nonsense! The Grand Central will pay for itself one day, my dear, and when it does, your father's share in it will flow to your family. But in the meantime, Paulo vowed to take care of the three of you, and I assure you he intends to keep that promise. But . . . he wishes to do something *more* for you."

She realized suddenly what Slowslop was about to say. Word of her desire to enter the Academy had reached Paulo, and he was going to use his power to secure a place for her. She would be even more deeply in his debt, and yet . . . she would not turn down such an offer. Although she wanted to gain entrance to the Academy program on her own merits, she also knew that merit was only a fraction of the real consideration. The main, and nearly insurmountable, obstacle was that she was female. And this obstacle no amount of intelligence, discipline, or dedication on her part could ever surmount.

But with Orlovsky's help, with his backing—even more than that of George Tessera—she knew the doors of the Academy would open to her.

She waited for Slowslop to offer this gift on behalf of her benefactor, Paulo Orlovsky.

"You know," he said quietly, leaning closer now, with a sense of urgency threading through his words, "Orlovsky has a great future. I have seen it, Elena, believe me, or I would not have allied myself with him. He relies on me to achieve the physical accomplishment of his dreams, but the dreams themselves are his, and without them none of this would come about. None of this glory.

"Paulo believes you deserve a special place in that future. Your family, too, of course—but for you, a particularly prized honor. One he hopes your father would have approved."

In the center of her being, at the core of her hopes and fears, a cold lump began to congeal. She opened her mouth to speak, but nothing came out; only a chill breath that felt as if it must have emanated from some void that had never known contact with a living being.

At that instant, looking up, she saw Paulo Orlovsky himself, standing behind the steamed glass, between the greenhouse and the kitchen. He was looking her way, smiling fondly, but his eyes did not seem to be on her, quite. His attention seemed to be wandering. For her own part, she felt herself unable to turn away. It was as if Slowslop were a ventriloquist's manikin, mouthing words that were forming in Orlovsky's brain at this very instant.

"For you, my daughter . . . child . . . a very special place at Paulo's side. A place in a noble line. The conjunction of two great families that will give rise to a greater one."

"No," she whispered, uncertain if she really spoke.

Through the sweating glass, she saw Lord Orlovsky extend his hand.

"We come to ask, then, Elena, if you would consider taking the title of Lady Orlovsky."

There were no words for what she felt. As she stood, the metal chair clattered backward into orchid pots. She moved away from Slowslop, whose mouth was like a bloodless wound; and although Lord Orlovsky was directly in front of her, she pushed the door open, nearly toppling him as she hurried past.

Orlovsky sank back, looking shocked and fearful, raising one hand as if to ward off a blow. Glancing back, seeing him in such a pathetic stance, she found the nerve to turn and face him. Now she realized why he had taken such care of her family; not for her father's sake, but in hopes of securing *her*. In rejecting him, she imperiled her family's safety; but it was illusory, worthless, if this was its only foundation.

"Never!" she spat at him. "Never, never, never!"

"Child," he began.

"Yes, I am a child, compared to you. What you've done, what you ask, is disgusting. I will never agree. Never!"

"I *ask* nothing," he said, straightening now that he realized she intended him no physical harm. He seemed to rise out of himself, continuing to stiffen until he was taller than she had ever seen him, as if something of enormous power and cunning had camouflaged itself in an old man and now stepped forth to display its full strength. She wondered if anyone else had ever seen this Orlovsky, so calculating. So evil.

"I command," he said. "I *command!*"

Elena turned and ran through the kitchen, through the house, down the drive. Cars were still coming in for the party, so the gates were open, and out she rushed into the street. For a long time she did not know where she was running, but gradually she realized that there was only one place to go. One place where she felt safe. She saw with total clarity the ruin of her career, of her life. Saw that she would never gain admission to the Academy now, for any number of reasons, all of which might be attributed to Paulo Orlovsky.

How long had he been planning this? Since before her father's death? Planning and plotting and waiting, yes; for she knew love played no part in his scheme. He wanted her, but not for love.

Gradually, as she approached the grounds of the university and the National Academy, she slowed to an exhausted walk.

It was some consolation to realize that no matter what choice she made, it would all end the same way for her. If she agreed to wed Orlovsky—hideous thought!—that would mean sacrificing her career as well. At least she had been honest. She tried desperately to discover some way out of the trap, but the more she thought about it, the more she realized that it had been constructed around her for years. It had no doors.

What was to become of her now? What of her brother? What of her mother, the manor, and the name of Hausmann?

As she crossed the damp lawns of the university, she could not help wondering if this might be her last trip across the grass. The huge gray buildings were dark and quiet. The Academy, an enormous cube wrapped in bare girders, was even quieter and darker inside, and the air itself felt ponderous. She hurried down the corridors, followed by the echo of her footsteps, and into the basement. At the last moment, standing in the hallway strung with bare lightbulbs, she panicked; but then she found the key to the laboratory in her pocket, and hope flared again.

Maybe George can help me, she thought. *He's brilliant; he knows everything. Surely this is a problem just like all the others he's solved. There must be an objective solution somewhere, and he will help me find it. He'll fight to keep me on, won't he? He can't just let me go. Orlovsky has no power over him. The scientists are loyal only to truth.*

She put her key in the lock of the office door and pushed it open. The inner offices were all dark. She had never seen the place completely deserted.

Standing in the darkened room where she had spent so many hours, she felt her confidence begin to return. *Paulo can't stop me,* she thought. *It's paranoid to think he has such power. My place is here, and he can't keep me from it.*

Elena wandered past the scientists' small offices; some looked as if their occupants had been snatched away in the midst of a cataclysm; others were so tidy and organized that it was hard to believe they had ever been occupied. George Tessera's was moderately cluttered. She had come seeking his guidance, but in his absence she had to content herself with sitting at his desk, wondering what he might have told her. She touched his books, his pens, thinking that Louis had not been so far wrong after all. Only it had not been George Tessera who felt an "affection" for her.

She almost could have laughed at the situation if it hadn't been so horrifying. And if the implications for her future had not been so grim.

The upper drawer of George's desk was unlocked; she slid it open an inch. How little she knew of him, really; as a teacher he was thorough, methodical, but revealed little of himself. How she wished she knew him better! It was difficult to imagine what he might tell her. Seeking clues to his nature, she opened the drawer another few inches.

Coins and clips and pencil shavings; twists of wire and electrical components; notes scrawled on foolscap, the ink-encrusted nib of a fountain pen; and a key.

Without another thought, she snatched up the key and hurried out of George's office to a solid metal door at the back of the main office. She jabbed the key into that door, twisted—

And the door opened.

Heart hammering, Elena backed away. She listened for any faint sound from the outer corridors, but for all she could tell she was the only soul in the building at that moment.

The cold glow of a single utility light shone out from between the crowded aisles of equipment in the room beyond. In the center of the room sat the Beam Machine.

The Beam Machine was huge and cumbersome; it had been built in this room and could never be moved without first being dismantled. The crux of the device was a huge hollow sphere studded with lenses, mounted so that it could rotate in any direction. The enormous metal framework that held and powered the sphere reminded her of the skeletal chassis of one of her father's Alpha model locomotives, when she had seen them under construction in the train yards. Facing the sphere was a seat, actually part of the Beam Machine itself. She had never seen anyone sit there during the trial runs, but she knew that every member of the team had at one time or another occupied the chair. Charles Reif kept logs of the Beam team's experiments under lock and key.

Power cables ran over the walls and across the floor, linking the Beam Machine to the generators and transformers and huge cabinets and controls that packed the room. She had assisted in adjustments and repairs to many of the devices; she had worked on fine-tuning the Beam Machine itself, under the supervision of Thomas Reich, its chief engineer. She had seen the machine powered up for dry runs, but she had never seen it in operation. She was still uncertain what it was meant to accomplish. The chair was there for a reason, but it was one none of the scientists ever discussed in her presence.

If Paulo Orlovsky had his way, she would lose all her privileges here. She might never get another chance to try the machine.

She stepped inside the room and locked the door behind her.

On one wall was a clipboard holding pages of a log sheet. Dates of trials, critical power settings, and other notations were made in various hands. She recalled an afternoon of the previous week when George had been very pleased about the prior night's experiment; Charles Reif had remarked that the settings were extremely promising.

She found the date, and the settings, then she began to move about the room, restoring the various devices to the indicated positions. Most of the switch settings were permanent; only a few were ever altered, and it took several minutes to make the adjustments. She had assisted numerous times in the various operations involved in bringing the machine up to power, but never before had she done all of them herself. It was thrilling to be alone with the Beam Machine, to bring it to life single-handedly.

At last she could learn its purpose, its effect. She had no fear of harm, for all of her teachers had willingly seated themselves in the chair at one time or another.

She pressed a milk white button that began to glow murky yellow. The cabinets hummed; electricity uncurled through the wires. The core of the Beam Machine, a transparent chamber with a laser at its center, began to glow with a thin bluish white radiance. The light had a pulse, it brightened and dimmed; and in brightening seemed to set fire to the metal sphere, for now the glow kindled and condensed beneath the clustered lenses.

Elena climbed down into the seat, facing the sphere, peering through the lenses as if they were portholes into a furnace. She set her feet on the metal rests and reached for the final switch, this one hidden in the body of the Beam Machine itself. As she sank back into the chair, gripping the armrests and gazing into the lights, the sphere began to revolve.

Her first impression was of pain. The rays from the Beam Machine swirled in through her eyes, feeling like large hooks spinning and casting about inside her skull, loosening membranes, chittering against bone. Fire spread from the center of her forehead, reaching clawlike around her head, stabbing down into her face as if her cheekbones were fracturing. The mesh of pain was so exquisite, and so very tenuous, that she could not quite believe it was physical. It came and went like an *impression* of pain, an idea that kept occurring to her and then fading away again.

As the sphere spun faster, the loops of flung light began to describe more complicated patterns on her retinas. She tried to shut her eyes and discovered they were already shut. When she tried to open them, the room itself turned inside out.

She could never remember, afterward, exactly what came next. On occasion, without warning, a shard of memory might return, as sharp and intense as something experienced in great detail but which she could not place as actually having happened in her life. These images had something of the quality of dream memories, but she always felt they had come from the session at the Beam Machine.

The most recurrent image was that of a swamp. A swamp in which *things* lay abandoned, in utter decay. She could never see them clearly. Shapes eaten by rust, submerged in oily water that rippled with weird colors. The water itself was perhaps not water but a form of light. She could not move; she was nothing but a witness, a pair of disembodied eyes, a form of pure consciousness embedded in the mire of the place, as if her mind had been caught here like all these shapes of machinery. She sensed there were bones beneath the surface, preserved in the mud, but they were beyond her sight, beyond her knowing. She had no way, no wish, to excavate them.

Ancient trees grew up twisted from the swamp, deformed hybrid growths like willows with gingko leaves. They looked quasi-mechanical themselves, with angular branches, the geometrical leaves snipped out through some process more artificial than natural selection. The strange trees were the only things that lived in the swamp.

Sometimes she remembered lights, discrete balls of luminance, will-o'-the-wisps that floated through the branches singly and in groups. Her most chilling "memory" was of many such lights coming toward her through the dense tangle of trees, as if they had sensed her watching. They massed around her, probing the dark swamp with radiance, catching her in a net of scrutiny she could not escape.

These were all fragments, pieced together over years of recollection. The swamp was the most coherent image, the only one she had been able to assemble into anything like an actual place—although it was unclear to her whether the balls of light had been an afterimage of the Beam Machine, coming at the beginning of her self-experimentation, or if they had come only in the instant before she was awakened. The very concept of sequence seemed meaningless. There was no swamp in the Empire, no place she could have visited as a child; she must have assembled it out of fantasies.

She remembered a glimpse of sky—black and choked with ash.

She remembered a nightscape, charred and fuming as if riven by earthquake and volcanoes, with sullen green embers lying deep in the black earth, throbbing.

And another image, unrelated, of herself, distinctly in physical form, high in the air atop some kind of tower, as a shadow drifted over her, too dense to be a cloud, too vast to be a bird passing across the sun. It rolled on and on, dimming the sky, as if bringing on evening; but she could not bring herself to look at what would cast such a monstrous pall. When she thought it had grown too enormous to ignore, she squeezed her eyes shut and brought her head down between her knees with her hands and arms wrapped around her skull.

And that was the image she had carried into consciousness, as the Beam Machine whined down into stillness and silence.

She waited there, curled into herself, wondering if she had blown a fuse or somehow overloaded the circuits of the device. How long had it been on? The team's trials were limited to runs of five minutes; never more than eight, from what she understood. How foolish and selfish of her to put the entire project at risk. What if she had damaged the mechanism?

As she huddled there, fearing the worst, she heard the scuff of a footstep. Someone cleared his throat.

She froze, absolutely unable to straighten or lift her head to discover who had caught her. Elena was mortified. She did not deserve George Tessera's mentorship. Her career was certainly at an end.

"Child," said a voice she did not know.

She lifted her head, half expecting to find a custodian. But the man facing her, with his hand on the frame of the Beam Machine, wore the long, white smock of a lab scientist. He was white-haired, balding, with a stern face; he looked familiar, but she was not sure why. He must have been some senior member of the Academy, an associate of George Tessera's; he seemed vaguely familiar although she could not place him.

"It's all right," he said. "But you must never do that again."

His measured words had a calming effect. Elena's shock faded slightly, but it took time for her to realize what had occurred. Already the images from her session were gone, everything but the fading impression that she had traveled great distances.

"Is the Beam Machine all right?" she asked.

He nodded. "I think so. I shut it down in time. But I wouldn't be surprised if it's in need of recalibration. You had it perilously close to overload. It needs an operator as well as a subject."

"You . . . you know what it does?"

"Oh yes. George and I have worked closely on this. Very closely."

"You are . . ."

"Dr. Frost," he said, extending his hand. "Horselover Frost." She took his fingers, found them warm and reassuring. He helped her out of the chair.

"He's never mentioned you," she said. "You're not part of the team."

"Not officially," said Dr. Frost. "There are good reasons why I have played an anonymous role in its development. I did not intend to come forward to you, Miss Hausmann, but you would have come to great harm if I had not."

She looked at the Beam Machine, idle now, ticking as it cooled. "I was foolish," she said.

"Well . . ."

"You could have shut it down and slipped away without revealing yourself."

"No. The harm I mean to warn you about is not from the Beam

Machine alone, my dear, although you will do well to avoid it—and particularly its future incarnations."

"Future?" she whispered.

"Elena, I know of your hopes and dreams for a future at the Academy, a future with George and his associates. But you must put them behind you now. Put your dreams somewhere very far away, where they cannot torment you."

"I don't understand."

"And you won't, for some time. But I am warning you—stay away from here. Changes are coming, my dear. Cataclysmic changes. And this place, this device, will be very close to the epicenter of disaster. I do not believe George, or any of the other men associated with this project, can survive these changes without . . . *compromising* themselves. They will have to make difficult choices, but at least they have gained the knowledge they need to make their decisions. But at this time, at your age, it is hopeless. You would be crushed. There is simply not the time to prepare you, or I would. We would. Instead, my dear, I ask you, I beg you, to abandon your plans. Even though we have not met until today, you must trust that I know you; you must consider that I speak for my friend George Tessera."

She listened in horror. Horselover Frost, although a stranger, spoke with such authority and sincerity that his words somehow meant more to her than if they had come from an old and trusted friend. The scenario whose imminence he suggested was terrifying enough, but he did not deliver it like some mad old prophet. He sounded very reasonable, very deliberate, concerned mainly for her safety. And because she did not know him, he seemed an objective source of information.

"What—what is going to happen?" she asked.

He shook his head. "In precise terms? No one can say. I see only the shadows of ominous events—whatever casts those shadows is too dark to discern. But I see Orlovsky and his minions at the edge of the penumbra. I see Slowslop's hand in this, too. There is talk of revolution."

"Revolution?"

He looked up suddenly, as if listening for a sound from the lab outside. "I can't say more, Elena. You will learn, we all will, soon enough. But think on what I've told you. Take my warning, if you can."

She did not think it wise to tell him that, whether she wished it or not, she was already well on her way to losing her place at the University. As for her dream of joining the Academy, that already seemed no more than a fantasy. It was as if her entire life had been a dream, up to the point where she sat down before the Beam Machine. Only now, with the device switched off, was she truly awake.

Horselover walked her to the door. As she passed the threshold he caught hold of her hand and squeezed it gently.

"Be careful," he said. "You will find another way, I am sure of it. And perhaps we will meet again on that path. Perhaps there will come a time when you are strong enough to face the shadow."

For a moment she thought he was speaking of the shadow in her trance, the one she had glimpsed before the machine shut off, but how could he mean that one? No, he meant the shadow that threatened the nation.

She nodded. "Goodbye," she said, and Horselover Frost closed himself into the room with the Beam Machine.

It occurred to her that everything he said might have been lies; he might have come to sabotage the Beam Machine.

But no, he had already saved it from damage at her hands. And he had saved her from some other form of harm she could not clearly envision.

She returned George Tessera's key to his desk and then went out into the corridor. Before the door shut, she turned back to the room.

"Goodbye," she said, taking a long look at the darkened office. A long, last look.

SEVEN

IT WAS NEARLY MIDNIGHT WHEN SLOWSLOP FINISHED his inspection of the West End Hotel. The third-floor corridor was quiet, the latest batch of prisoners quiescent. A telltale light seeped out from under the door of Room 306. He was particularly aware of the resonance of the Sensorama as it engaged the full power of its meteoritic storage cell. Even in his suites in the subbasement, he always knew when the device was in operation, because of its characteristic sound—like a luminous bell, glowing and ringing so that one could almost hear its colors. But tonight the Sensorama sang for only a very few seconds before falling silent. Charles Reif was merely tuning the device.

Oskar Gondarev reported to Slowslop's private chambers at precisely midnight, bringing a summary of the day's experiments. They were still distinctly unpromising; there seemed to have been a decline in results since the first dozen, which went against both experience and expectation. Reif should have learned enough from their first round of experiments to have been able to show improvements by now; yet things were quite the opposite. The patients seemed to break down sooner, and recover more slowly.

Oskar seemed nervous as he presented the findings, written in

Reif's neat hand and initialed by the captain. Gondarev might have suspected that he would be judged personally on the strength of these results, yet the poor showings did not surprise Slowslop. They merely demonstrated that the human mind was incredibly weak, and so inextricably bound up in a frail physical constitution that the two could scarcely be teased apart without permanent damage to both.

The first round of prisoners was living proof of that—if you could call them living. Shambling wrecks, mindless lunatics, utterly useless to the Empire. Small consolation to think they were equally useless to the resistance—the Third Force, as it called itself. A grandiose name, as if the underground were a serious enough threat to rank itself somewhere in the power struggle between the Empire and the Republic. They were not the Third Force—they were the Nth Force, completely negligible. The true Third Force, whose hand could be seen in every round of revolution and counterrevolution, in every omen of progress or decay, lacked such a simple nature. It should be called, rather, the First Force. All the others were merely derivative powers. The historical conflict between Empire and Republic, important as it seemed to those involved, was but a small fire caused by embers falling from an immense and distant conflagration.

When Gondarev had withdrawn, his gruff manner unable to completely veil his dread of the Supreme Commander, Slowslop's final duty was to Lord Orlovsky.

The deepest level of the West End Hotel had once been a wine cellar, but this had been converted to apartments that were the most luxurious, as well as the most secure, in the Empire.

Paulo bade him enter at the first knock, but he held up a hand to keep Slowslop from speaking while he went on with whatever thought he was trying to put down on paper. His fountain pen was gold, as was the ink that flowed from it. His large, lustrous desk sat beneath a high arch remaining from the original cellar. The wall at the Emperor's back was covered with painted and photographic portraits, many of Paulo himself. There were images of the scientists originally associated with the early versions of the Sensorama; most of these men were now scattered around the Empire, their cabal broken by distance and unrelated projects. Slowslop always examined the photographs of Horselover Frost with partic- ular care, for he had a suspicion they'd been doctored.

Orlovsky finally sighed and capped his pen. He looked weary but in good humor. He always seemed better, more stable, after a good session spent developing his thoughts.

"Further mentations?" Slowslop asked.

"No, no. I have embarked on my masterwork—my treatise *On the Unicorn.*"

"At last."

"Yes, it should find a wide and receptive audience."

"I'm sure it will."

"Speaking of which, what about Elena? Have we heard a thing yet?"

"No, my lord."

"I spoke to Louis. I assumed you had as well."

"These things take time, my lord." As always, Paulo grew flushed when Slowslop urged patience. His childish behavior in matters concerning Elena Hausmann had already caused unfore- seen and, in truth, regrettable events. Slowslop had contributed in that first instance, but he knew better now. He had been uncertain of the girl, uncertain of himself, uncertain of what was expected— and so he had bent to Paulo's wishes and engaged in activities that had seemed, at best, unadvised.

Never again. He had learned to forestall Orlovsky without appearing to oppose him. He was determined that this time, things would go as he wished. He had sources of power unavailable to him before the Revolution. Things were very different now.

"Well, how long am I supposed to wait?" Paulo asked. "I am an old man already."

"And at the height of your powers and prowess, my lord. I am sure you have many years ahead of you in which to enjoy the fruits of your efforts."

"Yes, well . . . I should have had her years ago, Theodore. Would have, too, if you hadn't been so incompetent."

Slowslop made no comment; he refused to be drawn into this game.

"There are other matters, my lord, of which you might wish to be apprised."

Paulo had gone into a sulk. He sank back into his chair, glaring at the polished surface of his desk, and made a brusque gesture. "Tell me."

Slowslop ran down a short list—nothing too detailed. Orlovsky could not be bothered with any but a few pet projects. Since Slowslop had never mentioned the appearance of the boy in the Restricted Zone, he said nothing about having dispatched Louis Hausmann to visit the Army Hospital that morning. But it was the only event in the day's chronology that meant a thing to Slowslop himself.

"You seem to have everything in hand," Paulo said when he had finished his litany. "Now if you'll excuse me . . ."

He made a show of uncapping his pen.

Slowslop bowed slightly and withdrew from the room. It was somewhat troubling that less and less of Orlovsky's attention went into the administration of the Empire these days, while the bulk was consumed by his "literary" projects. The knowledge that every citizen was required to carry and study a copy of the *Mentations* seemed to have inspired Paulo to pour out further and more elaborate sequels. This latest project, with its emphasis on the unicorn that obsessed him, could easily usurp the rest of his energy.

In a way, this could prove beneficial, as it left Slowslop free to follow his own agenda. But it would not do to let the Emperor withdraw completely, or else he might never be accessible again. It was not difficult to imagine the old man crossing completely over the threshold of madness, useless even as a figurehead. He must involve Paulo again, somehow, in the daily operations.

One level above Paulo's chambers, Slowslop let himself into his own suite of rooms. The outer room, where he conferred with his staff, was comfortably furnished in the style of the hotel above. Beyond that, however, was his private chamber, which was as austere as a monk's cell. A bed, a small desk, a wardrobe, and a bureau were the only furniture. There were, however, objects of great importance inside some of these.

He went first to the bureau, which was locked, and took a small key from his pocket. The lowest drawer was compartmentalized into several inner boxes, each with its own combination lock. He spun the dials on one of these and flicked open the hinged lid.

Inside was a glass storage flask, sealed on both ends with polished metal caps, and further reinforced with metal bands. It resembled a ship's lantern. In the light of the room's solitary shaded lamp, the bit of matter sealed inside the capsule seemed to glow like a bit of greenish flame.

It was not fire, however, that the capsule contained; it was a roughly spherical crystal of refined meteoritic ore, a pure nugget of the element that George Tessera had named *xenium*. The nodule seemed to float in the center of the flask, held by a network of fine wires.

He set the flask on the desk beneath the small lamp, where it caught the lamplight and gave off shimmering interference patterns as he moved.

He unlocked the wardrobe and reached through the dangling trouser legs of several glossy black suits. Seizing a handle hidden among the clothes, he drew out a shockproof silver suitcase and set it on the bed. Flicking open the latches, he revealed a thickly padded interior, with hollow niches carved from the foam to exactly accept the shapes of five specific objects, four of which were presently missing, in use throughout the Empire.

There was room for a pair of binoculars, no longer in his possession. Another empty niche was cut to hold the xenium battery which now powered the Sensorama. A third nest had carried a long laser tube, currently in the hands of George Tessera at his research facility in East End.

The capsule of xenium ore would have fit precisely into a fourth niche, but he was not yet finished with it.

The fifth and largest object, and the only one in the case, was the three-dimensional scanner, which he lifted from its foam bed and set on the desk beside the xenium flask. He'd had no chance to inspect it since that afternoon. He regretted that he had not debriefed Hausmann personally about the mission.

It would be valuable to get Louis's impressions of the boy, as well as those contained in the scanner. He was also curious to learn what Constantine Wallace might have been up to.

But for now, the scan itself would tell him enough about the boy. In a sense, it would tell him everything.

He switched on the scanner and, when it had warmed slightly, checked the indicator screen. Instantly, he saw trouble. The scanner had absorbed a full spectrum of the expected emanations, but at levels far below the critical threshold. The device contained merely a *trace* recording, just enough to destabilize the source. The bulk of the field, the boy's essence, had eluded capture.

He switched on the opalescent screen, but only a ghost of the boy's face appeared there. The features were stiff, swollen, somnolent; the shut eyelids seemed to contain—barely—a radiant seethe of xenium light. Slowslop felt a deep, even a bottomless, gulf open within him at the sight—a new face, freshly pressed, but horribly familiar all the same. He recognized the *true* face that hid behind this mask of seeming flesh.

The image flickered, erupted in a glare of green static, and died out.

Even now, poorly captured, the field was dissipating. The spectral indicators were falling, for the act of operating the scanner itself degraded the recording.

He shut off the scanner, opened the desk drawer, and removed a small set of tools. Disassembling the two halves of the scanner was a delicate task, but he had performed it often enough that it took no more than two minutes. He pulled away the curved power canister, revealing an iron-sheathed inner compartment holding both the battery and a core crystal of xenium imprisoned in a glass vacuum tube, between two filaments of meteoritic wire. The crystal looked dark, tarnished, inert. Slowslop knew it was anything but. Carefully, he worked the tube out of the scanner and picked up the capsule of refined ore. One end of the scanning tube locked snugly into the metal cap of the ore capsule; with the pieces thus joined, two iridescent spots of fused xenium in the tip of each component made full contact.

The circuit required one more element for closure: a conductor.

Slowslop lifted the combined units gingerly, pressing the tips of his forefingers against the free ends of the ore capsule and the scanning tube, lightly stroking the xenium contacts, then coming down firmly upon them.

Slowslop stiffened, his eyes rolling up under his smoked lenses. To an observer, he would have seemed dead to the world, making no move for the better part of an hour.

Suddenly he lurched forward, twisting the scanner tube from the capsule, setting both pieces on the desk, rising from the chair. He moved slowly, dragging one leg, pulling himself to the bed. He crawled past the open suitcase and lay flat, facedown, breathing raggedly. After a while, his breathing normalized. He rose and went into the bathroom and twisted the cold water tap, then held his wrists beneath the cold stream for several minutes, watching himself in the mirror. He cupped some water into his mouth, then spat.

Still dragging his leg slightly, he went to the phone and punched a button. It buzzed several times before a voice responded.

"Prepare my car," he said, his voice leaden, that of a man roused from deep sleep. "I'll be up in five minutes."

He seemed to listen for a moment. A nervous tremor shook his entire body, but as it passed, his eyes seemed brighter. He took a few steps, the limp gone now.

"To the Restricted Zone," he said. His voice was strong and clear.

■ ■ ■

Slowslop had not visited the Restricted Zone in more than a year—not since the completion of Thomas Reich's armored excavator and the commencement of full-scale mining operations. As the car slowed, approaching a structure apparently made of symmetrical lights, he strained for some glimpse of the surroundings. The muddy road into the mountains had spattered the windows until they were all but opaque; and although the rain was only intermittent, the clouds had smothered every trace of possible moon- or starlight. Dawn was an hour away, but seemed to Slowslop as if it might never come.

He knew for a fact that ordinarily only one guard occupied the booth, but news of his arrival must have gone ahead, for now a contingent of three men waited to greet the car. They accepted the driver's word as to the identity of his passenger, and waved the sedan through the open gate, trying to peer inside as it passed.

Beyond, industrial lights cut through the filthy glass; in the glare he could see high gantries and power poles, a muddy wasteland crammed with machinery and rude metal sheds. In the distance, spotlights held aloft in a tangle of barbed wire shone along the edge of the workers' barracks. Dogs barked at the approach of the car. Soldiers crossed through the headlight beams.

Ahead, a tangle of bare trees raised their limbs against an arch of harsh lights. Immense tractors sat abandoned, gleaming in the rain. A small barracks station squatted just before the arch of lights where the earth gave way at the entrance to the mines. A line of overhead lights dwindled out of sight into the exploded mouth of the mine shaft. Tubes, hoses, and power cables snaked away into the depths like life-support equipment threaded down the throat of a hospital patient.

The driver pulled up beside the barracks and shut off the car. Still, there was no silence here. The earth vibrated with a deep thrumming, as of something steadily grinding away beneath the tires. Generators clattered beyond the barracks. From the tunnel itself came clanging sounds, the crash of metal on stone.

Slowslop waited for his door to be opened, then stepped up under the dripping tin eaves of the barracks and hammered on a warped plywood door. From inside came an angry cry; Slowslop knocked again.

This time the door flew open and a man thrust his face out, in a rage at having been dragged from sleep. Slowslop was recognized in an instant, but the soldier or miner must have thought he was still dreaming. He blinked and gaped and said nothing.

"A boy was found in the mines on the night of December first. I want to see the men who discovered him."

Still in shock, the man leaned back into the room, where several dozen cots were arrayed along the walls. "Stirck!" he called. "Milo!"

"Go to hell," someone muttered.

"It's the Supreme Commander!"

"Take him with you."

"Excuse me, sir," said the man at the door, aghast, as Slowslop entered and stood just inside the doorway. He watched as the man strode quickly down the row of cots and stopped at one, lifting his

leg to deliver a powerful kick to the ribs of the man lying there;
then he overturned the cot. He dragged the man off the floor,
swearing and gasping, and pointed him toward Slowslop, who
stood just where his face caught the slant of light from the tunnel
entrance.

"Holy—"

"Get moving! Milo, you too!"

Two men eventually came to the doorway, trembling in their
underwear but too terrified to complain about the cold. One was
short, balding, with grizzled cheeks and a red nose that looked
ready to burst; the other was young and blond, thin to the point of
starvation, a greenish tinge to his downy cheeks.

"Sir?" said the dark one.

"You found the boy in the mines?"

"Milo and I, yes sir." He hugged himself in bare, goose-pimpled
arms. "The name is Stirck."

"I wish to see the spot where you found him. Which of you can
take me there?"

"Either of us, sir. Or both. As you wish." His teeth clenched suddenly as he repressed a cold shiver. "Pardon me, sir."

"Get dressed. Both of you. I will be waiting just inside the
shaft."

"Sir!"

Slowslop strode away from the barracks building, through the
drizzle, stepping on a plank boardwalk thrown down on the mud.
The trees looked as if they were being murder by the incessant
light. He passed under the high arch of lights and into the shelter
of the tunnel, remembering this spot as it had been the first time
he visited, in company with George Tessera and Wilhelm Draun.

At that time, in the first days of the Empire, the mine in the
mountains had lain unworked for many years. Immense heaps of
red, iron-rich earth, eroded by rain, had slumped down to choke
the mouth of the shaft, partially covering the rusted rails and
abandoned barrows. The land had long looked poisoned and sick,
but there had also been marks of fresh injury—pits of fused earth,
freshly filled with mud and water.

When the meteor showers had been reported days before, he

had taken it for a sign. A good omen for the new Empire—and for himself. He had ordered a search for the impact sites and dispatched George Tessera and Wilhelm Draun to make the initial survey.

Tessera and Draun had gone to work alone, making preliminary excavations, literally digging up meteoritic fragments by hand, prying them from the mud. For a time they had failed to file official reports, confirming Slowslop's premonition that they would find something of value. He had gone to the site himself. The scientists had tried unsuccessfully to hide their excitement, but Slowslop recognized the significance of the glimmering greenish-gold ore embedded in the calcareous matrix of the stones from space. He was only surprised they had been so long in coming.

The small new meteorites were only a sign, of course; and while ordering their continued excavation, he had commenced a large-scale search of the area, resulting in the reopening of the mine. Within a matter of months, a vast new seam of ore had been discovered, just beyond the limits of the archaic iron mine.

The newfound deposit proved to be composed of the same substance that speckled the meteorites, but in much richer concentrations.

Such a fall of meteorites *should have* caused disastrous dust-flumes, climatic changes, and other unpredictable effects; instead, it was as if they had come down at a rate precisely tailored to prevent harm to the Empire. Nor was it credible that they should have fallen in such a concentrated region, so near the site of an immense and ancient deposit of the same stuff—unless the older ore had somehow drawn the small fragments to it by an inexplicable kind of magnetism . . . or unless they had been aimed so as to lead the Empire's attention to the site. And how was it that the early miners had come so close to discovering the seam themselves? If they had only pressed on a little farther, what then?

It was just as well they had not, from Slowslop's point of view; for then he would not have had full control of the excavation. No, everything had occurred at precisely the proper time.

While the scientists marveled at the improbability of these coincidences, Slowslop merely found them satisfactory.

"Sir!"

He was polishing the smoked lenses of his spectacles on a sleeve; his garment sucked the raindrops from the lenses and left them sparkling. His suit showed not the slightest mark of rain. He donned his glasses before turning to see the two miners, Stirck and Milo, hurrying toward him through the mud, damp and disheveled.

"Sorry to keep you, Mr. Slowslop!" Judging from Stirck's rumpled uniform he was a civilian, pressed into service in the mines. Still, he knew enough to treat Slowslop with deference. "Weren't expecting a visit from the Supreme Commander himself!"

"It's a pleasure," said Milo, extending his hand. Slowslop turned away, walking deeper into the tunnel. The men hurried to join him. Stirck went ahead, talking back over his shoulder; Milo followed just behind.

"We were down here by accident that night," Stirck said. "Milo here dropped his lucky piece during the day, and I volunteered to help him find it."

"It's a piece of ore," Milo said timidly. "Shaped like—like a little star. Dug it right out of the earth like that; just like someone had carved it. Never did find it."

"No. We found the boy instead."

Deeper down, the mine diverged into secondary tunnels. They took the central path, finally reaching the edge of a vertical shaft. Looking straight down, over a thin bit of rail, Slowslop could see the mouths of other tunnels opening from the shaft, which ran down as deep as he could see. A railcar elevator had been constructed along one wall of the shaft, and the car itself waited at the top. Stirck motioned him in.

At the touch of a button, the car shuddered and groaned and began to lower itself into the depths. The two miners glanced at him, then at each other. Milo adopted a pleasant smile, then let it fade. They clearly thought they were in some sort of trouble.

"Uh . . . Mr. Slowslop," said Milo. "Some of the miners . . ."

Stirck threw Milo a warning look. "Just a few minutes and we're there," he said loudly.

"Some of us were wondering, sir—"

"Milo," Stirck growled.

"Well, sir, we were wondering about this ore . . . you know, we're breathing it a lot, and carting it about, and, and—"

"You're a superstitious lout!" Stirck said abruptly.

"It's not just me," said the younger man. He was suddenly seized by a coughing fit. Before he had quite covered his mouth, he ejected a large lump of sputum onto the metal floor of the elevator, barely missing Slowslop's toes.

Stirck looked mortified; he let out a slow hiss. Milo looked merely embarrassed.

"Sorry, sir, but . . . but there you see . . ."

The globule shimmered with the xenium light of the rarefied ore.

"It glows in the dark, sir," said the youth.

"Nonsense! Milo, you are disgusting!"

"We're just worried, Stirck—I'm not the only one. There's men taken sick with green lung already, and no one will tell us a thing. I only wondered, Mr. Slowslop, sir, if the scientists, the men who know about these things, if they're aware of any dangers."

"It's perfectly safe—perfectly safe!" said Stirck. "I apologize for the boy, sir! Do you realize who you're talking to, Milo? For God's sake—clean up your mess."

Slowslop, silent, unperturbed, stared down at the lambent sputum.

"There's a few been sent to the hospital already," Milo said, just above a whisper, "and we've not heard a word from them since."

"There is certainly no cause for alarm," Slowslop said. "The substance has been studied in detail. Greater men than yourselves work with it in quantity, and in close proximity, and have reported no ill effects. Nor would we risk the Empire's finest for the sake of a few rocks. I am confident that Drs. Wallace and MacNaughton at the Army Hospital are taking good care of your comrades."

Milo took a moment to digest this, then began to grin widely; he gave a vigorous nod.

"That's what I wanted to hear!"

"And it's exactly what I've been telling him, sir. Now if you'll get over your folly once and for all, Milo, you can pay proper attention to your work. Ah . . . here we are."

The car ground to a halt. When Stirck threw open the cage,

Slowslop saw they were now at the very bottom of the shaft, approaching the outer limits of the excavation.

The lowest level was a tangle of intersecting corridors and large open spaces cut from the rock. The sides of the shafts were slick and smooth, in places fused like glass. The tunnels were only sporadically lit, with large standing globes that flickered to life as they passed. Carts full of rubble, awaiting transport to the surface, lined the walls of several side passages. The rails here were bright as new.

"It was just up here we found the boy, sir. Milo and I have been working at the forefront, you know. Just behind the excavator, pressing into the newest deposits . . . so we'd come all the way down here looking for his lucky piece. We had our eyes on the floor, of course, and we nearly run into the boy right about here."

"Yes, right here," Milo said, pointing at an otherwise unremarkable point on the tunnel floor. "He was just . . . just standing here in the middle of the tunnel."

"Stark naked he was, Mr. Slowslop. Not a stitch on him. And at first I was just . . . well, so surprised I couldn't say a thing. And then I said, 'Hey there, boy. What the hell are you doing down here?'"

"You asked him which camp he was with," Milo reminded him.

"Hell, yes, I asked him everything I could think of. But he didn't say a word."

"Nothing."

"Just stared at us, as startled as we were, I'd say. Eventually, when I was sure he didn't mean us any harm—"

"He was unarmed."

"—I took him by the arm, and Milo got the other, and we started walking him back to the elevator. You could feel how cold he was."

"Deathly cold!"

"So the main thing, we thought, was to get some clothes or blankets on him. Then, you know, interrogate him."

"I thought he might be a spy."

Stirck gave Slowslop a weary, knowing look. "A spy, yes, that was Milo's theory. As if the Republic dispatches stark-naked twelve-year-olds to do their spying for them. Inconspicuous, wasn't he, Milo?"

"It was only a theory."

Slowslop meanwhile was staring at the place they had pointed out to him. Scanning the ground from side to side, looking up at the walls and ceiling of the shaft. As the miners talked, he began to walk deeper into the tunnel, his eyes still scouring the walls. They were mainly smooth, but here and there were irregular pockets, bubbles in the rocks, that had been opened by the excavator's enormous drill bit.

A few steps farther along, the texture of the walls changed further: streaks and seams of xenium, freshly cut, gleaming and polished, gave off a weak iridescence that might have been merely the cast-back glow of the standing lamps. Farther still, and the walls, ceiling, and floor were composed entirely of the stuff.

They were now in the heart of the ancient, long-buried meteorite itself. Slowslop's ears filled with a very weak yet sonorous signal, like the faintest imaginable echo of a million distant voices raised in chorus. His eyes fogged with green glare; he stumbled and went down on one knee. The two men caught him by the shoulders and helped him up.

"Are you all right, sir?"

"He feels it, Stirck!"

"Nonsense!"

"Look at him—can't you tell? He feels it, too!"

"There, sir. You tripped on the rail, that's all. He tripped, Milo, now leave him alone."

Slowslop tried to blink away the green glow. He steadied himself against the tunnel wall and felt as if he were putting his hand deep into the earth. He could feel the pressure of all the rock around him, but something else was there as well. Something which was keeping extremely still and inconspicuous in his presence.

The glow slowly seeped from his eyes, the voices receded from his ears. He looked at the men and said, "Remain here until I return."

"Be careful, sir," Milo said with concern. "Sometimes one gets faint in here. It may be gas . . . we're not sure."

Slowslop motioned him away, and walked a bit unsteadily down the passage. Now, just ahead, he could make out the bulk of the excavator, an immense machine the size of a locomotive, nearly filling the tunnel. It was cold and quiet now, but he had seen it in action, boring its way into the earth, ejecting pulverized rock behind it. The operator sat within, like a railway engineer, grinding his way through stone, quite comfortable; while those behind were responsible for gathering the ejecta, loading the shards into cars for transport to the surface, where the pure ore was separated from the matrix compounds. Here, of course, in the heart of the primordial meteorite, it was almost all pure ore, cold and green with feigned inertness. He wished he could find some way to trick it into revealing itself.

Perhaps if he came back with the "boy," he could convince the stone to reveal its purpose. If he could sufficiently endanger the courier, he might prompt revelations from the living rock.

His next stop, upon leaving the Restricted Zone, must be the Army Hospital.

The idiot Milo had come near the truth without catching the faintest glimmering of it. The boy was an agent, but not of the Republic.

Suddenly the green glare swarmed him again; there were specks in it, living motes of light that seemed to follow in the trail of his limbs. He swatted at them, taken by surprise, but they had already vanished. He looked back to make sure the men had noticed nothing; if they had, they pretended to ignore it.

There was hardly room enough for him to walk alongside the excavator. He mounted the carriage, squeezing against the tunnel wall, walking his fingers delicately over the rock. He felt he must be close to the proof he sought, the confirmation of his suspicions.

And then his fingers slid into a pocket, a cavity opened by the excavator's drill. This one was smooth and softly curved inside, and felt almost moist to the touch. He drew his hand out and peered into the crevice, but it was dark, too dark.

He explored the edges of the crack with his hands and eyes. It ran several feet from end to end, like a slightly curled scar, and seemed to contain a pocket of varying depths.

Finally he called to Stirck and Milo. They came running, clattering through the stone shards, till they reached the rear of the excavator.

"Do either of you have a lantern?"

Milo nodded, reached deep into the pocket of his overalls, and pulled out a small flashlight. He tossed it up to Slowslop.

"All right," he called down. "That's all for now. Wait for me at the elevator."

They backed away reluctantly. Once they were out of sight he switched on the flashlight and aimed it into the fissure.

Inside, as he had expected, the cavity's lining was smooth, glazed, and bore a dewy coating. He probed with the light into small egg-shaped concavities, gentle depressions. Then he directed the beam straight down, and his mouth twisted.

At the bottom of the cavity, out of his reach, some of the gelatinous film had gathered in a few shallow pools that distorted the lines of the hollow.

Even so, it was clear enough what imprint was borne by the green untapped xenium ore, pressed there as if in a mold.

It was the concave impression of a face.

The same face he had seen in the scanner earlier that night.

The face of a boy.

■ ■ ■

"Where is Dr. Wallace?"

The nurse looked up sleepily at Slowslop's voice; then her eyes filled with terror. "Doc—"

"Constantine Wallace. Call him now."

She fumbled for her telephone, nearly dropping it as she jabbed the buttons. "Find Dr. Wallace—no, now! Supreme Commander Slowslop is here to see him. Yes!"

She dropped the phone and stared at Slowslop, pale and speechless. He moved away, and stood listening to the sounds of distant commotion in the corridors. Within moments, Constantine Wallace burst into the receiving area, his white coat thrown on over rumpled clothes. He showed no surprise—only loathing. Still, it was a pleasure to see him. Wallace had a very fine, rich mind.

Slowslop had deeply enjoyed all the time spent overseeing his and John MacNaughton's interrogation.

"Doing your own dirty work now?" he said.

The nurse, horrified by Wallace's insolence, appeared ready to throw herself under the desk.

"I want to see the boy."

"Of course you do. You might as well see him now. He was dying last night."

"Dying?"

"You sent Hausmann to finish him off, didn't you? Crude, our lieutenant, but apparently effective. I left John MacNaughton with the boy. I guess he's still alive or we'd have heard."

Wallace led Slowslop to the elevator and brought them swiftly to the locked ward. The ward was just as Slowslop remembered it, except that today he sensed a new form of interference—something coming from the room at the end of the hall. A strange emanation. Surely not the boy . . . ?

The doctor opened the door for Slowslop. John MacNaughton sat dozing in a chair beside the bed. The source of the energy he'd detected was not in the bed itself but running all around it, a complicated arrangement of vacuum tubes and instruments whose function was not immediately apparent.

The bed was empty.

As they entered, MacNaughton woke with a start. His first glance was at the bed. He leaped to his feet, only then noticing Slowslop. But the sight of the Supreme Commander seemed not to register; instead he gave Constantine a panicked look.

"Where is he?" Wallace asked.

Slowslop put his hand on the bedsheets. They were cold, colder than the background temperature, as if chilled.

"I must have drifted off." MacNaughton looked about in desperation. "He couldn't have left the floor. Not without . . ."

"He's somewhere in the hospital, or on the grounds," Wallace said.

"He was dying!" MacNaughton said. "He couldn't . . . couldn't even . . ."

"We'll begin a search," said Wallace.

Slowslop walked to the window, looking through the thick old glass at the grounds of the hospital, the high security wall surmounted by barbed wire. His hand rested lightly on one of the vacuum tubes above the bed. As he scanned the compound, the hunched shapes of the sodden willows, his fingers tightened inadvertently and the fragile glass shattered in his hand.

"It's the Army's fault if he slipped away!" Wallace said. "We're not here to provide security. We're doctors! You can't hold us responsible!"

"That," said Slowslop, "remains to be seen."

EIGHT

LATE IN THE AFTERNOON, ELENA WAS AT THE MAIN
counter of the library, assisting an old woman who could no longer
remember the name of a book she had read in her childhood. She
wanted to know if it might conceivably be forbidden. "I remember
there was a young girl in it," she said hopefully.

"Yes?"

"And . . . and something to do with a hedge."

"A hedge?"

"Either a door in a hedge or someone wanting to do something
to a hedge. It might have been a dream."

"You mean, you might have dreamed it?"

"No, she might have dreamed it."

"The hedge?"

"No, the girl."

A flicker of brown outside the glass of the main doors caught
her eye, and there he was again. Immobile, rigid, as he had been the
other night—but more startling in daylight. The boy stared
straight at her.

She signaled her assistant, who was working her way through

catalogue cards at the far end of the counter. "Alice, could you help madam for a moment please? She's looking for a picture book."

"What kind of book?"

"Maybe it was a ledge," the old woman said as Elena made her way toward the door. The boy's expression did not waver. It was not exactly sad; it was not exactly anything. His face was aimed precisely in her direction, but his eyes were so enormous, and seemed to take in so much, that she must have been an insignificant fragment of all he saw.

Maddeningly, he drew back as she approached the door.

Not again! she thought.

It was like the other night. As she hurried to open the door, he slowly rotated away from her and began to glide along the long path toward the Imperial Museum of Science. His feet scarcely seemed to touch the ground. She felt quite certain now that he was, in a very real sense, unreal. Yet she found herself unafraid. Intrigued, mystified, yes—but not afraid. Not of the boy, anyway.

It was a strange feeling, one she had not known since her days in the university, when she had felt a constant sense of revelation, as if the cosmos were eternally unfolding before her. It had been a daily certainty that there was no end to mystery, once you truly took hold of something important; the real questions, the ones worth asking, had limitless answers. Science was not about technology, progress, applications . . . it was a quest for the sake of questing, an endless love affair with strangeness and beauty and truth.

Now, as the boy vanished through the grand entrance of the Imperial Museum, she felt that old thrill again. And as she followed inside, it was as if her mind had become fully engaged, at long last, with the rest of her being.

The main gallery of the museum was a vast enclosure several stories in height, devoted to relics of science and industry. Rows of glass display cases occupied most of the floor, containing gears and vacuum tubes, experimental calculators, and other oddities. Old aircraft and outmoded ground vehicles stood at the far side of the room. The light was a strange mixture of fluorescence and daylight, for the ceiling was partly composed of a high glass skylight. As a child, she had spent many gloomy days roaming the museum—

particularly its basement corridors, full of experimental gadgets, obsolete technology, and practical demonstrations of physics. It was here, in fact, that she had first fallen in love with science.

Across the room was a curtained theater containing several projectors, where she had watched compressed-time films of seeds germinating, flowers blossoming, mushroom stalks sprouting through damp soil and opening their caps to drop powdery spores. Several other similar enclosures marked special exhibit rooms, but there was no indication now of what they held.

The museum, today, was as empty as the library; if anything, it had even fewer visitors, for countless objects had been removed from public display after the Revolution. Unless they somehow reflected on the glories of Orlovsky's research programs, most of the old marvels had been hidden away. The Emperor was obsessed with erasing all traces of history prior to his rise. All the grand discoveries and inventions of humanity were worthless in his scheme, unless he could somehow claim credit for them.

She moved quietly among the cases; her silence was second nature from practice in the library. She thought someone was standing behind one of the displays, watching her, but as she drew closer she saw it was a mechanical manikin, a primitive robot torso. A reflected movement in the beveled prism edge of a display case caught her eye. Turning, she saw the boy standing just outside the thick red velvet curtains of an exhibit room.

She rushed toward him, wasting no time. He backed through the curtains without stirring them. There was no separate entrance. At last she had him!

As she put her hand on the curtain, she heard someone cough inside. He would not vanish again.

She pulled the heavy drapes aside and stepped into the room. It was dim inside, but beams of colored light bounced between a complex arrangement of mirrors and lenses. In the midst of the mirrors, for an instant, she thought she saw the boy. It was impossible to be sure, for really there was only a blur of colored light suspended in midair, losing shape and consistency even as she watched. The bright patch dimmed, grew translucent, and vanished more thoroughly than smoke.

As the mirrors darkened, a man stood up from beyond a control console, where he had been kneeling to adjust one of the many thick cables that joined the mirrors. Seeing Elena, the man jumped visibly and she let out a startled gasp. He was tall, stocky, and balding.

"Sorry," she said. "I was looking for . . ."

He stepped forward, into a narrow beam of light that fell upon the console.

"Elena?" he said, coming briskly around the console. "Is that you?"

She couldn't speak for a moment. Then she stammered, "Dr. Tessera?"

"George," he said, taking her hands. "Call me George."

■ ■ ■

"You were looking for Charles Reif?" he asked, leading her downstairs into the basement galleries.

"Dr. Reif? No, I . . . I was just following a whim."

"Charles was stationed here, but he's gone missing. That's the official story, at any rate. Missing."

He paused at the bottom of the stairs. The corridor ahead of them, lined with glass cases, was only partially lit. A grilled gate had been pulled across it, thoroughly chained and locked. Recalling how she had once skipped happily down this hallway, looking for new exhibits and treasuring the old, she felt as if the lights had been shut off in some portion of her soul. Still, in George Tessera's company, she did not feel as depressed as she might have otherwise.

"This way," he said, tugging her along in the opposite direction. "Charles kept an office here."

"I know he was the curator," she said. "But I never visited. I felt very strange about seeing any of you again, after I . . ."

"If you were afraid of disappointing us, you could not have been more wrong, Elena. We were all greatly relieved by your decision not to stay with the project. It was a very dangerous time."

"It wasn't entirely my decision."

"I know about Orlovsky's proposal."

"You know?"

"He turned from your champion into your destroyer in the course of one day. It was not difficult to guess what designs he had on you." He pushed open a door into a cluttered office.

"It wasn't just Paulo," she said. "Your friend Professor Frost also persuaded me."

George gaped at her, panic-stricken, then seized her by the elbow. "Get in there!"

He hauled her into the room and slammed the door. There were two chairs, one piled with papers—old books, old journals, since nothing new had been published under Orlovsky's reign. He seated her in the empty chair, then cleared the other for himself. He leaned forward to take her hand.

"What do you mean?" he said with frightening intensity. "Who did you say spoke to you?"

"Professor Frost," she repeated. "I'll never forget his name, though it was—what, ten years ago? Horselover Frost. Where is he these days?"

"Where . . . ?" He looked around the room, and she suddenly understood his paranoia. The museum must be wired. Perhaps Frost had fled the Empire, his whereabouts a secret, his name never mentioned. She made a gesture that every citizen knew, tapping her ear, then pointing to the corners of the room.

"No," he said. "We can talk here. It's just that . . . you say you . . . Horselover Frost persuaded you?"

"Yes. We were in the laboratory, with the Beam Machine. He warned me that dangerous times were coming."

"Warned you *how?*"

"I don't remember his exact words."

"He spoke?"

"Of course. Professor—George, what is the matter?"

He looked as if he were about to weep, his mouth pulled down in a tense scowl, his eyes bulging. He leaned very close to her and whispered, "Horselover Frost does not exist!"

"But . . ."

"There is no such person, Elena, I assure you!"

"But I . . . I met him."

"Whoever you met, whatever they called themselves, it could

not have been Horselover Frost. I know this for a fact, Elena, because I created him myself."

"But he knew you," she said. "He . . ."

Slowly his statement sank through her mind, stirring eddies of confusion in the surface of her thoughts, but brushing against deeper concerns as it fell.

"Who was it then?" she asked, expecting no answer.

"My dear, can . . . can you describe him?"

It had been a long time, but she remembered him quite clearly. After her short session in the Beam Machine, everything had possessed an intense clarity; the memories of those surrounding days had never dimmed, but the memory of Horselover Frost was particularly strong and real.

"A high forehead . . . very white hair, receding . . . a pinched mouth . . ."

"Yes, yes," he said, growing more agitated as she spoke. "Elena, you have described the man I created as a . . . as a voice for the project. He was invented as a ruse, you see, to mislead those who might take too great an interest in what we were doing. We feared what was coming . . . the Revolution. We took steps to safeguard ourselves by creating a false identity for a seventh member of the project, who was to be our leader. That way we could deny ultimate knowledge, if any one of us were put to work against our will. Horselover alone knew all the secrets; the rest of us had only partial knowledge. We went so far as to create false photographs of Horselover Frost."

"I—I thought it was strange that I had never met him."

"We debated sharing the secret with you. Had you continued on as our associate, had the project not been abandoned during the upheaval, you certainly would have been told."

"But the man I met . . . the one calling himself Dr. Frost. Who was he?"

"I cannot imagine," George Tessera said. "An agent of the Empire?"

"But there was no Empire at that time."

"No. And Orlovsky seeks him still. Frost has led Slowslop's agents on an endless chase, for they can never capture a man who does not exist. In fact . . ." He gave a brief, wry smile. "In fact, your brother is in charge of the investigation. Very frustrating for him, I would imagine."

"Louis?"

George nodded. "I know your sympathies are not with your brother, or I would not confide in you, Elena. The truth is, I have long wished for your assistance in my current work. I would offer you a research position if I weren't wary of creating conflicts with your *other* allegiances. There are appearances to be maintained, I know."

"Professor, I am a librarian, nothing more."

"Nothing less, you mean. I would join the Third Force, too, if I could."

She tried to keep her composure at the name, spoken so casually. She tried to show nothing. But a good citizen would have displayed outrage, or pretended it.

"The fact is, I feel still other allegiances," he went on. "To my work. To humanity. I must monitor the abuses being made in the name of science. Someone must remember them, and tally the blame, and do what he can to prevent the worst from happening. That is what all of us have devoted ourselves to at this point, Elena. Even Charles Reif, in his private hell, doing the work to which they have put him. None of us knows where our efforts will lead; we have no particular agenda, nor do we hope for a second revolution to plunge us further into chaos. We only follow where the knowledge leads."

"You need an assistant?" she asked.

"I dream of it," he said, allowing himself a smile. "If you would consider it, and if there were some way to get approval, perhaps it would benefit all of us. I mean, your friends."

"How, though?" she asked. "Whose approval do we need?"

"There is but one source of authority these days," he said. "Lord Orlovsky. Which is to say, Theodore Slowslop. Given your relationship with Paulo, however, it seems hopeless."

"No," she said, thinking of Louis's invitation, and more darkly of Krystoff's glee. Everyone, everything, urged her to take the next step. Even the boy, she felt, had led her to George for one purpose:

so she would finally have selfish reasons to do what ought to be done for selfless ones.

"I think I can find a way," she said. "If you have a place for me, then I will join you. I have only to call my brother."

"Elena!" He clasped her hands, rising excitedly from the chair, pulling her up with him. "There is so much to share with you. To have a fresh mind, a new perspective on the old problems, would be of measureless value."

She nodded, and joy mixed suddenly with the dread that had haunted her for years. At last she felt the promise of real work again.

"Let me show you something," he said.

From a high shelf, behind a row of dusty mounted minerals and rodent skeletons, he removed a small glass bell jar that, unlike the other objects on the shelf, had been recently polished. She took it in hand and examined the jar, which contained a lump of greenish metal. The label, if there had ever been one, had long since fallen from the jar.

"Several years ago," he said, "a meteor shower fell in the area of an abandoned iron mine in the northern mountains. Wilhelm Draun and I were the first to inspect the site and conduct preliminary research on the meteoritic fragments."

He tapped the bell jar. "This is a bit of unrefined ore. You may recall that our plans for the Beam Machine ultimately collapsed because we could not find a suitable power source. Well, once refined and subjected to the proper stimulation, this little piece of matter revealed itself to be the source of a wealth of energy. Slowslop encouraged the development of a new technology founded on the ore, and since that time, there have been many strange developments, my dear. Very strange indeed."

"Xenium!" she said suddenly. George gave her a very pleased look.

"You do have sources, don't you?" he said.

"I—"

"No, you mustn't tell me any more. But you are correct. Xenium. The alien element. Alien not only because it came from far beyond this world—beyond our solar system, I believe—but because it lies beyond the other elements of the periodic table. I have been so far unable to test its atomic weight exactly, but indications are it possesses a number *beyond 180!* Do you understand what this means?"

"You always speculated there were undiscovered elements."

"Yes, certainly, but as one climbs the periodic table, they become ever more unstable, more dangerous, and with infinitesimal life spans. We suspected small islands of stability beyond elements 115 and 180, but it was literally inconceivable we might ever witness such things, let alone . . . let alone hold them in our hands! It's as if, my dear, as if this element were somehow stripped of its lethal properties, made stable and malleable before it ever fell to Earth. I still don't know exactly what it is, only that it is something completely new. And I'm not at all sure it could have been created by natural processes. But its properties are so very strange and wonderful that it pains me to see the uses to which the Empire wishes to put it."

As she stared down at the lump of pitted stone, the bell jar began to tremble in his hands. A drop of water as bright and clear as the glass itself suddenly splashed upon the jar. She looked up, amazed to see George Tessera's face streaked with tears.

"George, what is it?"

"It's horrible," he whispered, suddenly sounding very old, his voice ragged. He collapsed backward into his chair, and it was all he could do to reach out and set the bell jar on the desk beside him. "They are making us—making me . . ." He buried his face in his hands, and she moved to put her arms around him, to offer what comfort she could.

"George, what? What could be so terrible? What are they making you do?"

He looked up at her, pleading.

"God save us, Elena. We are building a terrible weapon."

NINE

LOUIS ARRIVED TO FETCH HER NOT LONG AFTER sunset, riding in the back of a long silver limousine. She watched from her window as the uniformed chauffeur held the door for Louis. Moments later she heard him on the stairs.

She was not eager to linger in the building, nor to have Louis in her apartment again, although Krystoff had taken the binoculars away to study them—not that she had voiced her suspicions about their properties. She rushed out of the room, locking the door behind her, and went to meet her brother before he was halfway up the stairs.

Other tenants, having seen the limousine through their windows, peered from their doors and came to the stair rails to watch. Louis took her arm with scarcely a word, sensitive to the attention he was causing, and walked her back down to the car. Only when they had been sealed into the limousine, with its smoked windows like dark portholes, did she feel safe. Cruising the streets she felt as if she were patrolling the depths of some drowned city in a strange silver submarine. The lights of houses flickered past and then the streetlamps ended, as if they were leaving the universe itself behind. Around them now was only a dark unpeopled realm, with West End somewhere in the greater darkness ahead.

"Elena," Louis said, as they rocketed down the unlit road, "I want to thank you for coming tonight."

"I'm not doing it for you," she said.

"I know that. But it may improve my position nonetheless. Lately, I have had some terrible problems laid at my feet. The blame for them, I mean. I'm afraid I need to salvage myself in their eyes. You know . . . Theodore's and Paulo's."

"I don't need to know any of this, Louis. I'm coming because I've been stagnating in the library. It's a crypt for knowledge now. No one can borrow a book without fearing for their lives. I want to return to the sciences. I want to contribute something. That's the only reason I've come. Maybe I can help my old mentor, if he'll have me. And if Orlovsky will give me his blessing."

"I hope you get everything you desire." He took her hand. "You know I do, Elena. I want only the best for you."

"Just as you wanted only the best for the family."

He withdrew his hand slowly, his face white with shame.

"I—I thought that by serving the Empire, I would help keep our position secure," he said. "I joined for the best of reasons, and Theodore has always been most fair—"

"Fair to you," she said bitterly. "Because you did everything he and Paulo asked. But what about Mother?"

"It's no one's fault what happened. It was just bad luck."

"Orlovsky swore our father's share would come to us, and then he cut us off. Now the railroads boom and what do we have?"

"The railroads are a government concern now. No one owns them any longer—no private individual can reap those profits! They run for the glory and in the service of the Empire."

"You mean the *Emperor*, don't you?"

"Everything changed with the Revolution. The old ways had to go. And the people who wouldn't change, it was a pity, but . . ."

"Yes, a pity. No more counts and countesses. But there are, I notice, still a lord or two around."

He turned away from her, staring out the windows or watching his sad reflection in the black glass—there was no telling which. It was a pointless argument, one they would never resolve, one they resumed whenever they met. She never intended to resurrect it, but the words always came out of her unbidden, in spite of her precautions.

Tonight she had other things to think about. She tried to let go of anger, but as soon as it cooled, something worse took its place.

Fear.

The suffocating thought of Paulo Orlovsky came to her through a distorting lens of ten years. Every memory she retained of him from her youth had been reinterpreted in the light of their final confrontation. His long history of kindness to her was seen only as a prelude to that horrible proposal, every small gift a covert bribe to win her favor.

It was anger she needed now, to keep her strong and determined in his presence. She must reveal nothing of her real emotion, apart from her honest desire for meaningful work.

A xenium bomb, she thought. What would Krystoff do with that knowledge?

Surely it would be safer in his hands, and in the keeping of the Third Force, than in the hands of the Empire. No wonder George Tessera despaired; to think of how Orlovsky's power would be magnified with such a weapon! But a bomb would mean real power for the underground; therefore it might mean freedom for everyone.

The streets of West End emerged from the night. The tall government buildings lined orderly boulevards of lights. Down the side streets she glimpsed the old estates, neighborhoods she had not visited in years. Her childhood home was not far from here, although it had been confiscated by the government, converted into administrative offices or perhaps inhabited by someone who had won himself a fortune in the Revolution.

The car slowed to a halt before the West End Hotel. Once it had been a grand and bustling hotel, with the flags of all nations hung above the entrance. Now its paired clusters of windows were mostly dark, showing no sign of life beyond the railed balconies. The limousine was the only vehicle at the entrance where once it had been common to see a line of such cars.

The driver opened her door and she slid out. Louis took her arm and led her up the steps.

The doorman stepped toward them as if to block their way: no nod, no tip of the cap. He didn't even make a move to open the door until he saw Louis's face, and then he turned and ran toward the entrance, blowing a shrill whistle.

The door was opened from inside by a red-suited bellboy. As they passed the doorman, Elena glanced back and saw him scowling after her; his hand rested at his hip, fingertips curled around the stock of a holstered gun.

The lobby was hushed; its emptiness swallowed up her footsteps. The dim golden lights, the old wallpaper, brought back claustrophobic memories of waiting at her father's side to greet some visiting dignitary or businessman. The place smelled the same: cold and musty, with a touch of mildew, and the faint aroma of cooking. She pulled her coat more closely around her, growing even colder as she heard her name spoken from across the room.

To her left, in a bright red armchair, Theodore Slowslop sat craning around at her. He rose as Louis guided her toward the chair. Elena hung back a moment, then reminded herself why she had come. She put out her hand, hoping Slowslop would merely clasp it; instead, he bent and put his cold, cold lips to her fingers.

"Elena, my dear. It has been too long. How we have missed you!"

"It has been a long time," she said. There would be no mention of their last encounter in Grand Central Station.

"But you look lovely. Lord Orlovsky is in ecstasy at the thought of your arrival. We mustn't keep him waiting another moment."

Slowslop slid his shiny, slick sleeve through hers, and led her across the lobby to the elevators.

"The hotel chef is a master," Slowslop said as they stepped in. "Paulo dined here so often that he decided to take a second residence."

"Really?" She looked for Louis, and saw him out in the lobby. Then the doors closed. She fought her panic. "Is . . . is Louis not coming?"

Slowslop inclined his head. "I'm afraid your brother is not in the Emperor's good graces at the moment. A prisoner escaped from his custody."

"A prisoner?"

"Yes, a wounded foreign agent who feigned traumatic shock to gain admission to the hospital instead of the penitentiary. Louis failed to penetrate his ploy and . . . the boy escaped."

The boy, she thought.

"Well, no matter." The elevator came to a halt and the doors opened again. Another bellboy waited for them. This one led them down the hall to a door, and rapped softly.

A man in a black tuxedo let them in.

In the center of the room was an immense table set with silver candelabra, glowing with dozens of tapers. Places were laid for three, with a chair at either end and one in the middle. She looked for Orlovsky, but saw only another tuxedoed servant who moved about the table adjusting silverware and checking the folded napkins.

"Come, Elena," Slowslop said, urging her in.

At her name, the servant at the table turned suddenly and came toward her, grinning. It was not a servant after all, she saw. It was Lord Paulo Orlovsky.

"My dear, dear, *dear* Elena!"

His hands closed around hers; her skin crawled at his touch. She felt, as she pulled her hands away, that his flesh might slide from the bones like overlarge gloves. He wouldn't let go of her that easily, however; he made little snatching gestures and caught her hands again, then her arms, leading her toward the middle chair, drawing it back for her.

"Please have a seat, my darling Elena. I hope you are quite famished. My chef has prepared an exquisite feast in your honor. But first—wine!"

The servant appeared at her side with a bottle, pouring as she sat. Orlovsky bent close, his face alongside hers, so that she could hardly avoid the sight of him grinning as he waited for her to take a first sip.

"Well? Well?"

"Excellent, thank you," she said. "Please, why don't you sit?"

"Yes! Theodore! And you!" Orlovsky waited until Slowslop had walked around to one end of the table, then took the third chair for himself. "Elena, it is such a pleasure to see you, I may not be able to eat a bite. How long has it been?"

"I'm not certain I recall, exactly," she said.

"Five years? Six?"

"Something like that," she said.

Slowslop, who surely remembered, kept a diplomatic silence.

"Well, your absence has been sorely felt, especially by me. Elena, I must ask—have you read my book?"

"Of course, Lord—"

"No, no, call me Paulo! You're a grown woman now, anyone can see that. I fear I treated you like a child for far too long, but let's get past that now. I understand you've had a career in the sciences?"

"The sciences?" she said, horrified.

"I believe he means library science, my dear," said Slowslop.

"Oh, yes . . . at the Imperial Library."

"And is my book very popular there?"

"It is our single most requested volume."

"Astonishing! Do you hear that, Theodore?"

"Yes, my lord. Most gratifying."

"It's true, Elena, that while my main energies are devoted to the course of the Empire, my books are of special importance to me. I have embarked on a new one, as well."

"How wonderful."

"And . . . and with your permission, my dear, I would like to dedicate it to you."

She could feel herself growing warm with the wine. "To me? I don't know what to say."

"Say yes! It is a treatise on the unicorn. Nothing unfitting, I assure you."

"As you wish, my lord. And perhaps in exchange you would grant *me* a small favor."

"A favor? Why certainly, my dear. Anything in my power."

"It's only that . . . I feel I am wasting myself somewhat."

"Dear, dear."

"In the library, I mean. You may recall I . . . at one time, I had other ambitions."

"Did you, Elena? I don't really remember. You were always an active young girl, weren't you? Sewing, needlework. Interested in everything."

Had he lost his mind and memory? Confused her with someone else? If so, it might be to her advantage.

"I only fear that I've grown a bit stale in the library, and I would like to give myself more of a challenge."

"I'm sure you can do anything you put your mind to."

"Yes. I wish to serve the Empire in more important ways."

"Custodianship of the archives is not an unimportant task, my dear, nor without its dignity."

"Certainly not. Yet—"

"Pardon, my lord," said Slowslop. "I believe Elena might feel her talents are being wasted in a position which any number of others might be able to fill. She seeks a place more suited to her abilities. Is that correct, Elena?"

"Yes. In fact, I ran into my old professor, George Tessera, yesterday. And it seems he is in need of an assistant."

"Tessera?" said Orlovsky.

Slowslop grew very still, his dark lenses fixed on Elena.

"What is he working on these days?" Paulo asked.

"Something very remarkable, I understand," she said. "Investigation of a new element. He would tell me very little unless I had authorization, but I felt that . . . that I was meant for this work."

"Fated for it, you think?"

"Yes, my lord. And now I have come to beg you to give me this opportunity."

"Well, my dear, you needn't beg. If Tessera needs your assistance, he shall have it."

"My lord," Slowslop said cautiously, "I'm not certain that is a position suited to Miss Hausmann."

"What?" Orlovsky seemed not to hear.

"I understand there is some danger, not inconsiderable, in working with this substance . . ."

"She's a grown woman now, Theodore. Let's not treat her like a child. She can make her own decisions. And Tessera is not the reck-less type, is he?"

"George was my mentor, back at the university. I trust him completely. It would be an honor to join him."

"There you are," said Orlovsky.

"My lord—"

"Not another word, Theodore. Elena, you have my full approval. In return, I ask but one more favor."

Warily, she nodded.

"Come visit me occasionally," he said. "Grant me your com-pany, that we can again rekindle our old friendship. It's lonely in this cold hotel, with nothing but the tasks of state to occupy me. You warm us all with your presence."

"I would be glad to, my lord."

"Paulo!" he scolded.

"Paulo. I will visit you every chance I get."

"Excellent. More wine, if you please! And now where is that soup? Jump to it, boy—or I'll send Slowslop to speak with the chef."

The servant hurried from the room, and within seconds held open the door to admit another man carrying a large tureen. Elena glanced sideways at Slowslop, wondering what was going through his mind. Sensing her gaze, he lifted his head and smiled; but it meant nothing, it was like a nervous rictus. And his eyes, as always, were completely hidden.

■ ■ ■

Afterward, with the richness of so much wine and heavy food swimming in cream sauces, followed by a sherry trifle, Elena found herself feeling ill and rather dizzy. She could not remember the last time she had enjoyed such a meal—although tonight "enjoyed" was not the word she would have used to describe the experience. The two men had watched every movement her fork made travel-ing from the plate to her mouth. Now, still under scrutiny, she felt vulnerable, as if her slight nausea and drunkenness had put her at a disadvantage.

A waiter entered with a bottle of green liqueur, but before he could pour for Slowslop, there was a rap at the door and a heavy-set, balding man peered into the room. She recognized Oskar Gondarev from surveillance photographs taken by Third Force agents.

Slowslop excused himself and joined Gondarev in the hall. She had covered her own glass to keep it from being refilled, but Paulo drained his in a single swallow, then pushed back in his chair.

"Let us move to a more comfortable room," he said, coming to pull back her chair.

Next door was a small parlor reeking of stale cigar smoke, containing several plush armchairs and a small leather sofa. Ancestral photographs hung on the walls, and there were shelves full of books. Old books, real books, with distinctive spines. Testing her liberty, she plucked a volume from a shelf, certain it must be one of the forbidden volumes. Orlovsky watched her with scarcely veiled amusement.

"You're welcome to borrow anything you like," he said. "I promise not to tell."

The book fell open to a color plate, a detail from an old tapestry, all the colors delicate and subdued. It was an image of a young woman seated on a green plain studded with stylized tufts of embroidered grass; she sat cross-legged, and beside her lay a unicorn with its head in her lap. It was a peaceful scene, the woman's eyes resting serenely on the trusting unicorn, and Elena turned the page expecting more of the same.

But here, in what must have been another detail from the same tapestry, the same young woman lay on her back with her arms around the unicorn's neck, one of her fists gripping its polished horn. She was disheveled, clothed only in shreds, and the unicorn stood over her with its male member enormous and erect against her bare belly.

Elena nearly dropped the book. Instead, more ill than before, she shut it quietly and slid it back onto the shelf.

Orlovsky watched her keenly, but she was careful to let her face reveal nothing.

"Please," he said, "please have a seat. Let's sit and talk. So much time has passed. Let's remember the old days for a while."

"I—I'm afraid I'm rather exhausted," she said. "I haven't been well."

"No? All the more reason to take a rest before the long drive back. You live Downtown? Not in West End?"

"That's right," she said, still reluctant to sit.

"That's a shame. Your old manor sits empty, you know. Perhaps something could be arranged?"

"I'm comfortable where I am, thank you. And—that place is too full of memories."

"I understand." He sat on the couch and put his hand on a thick volume which rested on the low side table. "Come take a look at these."

For a moment she expected more pornography, but then she saw that it was an album of old photographs. In spite of herself, she found herself craning around to examine the pictures, and recognized herself and her brother, as children. There was her father in the severe dark suits she remembered, his bowler hat and his ornately waxed and curled moustache. Her mother, proud and beautiful, looking much younger than Elena could remember her. And Theodore Slowslop, standing among them at family occasions and picnics, looking exactly the same as he looked this evening, his odd shiny suits catching the glare of the magnesium flash or the noonday sun.

"Here, dear, sit beside me." He patted the couch but Elena kept her distance. He turned the page to pictures of Elena herself—photographs she could not remember posing for, or ever seeing in family albums. There was young Elena looking surprised in the display room of the National Museum; Elena at a birthday party; Elena sitting on a rock at the edge of a pond, and strolling in the park. Elena in her bedroom, at the edge of her bed; Elena as a young woman, standing at the window combing her long hair. Page after page of Elena growing older. As she watched the pictures slipping past, she grew increasingly certain that she had been unaware of the photographer—that they had been taken from great distances, furtively. Some had the grainy look of extremely fast film. These were sepia-toned surveillance photographs.

"Those were happy days, my dear, happy days indeed. But then, these are fine days, too, and it pleases me greatly to think of you working more closely for the Empire. I have long hoped that you would find a special place here. Arrangements could be made, you know."

"Paulo," she said softly, with a smile, "let's not speak of that now. Not too much, not all at once."

He let out a sigh. "You're very right, my dear. I fear I'm being very rude. If you are as tired as you say, I should let you go."

"I'm so sorry," she said. "You've been a wonderful host."

At that moment Slowslop entered the room. "Excuse me," he said. "A minor administrative problem . . ."

"Elena was just leaving, Theodore. Perhaps you could see her out?"

"I would be delighted," Slowslop said without emotion.

Orlovsky kissed her hand once more, beaming. He bowed as she stepped out through the door Slowslop held open.

Theodore walked her to the elevator. Before summoning the car, he started to speak, then fell silent. She felt as if he were withdrawing into himself, waiting for some signal to come forth.

"Is something the matter?" she asked.

"I'm sorry I had to leave you alone with Paulo."

She nearly laughed aloud; instead she sniffed and covered her mouth. "Theodore?"

"Believe me, Elena, I know how you must feel toward him after the events of your last meeting. Believe me also when I say I feel infinite regret for my own part in that affair. It was inexcusable, and therefore I make no excuse for myself. Only that . . . I wish to ask your forgiveness. I have hoped for this opportunity for ten years, for the proper moment. Of course, I cannot blame you if you refuse to accept—"

"Of course I accept, Theodore. That was a very long time ago."

"Not to me. Had I known, had I understood the impropriety of the situation . . . My actions were unacceptable."

"It's not your fault, but thank you anyway. And of course I forgive you."

His mouth tightened, as if he were repressing something he feared to release. She had the distinct impression that Slowslop was fighting back tears. It was a ridiculous thought, but no more so than the rest of his confession.

"You must understand that although I serve Orlovsky, I am my own man."

"Of course you are, Theodore. No one has ever doubted that."

"Thank you, Elena. Thank you."

With that, seeming to stand several inches taller now, he pressed the button and the doors flew open.

■ ■ ■

In the limousine, Louis sulked. There was no other word for it. He was like a child again, and she a big sister enjoying her moment of success. But she had not meant it to be at his expense.

"I will be working for George Tessera," she said. "At his laboratory in East End."

"I'm happy for you," he said without sincerity. "Your star is rising."

"Louis, can we stop the car?"

"Why?"

"So we can talk. In private."

He gave her a curious look, then leaned forward and rapped the driver on the shoulder. "Pull over and wait for us."

"But sir—"

"Do as I say."

The car slowed to a halt. Louis, this time, came around to let Elena out.

For a moment, looking up, Elena thought she was hallucinating. Then she realized they were merely at the edge of West End Square. Paulo Orlovsky stood above the car, an immense figure gazing east across the Empire, his arms held out with the palms cupped upward as if to receive gifts from heaven. The metal monstrosity was painted in lifelike colors and fixed in the glare of a hundred spotlights which only added to the figure's ugliness.

Orlovsky had proclaimed victory and named himself Emperor on this very spot. When he had proclamations to make, it was here he stood, at the base of his gargantuan memorial.

Still, the statue was deaf, and the square at this hour was deserted. She walked a short distance from the car and Louis followed.

"What is it?" he asked.

"If you don't want me working near you, I wish you'd say so."

"What? Elena, I'm glad for you, really I am. You'll be in East End, after all. It's not as though we'll be in each other's way."

"It's only that . . . I think Slowslop suspects me of other alliances. I'm not sure he's altogether happy with my appointment."

"He has never said anything but good of you."

"That means nothing. If he considers me a risk, then your position might be compromised as well."

"Elena, your coming here only improves my position. I was in trouble tonight." He smiled. "I feel like a little boy admitting that, but there you are. I was in trouble. It helps to have you here, really it does. You're back in the fold."

She kissed his cheek. "I'm glad to hear you say so, Louis. I have missed you. Maybe we'll see more of each other."

"I hope so. Is that all?"

She nodded, and he started to lead her back to the car.

"No, Louis, I think I'll take the train tonight. I need time to myself."

"Are you sure? Slowslop would never forgive me."

"He'll never know. The ride will be restful. I love the trains, you know."

His smile grew sad, his eyes distant. Thinking of their father, she knew. But then he squeezed her arm and let go. "Very well, then. We'll talk tomorrow. At least let me see you safely across the square—there are vagrants camping out here lately. People who refuse to take what the Empire has to offer."

"No. I'm fine. Get back to the car, Louis."

He stepped back, waving, and climbed into the limousine. She watched it pull away, saw him looking back at her. Then she turned and faced the square. The monstrous Orlovsky gazed over her. Fearful as it was, it did not hold a fraction of the horror evoked by the tiny original.

Looking up at it, she thought: *I know the first thing Krystoff would topple if he had a bomb.*

And then a more terrible insight followed:

I would do it myself.

She hurried toward the monument, walking quickly in the brisk night air. West End Station beckoned at the far edge of the square, tall and glowing from within like an enormous greenhouse full of metal flowers.

As she passed the base of the iron emperor, someone whispered from the shadows and came scuttling toward her, shoving a scrap of paper in her face. She shied away, her heart leaping, and nearly shrieked. She tried not to show panic, tried not to run, in case that might provoke him. But the skulker showed no inclination to follow, and instead squatted there mumbling and calling to the night wind. When she looked back, just short of the entrance to the terminal, he had vanished back into Orlovsky's shadow.

A train whistle shrilled. Glancing up at the station clock, she realized she was just in time to catch the last train east.

The whistle deafened her temporarily, and it must have had other strange effects as well, for as it faded she thought she could hear someone out in the square, in the shadows, calling her name again and again. An hallucination, she told herself. Then she had to hurry for a ticket.

TEN

IN WEST END SQUARE, IN THE SHADOW OF PAULO
Orlovsky's iron heel, the old man huddled and mumbled, hoarse
from calling after Elena Hausmann, wondering if it had been she
after all or merely another hallucination.

Hardly a moment passed these days that was not full to burst-
ing with visions. Waking and sleeping, his eyes were blinded by
explosions of color, scenes from impossible futures and nonexis-
tent pasts. Perhaps that was all she had been, another signal of ill
omen catastrophically linked to the railroad. What did it signify to
see Elena Hausmann's specter hurrying into West End Station?
What did it mean for all of them?

There must be some meaning to the vision, if only he could find
it. He felt the sight of her had come with a certain cadence that
demanded words, a poet's phrasing. Many messages were meant to
be shared in their raw form, as pure delirium, but others must be
polished for wide dissemination; this was his duty, as prophet to
the Empire.

Scraps of litter tumbled across the square, blown in place of
leaves now that the trees were bare. Some became caught against

the base of the statue, or tangled in his hermit's nest; he flattened them, ironed them, dried and collected the finest scraps.

He dug a pen from his pocket and began to scribble the latest installment of his prophecy on the back of a handbill. There was plenty of light from the numerous lamps that cast their glare on the monument, but still his eyes grew weary. He wrote for what seemed like hours, filling scrap after scrap. Some he tucked into his pockets, or weighted down with chunks of broken masonry, or rolled up and shoved into the rag bundle that served him as a bed. Others he dispersed on the wind. He wrote without feeling he was getting any closer to the truth—and yet he knew he was no judge of truth. Leave that to others; let them pick sense out of his words. Only much later, when his fingers were quite numb from scribbling, his eyelids beginning to droop, did he feel he was finally coming to the point. It seemed inseparable from dreams. Then something darkened his page, and he looked up in irritation to see a silhouette standing over him.

"Get out of my light!" he snarled, although really all he wanted was to sleep. "Go on—-get!"

"Diaghilev," said a voice he vaguely knew. "Guess who?"

The man crouched down, and his features took shape in the shadows. He was filthy, cloaked in rags as poor as those Diaghilev wore. He was younger, though, and much taller. And the old man remembered him from somewhere—yes, a distant time, a distant land, perhaps. They were veterans of some long campaign against evil.

"I knew you once," he finally admitted.

"So did I!" the man said with a laugh. He dropped down beside him. "Gregor Stillson. Remember now? No? Well, I enjoy your story," he said, gesturing at the scrap in Diaghilev's hand. "I pick up every bit I find. They say it's madness, but it makes perfect sense to me. I've seen the Ark, my friend."

"The Ark," Diaghilev repeated.

"Yes. And I await that glorious day!"

"What do you mean, the Ark?"

"And the sky was full of ships! And the land was gray as corroded tin, and the trains rolled from their tracks and drowned in the quagmire the Empire had become. The mountains turned to liquid and to dust, and rivers deserted their beds for deeper domains, and the only reason we did not die was because we were already in the tomb of the world. Better yet, we had reserved seats on the Ark. All aboard, the conductor called. All aboard! Tickets! Tickets! Do you have your ticket yet, Diaghilev?"

"I'm still saving up for mine," the old man said, thinking this fellow was insane. There was no Ark, no escape from the end of the world. Some might be saved, but not the likes of them.

"Come with me, then," Stillson said. "Hurry now, hurry, and we'll pass the hat around. We'll pool everything we've got to buy your passage. You're one of us, old man, and you should know it."

"I live alone," Diaghilev said.

"Of course you do. We all must! But at times we gather, and this is one of them. That's why, tonight, I've come for you. We agreed you should have the chance."

"We? Who's 'we'?"

"The others. The chosen. The lottery winners. Raise up your ticket on the eve of judgment, so God may read your winning number. No one else can hope to be spared."

"I don't want to be spared," Diaghilev insisted. "When the end comes, I shall embody it. I shall claim my immortality there. It is the climax of my poem, and I must be on hand as author of the event. To lend my signature, if nothing else."

"Come with me anyhow. Don't decide now. You can still be on hand. But come."

"No."

"Diaghilev, you old fool! Don't you know the days are rushing on apace? The Empire, the Republic, the Third Force—what are they? Useless! Nothing! It's all down to us, old man. Be a prophet, if you wish—but be *our* prophet."

"I belong to no one."

"You belong to *this*."

Stillson reached deep inside his tattered coat and brought back his fist, tightly clenched. A faint green light leaked from between his fingers.

Diaghilev rose slowly to his feet.

"There we go, that's right." Stillson waved the glowing handful under the old man's nose.

"Where—where did you—?"

"Yes, that's it, up, up!" Stillson pulled his hand back, a luminous lure.

Diaghilev reached for it, nearly stumbling as Stillson danced away, saying: "Aha! You see, I know your allegiance."

"Let me see it."

"Not yet—not here! There's more, plenty more, if you'll follow me."

Diaghilev stuffed the last scrap of unfinished thought into his pocket and hobbled after Stillson, who led him across the square toward West End Station.

Warm air gusted from the open doors, bearing the scent of machinery, oil and dust, steam and smoke. At the smell of the trains he panicked, stepping back. He would not go through those doors for any price. But Stillson caught him by the arm and dragged him down the steps. Diaghilev's protests echoed through the station, seeming to fill it from wall to wall. The place at this hour was deserted. The station clock showed the time to be two in the morning. The tracks lay ahead, down several flights of stairs. One train waited in the station, beneath the high triple arches of glass and steel, ticking as it cooled like an enormous, slowing clock.

The tracks led straight out into darkness. The ticket office was vacant, dark, but the station itself was bright and gleaming. The tall black girders seemed to sing like a polished steel chorus, their song reverberating from the cold tiles of the floor and the colder skylights full of infinite night.

"We'll be arrested in here," he muttered.

"And so? A warm night in a warm cell? Or is it Grand Central Pen you fear? You've already seen the worst they can do to you, old man. Now they fear us! Come on."

Halfway across the station floor, they passed a locked gate with stairs running down to a defunct platform. Or supposedly defunct. In truth, it serviced the Nova Express, a military train. Officially, it never ran; it had no admitted purpose and was by decree of the

Grand Central Railway Authority perpetually out of order. And yet at odd hours, far below West End Station, you could hear its churning thunder. The Nova Express came and went, came and went, and Diaghilev, obsessed with schedules, had tried to track its times, to discover a pattern, but without success. It was Slowslop's train. Noble Slowslop! Builder of railroads, builder of empires, on whose shoulders all progress was borne!

"Hurrah," he said weakly, as colors flared and ebbed across his eyes. He seemed to see Slowslop's face engulfing the station like a great pale balloon full of golden green gas swelling to incredible proportions. Then Stillson pushed him toward the long flight of metal stairs to the main platforms. He held his silence because he did not want to attract the attention of the railway police. They would beat you senseless and throw your body from the running train—into woods or swamp or desert . . . or into the great abyss. It was all the same to them. Whatever disrupted the trains must be destroyed.

Diaghilev's horror grew as he realized Stillson was hauling him, with braying laughter, straight through the turnstile toward the sole train in the station. It was a Sigma-type locomotive, the very latest. Sleek as a missile, but tied to the earth, its nightmarish shape sparked a host of apocalyptic visions—so many that they blurred, indistinguishable, and he was forced to cover his eyes.

"How do you dare to meet here?" he asked.

"We won't be here for long," Stillson said, forcing him up the steps into the engine car. It was a steep climb, but halfway up another pair of hands took hold of him. He found himself hauled into the middle of a crowd of his fellows.

His fellows . . .

"Well, well," said one. "We meet again."

"I told you he'd come," said Stillson. "Now we're complete."

They were a dozen now, including Diaghilev. They had met once before—perhaps aboard this very train—on the ride from Grand Central Penitentiary. They were all in much sorrier shape now than they had been even then, after months and years in prison. Some he had seen in the streets, in the parks, living furtively in West End, in the shadows of the great public buildings and ruined manors.

"There will be time for this later," said a man with a thick black curling moustache. "Let's get moving."

"Moving?" Diaghilev croaked.

Several of them grinned. Stillson slapped him on the shoulders. "Yes! Perplies can drive the train single-handed!"

"It was part of my officer's training," he said. "Not this model, of course."

"Look closely at the engine," Stillson urged Diaghilev.

The old trains, the trains of his youth, had run on coal; in the great days of experimentation and expansion before the Revolution, there had been models that ran on gasoline and even electricity. But here, in the center of the helm, where one might have shoveled coal in an old-style train, was a round hatch set with a crystal portal. As the extravagantly moustached Perplies began to twist the knobs and pull the levers that summoned the engine's powers into being, a cold and brilliant light began to glow beyond the little hatch. It seethed and flared with lovely oranges and golden greens, with traceries of blue fire and emerald flickering.

"My God!" he gasped.

"It's a hybrid engine," said Stillson. "The Nova Express has run strictly on the new fuel for some time. This train shouldn't really be here."

"But then neither should we," laughed another.

Perplies let out a groan and pulled back on the largest lever. The train, with a shudder, began to back out of the station.

"This is insane," Diaghilev cried.

"Yes!"

West End Station slid away, and they were soaring through darkness. He looked back almost wistfully at the high arches of steel and glass, a cavern of contained light. As the train continued to reverse, the station shrank away. Now nothing stood between them and the stars. On either side were the dark shapes of buildings, the back walls of towers and tenements, holding here and there a lit window, but most of them dark and many shattered. As they backed through the ruins of industry on the edge of West End, he realized that no one was going to turn the train around.

The locomotive continued to pick up speed. West End itself was now a cluster of star-specks on an unseen horizon, seeming to dissipate upward into the greater cluster of stars above. Then the actual horizon must have imposed itself, for the flecks vanished, and he was aware of reaching shapes, torn clusters of foliage groping at the dark. Someone must have touched the headlamp switch, for suddenly the streaming woods sprang out in harsh relief. The rails clattered away beneath them, into darkness; they dragged their trail of light behind, snagging on branches, throwing sparks from the track.

"Come down, old man," someone whispered, tugging him by the sleeve. He realized that he was alone at the windshield, staring backward. The others now sat on the floor of the dark cabin, clustered together in a ring, passing a glimmering flask. He sat, unable to recall the last time alcohol had stung his throat. The metal floor hummed rhythmically beneath him, and he was half entranced by the time they put the bottle in his hands.

It was no wine bottle. It was a fat tube sealed at either end with polished metal caps. Stillson twisted one end and three slits opened in it, and the glow of madness seeped out. He put the slit end to Diaghilev's eye, while twisting the other end as if it were a kaleidoscope. The interior of the tube was mirrored, multifaceted, and somewhere—difficult to tell where, exactly, for there didn't seem to be room inside for so much of the stuff—a bit of the strange bright crystal gave off its glow. The rays bounced and fractured and then began to spin, setting off reverberations inside the eye, traveling into the brain, shimmering loops and whorls and waves of light that continued to echo and amplify even when the next man's hands fumbled for the tube and tore it away.

Diaghilev sat stunned, regarding the interior of his mind as if it were another world. He was far out in space again, out in the void, moving through the night like a vast train barreling toward a dark and distant station in the heart of a wasteland. White bands of light streamed over him, stabbing into the engine car, the shriek of the train echoing suddenly as they streaked through Downtown Station in scarcely more than a second. Still accelerating, that green fire burning in the soul of the train, pushing them backward and forward at the same time. He could hear the light leaking from the eyes of the others, Perplies and Stillson, Lyphoudt and Chassagnac, Dvoris and Angouleve—the only ones whose names he had learned during their captivity. Outside, a regular thrumming of wind in trees, the forest spires flicking past. The rhythmic thoughts of the twelve, conjoined, filled the cabin:

"How shall we know the Ark?"

"By the sign of the seventh scientist."

"As it flies on metal wings!"

"As it bridges earth and heaven!"

"As it moves upon the waters!"

"As it ferries us to freedom!"

The kaleidoscope came round again and his eyes filled with greater glories. It was not an ark he saw, no such tiny thing; no such insignificant destiny lay in wait for Diaghilev. He knew a greater ship in the distant night, gliding toward him, toward this very train; he was receiving signals bright, clear, and terrible. A ship that came to rescue him, a ship full of promise. The Ark or Arks were motes of dust in comparison. How could they not know of its coming? How could they not know, as well, of the hideous end that awaited them all?

Another blur of light followed, so swift as to seem illusory, as if he had pressed his thumbs into his sockets. They concluded that it must have been Museum Station, but long before they reached agreement they were far beyond it, howling through the barrens.

He climbed from the floor, letting the cylinder pass him by this time. He felt in danger of falling into it. He was beginning to remember events best left forgotten: the days in the West End Hotel. It was the light that had triggered it, the same light into which he had stared day after day until he knew nothing . . . until he knew things he had never known. He had memories that did not seem to fit with one another, memories whose reality no longer convinced him. The trouble was he did not know which set of memories might be true. Even his memories of Grand Central Penitentiary and his journey to the West End Hotel rang false.

He was in no condition to judge, certainly not now, with the stars streaming above and the sand pouring away like foaming milk along the tracks and the others babbling away behind him, holding forth with their grand plans of insurrection. The moment will come, the moment is coming, the moment has come.

Behind him, Lyphoudt said, "There was a special exhibit at the zoo. It was the talk of the town. Everyone said, You have to go, you have to see the new display. But if you questioned them closely, it always turned out they hadn't seen it yet. Finally a group of them got together and said, 'That's it. We're going to the special exhibit.' They went out to the zoo, but when they got there, there was no zoo."

Bright bars thrust up from the sand, stabbing into the sky. A silver network, wires humming, click and clatter; the train floating and swaying between the bars of a whistling cage—all for a blurred instant, and then it was over. Gone. The bridge of his nightmare, his horror, his greatest loss . . .

If that horror had even happened.

Now he doubted everything. If the great defining moment of his life had not occurred, then what did he have left? What events had shaped him? Who was he really? He despised the Third Force, he had sworn himself to its destruction—but why did he feel that it had not always been so?

He turned and threw himself onto the floor, reaching so desperately for the tube that they pitied him. Someone held it to his eyes while another turned it and someone else cradled his head and whispered that all would be well, there was really no reason to cry . . .

And the train sped on and on, backward through the desert, barely a heartbeat marking its passage through Grand Central Station, still faster, while Lyphoudt the storyteller droned on:

"There used to be a fellow who owned a little shop where he sold junk. Any old piece of junk he found lying in the street or could buy for next to nothing. But he never sold any of it; no one was interested. One night thieves broke into his place and stole everything he had. He spent the rest of his life wandering the earth searching, and every time he saw a piece of garbage in the street he would pick it up and try to determine if it was something from his shop. He could never quite be certain. That's what finally drove him insane."

Diaghilev began to howl. Their speed was such that he feared this engine would tear something loose in the night, drawing something inconceivably massive from its orbit, bringing disaster down on all of them. The collision was approaching—the end of the line. They would strike East End Station and hurtle on through, soaring straight off the rails, straight out over the horizon into space, rushing out to meet that cold black body which even now hurried toward them.

They tried to calm him, but he would not be calmed. They laid him flat on his back on the cabin's floor and tried shining the light in his eyes, but then he saw the ceiling of National Observatory Station closing down like eyelids and he struggled aright, throwing off men much younger and stronger than he. Ahead lay Suburbia Station, and then East End—and certain death.

"Stop the train!" he cried. "Don't you see what you're doing?"

They looked at him with perfect understanding. They did see.

"I'm not part of this," he told them. "You can't do this to me."

"There's no escape," said dog-faced, mournful Chassagnac.

But Diaghilev would not hear it. He pushed his way to the back of the car and threw open the door. They should have been approaching Suburbia through the industrial regions, tanks and towers and pipelines, all edged with signals and indicator lights, guy wires singing in the night.

But there was nothing outside the car. No light. Not the faintest sliver of a single star. No sound of wind, despite the incredible velocity of the train. The other cars loomed ahead of them, hiding the future from sight, masking all trace of their destination. "There's a place for you!" he heard Stillson saying, but that place was oblivion—it was somewhere beyond all understanding.

He reached out for the car, leaning for some handhold, poised unsteadily in the utterly airless, soundless, motionless dark—

And fell.

He caught himself, regained his balance, landing in sudden light on a train platform.

It took him several moments of turning about to recognize the station.

Suburbia!

He turned around again and again until he was sure of it. He laughed, insanely relieved to be alive, then listened for the train, head cocked to the eastern tunnel into which the Sigma must have plunged. Soon, any second now, would come the sound of the great collision up ahead at the not-too-distant East End Station.

He listened.

Listened.

And heard nothing.

Nothing.

And then he heard a train.

It was hardly what he had expected. Another train, approaching. At the hybrid Sigma's rate of speed, there should have been a horrible crash by now. Instead, here was the predictable clangor of a Beta locomotive, its bell sounding nearer and nearer, one shriek of the whistle rising as it plunged through the tunnel into Suburbia Station. Light flared along the rails, creeping in just ahead of the train itself.

The Beta came in from the east, slowing. It emerged from the tunnel that had swallowed the Sigma. There was no way they could have avoided each other—and yet, here it came, easing along the platform, as if the other train had turned to mist somewhere along the line.

He watched without comprehension as the Beta drew to a halt beside him, disgorging passengers. They moved immediately toward the exit tunnel. Since he was at the end of the platform, none headed in his direction—but even so, one of them paused and glanced sideways at him.

He saw her face and let out a gasp. But she seemed not to recognize him; she glanced back once again, troubled, then apparently dismissed him from her mind and hurried into the exit tunnel.

Only then, broken from his trance, did he call after her, perplexed beyond measure: "Elena!"

It could only have been she. Elena, her face still fresh from his earlier glimpse of her that evening, in West End. Her red hair marked with its distinctive streaks of silvery gray—although her hair seemed less lustrous, as if the gray had spread from its narrow bands and speckled the rest.

He hobbled after, reaching the tunnel well behind the last passenger. The stairs were steep and he was weary long before he reached the station above. The footsteps of the other passengers had already faded away. He limped alone through the echoing lobbies until he finally surrendered to his infirmity and found a bench where he could watch the entrance doors.

Beyond, the night was as black as could be, save for a long row of streetlamps set just within a row of trees. The lamps lent a warm inner light to the autumn-colored trees, making them seem to glow from within, like muzzy lanterns of orange and gold and soft rust-colored glass. He had been aboard the train so long that dawn should have come many times over, he felt; but clearly he was disoriented and in need of sleep. He had survived the ride, and that was enough.

Above the station doors was a clock. As he sat with his arms folded, sinking into his coat and already drifting to sleep, he watched the hands, their motion barely perceptible. He noted the time as his last act before dreaming, and repeated it inwardly, wondering why it did not trouble him more, as he fell into a radiant greenish darkness: *Eleven o'clock. Eleven o'clock. Eleven o'clock.*

ELEVEN

AS ELENA PASSED DOWN THE LONG PROMENADE
from Suburbia Station toward her nearby apartment, a chill wind
reached through the trees lining the walk and brought a fall of sere
leaves down in her path. Autumn leaves, she thought, and an autumn
wind as well. It was scarcely September but frost already brittled
the meager grass and the iron breath of winter tainted the air.

Time seemed to move so quickly these days. She could hardly
keep up with her work, let alone phenomena of the outside world.
The short summer, the even briefer spring, were distant memories—hardly memories at all, in fact, considering that she had seen
little of the world apart from the converted water tower and adjacent laboratories where she had worked alongside George Tessera
for the last year and a half.

This was an early night for her. Usually by the time she was finished with work, or too exhausted to continue, the trains had
ceased running and she retired to a cot in one of the utility buildings that stood in the tower's shadow. That shed was her second
home—and sometimes felt more like her first. Uncomfortable as it
was, it was hardly less pleasant than the one that awaited her down
the long row of suburban towers.

At the end of the station walkway, the trees and small margins of grass ended abruptly; beyond, concrete held perfect and unbroken sway. The long avenues had been planned as if without human inhabitants in mind, so desolate that she rejoiced at the sight of a ragged weed thrusting up through a tiny crack in the pavement. The buildings were so tall, and on such narrow streets, that they appeared to lean and touch at their tips.

She had learned to count the buildings as she passed them, for the street numbers were poorly lit and in many cases absent, and the towers were practically indistinguishable. When she came to the seventeenth set of opposed towers, she turned and went into the one on her right. Inside, the lobby was a concrete floor like the apron of a garage, deeply stained. She came and went at such odd hours that she rarely saw another inhabitant of the buildings. Despite their incredible size, the towers were almost empty. Suburbia was an experiment that had failed. Her neighbors should have been engineers and chemists and technicians; instead, they were plumbers and welders and custodians. The industrial region was kept in adequate repair; it was maintained for some distant future of unparalleled productivity; but it was hardly put to optimal use.

The elevator had never worked, as far as she could tell. The stairwell was dark and silent, with a bulb on every other landing, entailing long climbs through dimness. At the twelfth landing she pushed through the door into her own corridor, uncarpeted, unpainted, unfurnished. Room 12-C-23 was a long walk from the landing, in a far corner of the tower, C-quadrant. Sounds carried well in the bare passageways, but it was never possible to ascertain their source. As she went along, slowing to peer cautiously around every corner, she could hear the distant bellows of a man and the shrieks of a woman. They grew fainter as she approached her own apartment, but she could not shake the echo. Once, hearing horrible screams after gunshots, she had tried calling the local security office. The phone had rung and rung, and eventually she had realized she could hear it ringing simultaneously somewhere far away in the empty tower.

Her door was like all the others; she had made no attempt to personalize the exterior of the apartment, not wishing to draw any attention to herself. As she fit her key into the lock, she forced herself to remain calm. Her sudden fear bewildered her, until a hand closed on her shoulder and another came over her mouth, silencing the scream that otherwise would have come.

"It's me."

She relaxed, but her dread did not leave her. His grip softened as she turned, her panic turning to anger.

"Krystoff!" she said, turning the name into a curse.

He nudged her backward, into her darkened apartment, then returned to shut the door across the hall. She had a glimpse of the opposite apartment, the floor littered with crumpled paper bags and cigarette butts. He followed her into her own apartment.

"What were you doing in there?" she asked, feeling for the light switch. He caught her hand and brought it back down to her side; his other arm went around her back.

"I've been waiting for you," he said. "Waiting two days now."

"You're lucky you didn't wait a week," she said. "I hardly use this place now."

"Busy, busy woman," he said, brushing his lips against hers, his cheek rough with stubble. She smelled cigarettes and something stale and fruity—probably pemmican, which he would have brought to feed himself during the long wait.

"My work keeps me away," she said.

"So busy you've forgotten who you're working for?"

"I haven't forgotten," she said, pushing away from him, finding the switch now. The room came into view around them, but it was not much of a revelation. A narrow bed, a dresser, little else.

"Then why no communiqués? Why no word for over a month?"

"There's nothing to report. Nothing of interest to you."

"To me?" he said, swaggering. "Don't you mean, to us? To all of us?"

"Things are going very slowly."

"I've heard otherwise," he said, dropping onto the edge of her bed, striking a match before he had even pulled a cigarette out of his pocket.

"What have you heard?"

"That you now have access to the ordnance factory. That you come and go from Army installations without a second glance from the checkpoint guards, they're so used to seeing you. You're no longer subjected to searches."

"There are plenty of detectors in those checkpoints, more accurate than a human guard."

"Even so, Elena, I'm sure you can find a way to outwit a simple electronic device. I'm sure you've been thinking about these things."

"I have been thinking about my work. Without constant devotion to that, without understanding what I am doing, I am useless to the Third Force. It takes all my concentration merely to remain useful to George Tessera's project. Once I am no longer important to the Empire, I will be terminated. And because I would be considered a security risk at that point, I believe 'terminated' is the appropriate term."

He watched her, unblinking, then exhaled a cloud of smoke.

"So tell me. How close are they to having a bomb?"

"It is . . . on the horizon. Something as massive as Orlovsky hopes, something capable of decimating the Republic and gaining their total surrender after one blow, will take a great deal of time. But it is a near certainty. The refining operations must be expanded, however; that is the bottleneck."

"But Orlovsky is a megalomaniac. Surely Slowslop doesn't think along precisely these lines."

She turned away, worried that he knew so much—perhaps more than even she. Krystoff had many sources. Like the Empire, with its omnipresent agents, the Third Force had eyes everywhere. Eyes fixed on her from every direction.

"Slowslop," she said carefully, "has his own agenda, I believe."

"I am told he has kept back a portion of all the processed ore, and that it travels to a separate, secret installation."

"You know this for a fact? Your source is reliable?"

"Our source," he said, "is Oskar Gondarev. He has been running an intelligence operation of his own, within Army Intelligence."

"Captain Gondarev's a double agent?"

Krystoff smiled. "He sends weekly transmissions to Onegin. We have been monitoring them for some time. Gondarev suspects

Slowslop of duplicity, but he has been saving the information until he can turn it to his advantage—to get closer to Orlovsky, I imagine. I fear, my dear, that he suspects you as well."

"Me? Of what?"

"He is not exactly sure, but he is watching you. He is the main reason I have been reluctant to ask you to make your move. In the meantime, we have learned something else from him—something that will make your work much easier."

"Go on."

"He has arranged for a breach of security. Several agents of the Republic, with his help, will make off with a large quantity of refined xenium ore and the plans for a ship Slowslop has been secretly constructing. With this information in Onegin's hands, the balance of power will tip very slightly toward equilibrium . . . both tyrants will gain an even tighter grip on their people. But we won't let things get that far. The ore has been set aside in a secret place while Gondarev awaits the right moment. We are going to seize it for ourselves. But first we must eliminate Gondarev."

"Explain," she said, irritated now to realize the real reason for Krystoff's visit. He wanted something of her, as usual. Krystoff took out another cigarette and handed it to her. She did not bother to remind him that she did not smoke.

"We are furnishing you with the frequency of Gondarev's transmissions. You are to supply them to your brother at the earliest opportunity, along with your suspicions about Gondarev. I assume he will be able to take care of the rest himself."

"How am I supposed to do this?"

"Tell him you accidentally came across one of the transmissions while investigating unused frequencies during your research."

"That makes no sense."

"Then contrive something that does! Make it convincing. You came across the transmissions, they made you suspicious, you decided to turn the information over to him. However you accomplish it is up to you."

She set the cigarette on the top of her bureau, turning away from him. "Krystoff . . ."

"What?"

"You don't . . . there is nothing left between us, is there?"

She heard him shift on the bed, and then he sighed. "Elena, how would you have it?"

"I don't know," she said. "I only—when I think about it, I think it must be over."

"How often do you think about it?"

She let out a small chuckle. "Not often, I admit."

"Well, then. That's evidence right there, isn't it?" He came up behind her, put his arms around her, and for a moment she stiffened—then began to soften, covering his arms with her own.

She turned toward him. He looked weary, as if it were costing him a great deal to focus on her for even this moment, when so many matters of greater importance weighed upon him.

"Elena, we still have the Third Force. We are comrades in that. When all this is over . . . who knows? But for the moment, I seem to have room for nothing in my life except the struggle."

She nodded. "I know, Krystoff. I only wanted . . . confirmation."

"I do love you, Elena. But exactly what that means, what it's worth, is beyond my ability to say."

She put her arms around him, laid her brow against his throat for a moment, then pulled away.

"I won't distract you any longer," he said. "It's already midnight." He kissed her on the forehead. "Get some sleep."

When he was gone, she sat on the edge of the bed monitoring her emotions, searching them for some clue as to what she felt. At a loss, she switched off the light and moved back to the bed. She took off her shoes, her clothes, and crawled under the covers. Somehow the room never seemed dark enough, there were so many sources of glare among the apartment towers. She went to the window to pull the blinds, and instead picked up the cigarette and began to tear it open, dropping thready clumps of tobacco onto the bureau. In the light from the window, she could see a string of figures, barely legible. Already her mind was at work on explanations Louis would not question.

A shadow blotted out the paper. She glanced up, wondering what could have crossed the window at this height.

Out in the air, silhouetted against a line of security lights that blazed from the rooftop of the opposite building, she saw an image she had nearly forgotten, and nearly ceased to believe in.

The figure of a boy, which quickly grew translucent, then vanished completely. It left her wondering why the dream had come again, just now.

Her eyes went for no particular reason to the sky above the line of glaring lights. She squinted, unable to see the stars, hardly able to see the night at all. But when she closed her eyes and pulled the blinds, the afterimages lingered so that she had a vision of blazing stars streaming down upon the buildings, and a sky full of white fire, and the boy staring at her with a fixed and urgent expression.

TWELVE

BEHIND THE DOOR OF ROOM 306, GONDAREV WAS
yelling at Dr. Reif, shouting in such a fury that Louis knew there
was no point in knocking. He would not have been heard. Instead
he opened the door quietly and let himself in.

"—utter failure! Do you realize how this looks to Intelligence?
You have failed to accomplish even the smallest goal of your project."

Charles Reif sat in a chair near the Sensorama device, cowering
under Gondarev's attack. "There are no guarantees in science," he
said faintly. "The whole project was an experiment. When you
interrupted us, we had only preliminary results. We were sure of
nothing."

"Nothing! And that's all you've accomplished. How do you think
it makes me look? This is *my* project, not yours; I am blamed for
your failures, your incompetence. An army of men we've subjected
to this gadget of yours, and every one of them shattered beyond
repair. You were supposed to imprint them with a new conscience,
with loyalty to the Empire, not make husks of them. What good are
they now? They're a greater burden than they ever were as citizens."

"Now, that's not completely fair, Oskar," Louis said, drawing
Gondarev's attention—and with it, his ire. "Look at Diaghilev, for

instance. He came in a collaborator with the Third Force, and went out an avowed enemy."

"You're only guessing, Hausmann. He was to have been a counteragent, but he's worthless now. You'll never convince me we planted coherent memories."

"This entire science is in its infancy," Reif said defensively. "We don't have the vocabulary we need to write completely new memories. The brain responses have yet to be charted. It's the work of decades, and you want results in months. If I had time to conduct even basic research, to analyze results, maybe things would be different. But you're bent on using this thing as . . . as a weapon. You have no respect for science. I can't be held responsible for the delays!"

"No? But I can."

"No one holds you responsible for the Sensorama's failure, Oskar," Louis said. "Not for that."

"What do you know, Hausmann? And why is this any concern of yours?"

"It's my concern because I am taking over the project."

"What are you babbling about? You're the ferryman, Hausmann. Go pick up another load of prisoners or beggars and stay out of my way."

"There's only one prisoner I'm interested in right now," he said, and seized hold of Gondarev's arm.

The other man met his eyes, holding in his scorn; but he must have sensed something in Louis's face, for gradually another emotion began to dilute his outrage. Was it fear?

"I would like you to read something, Oskar. Read it and initial it, if you would."

"Read what?"

"A statement. A transcript, actually. Of a conversation you had only last night."

Gondarev paled, looking down at the proffered paper. He clearly didn't need to see more than a few words of it. He wrenched his arm away from Louis, making no move to take the paper.

"I won't listen to this," he said. "You're concocting lies because you want my place."

"I don't need your place. I have one of my own. But since yours now falls to me, I must accept that responsibility, and relieve you to take responsibility for your treachery."

"Treachery? Why, I—"

Words failed Gondarev for once. He was trembling, uncertain of his next move.

"Reif? See what you've done?"

Charles Reif rose slowly from the chair, and backed into a corner of the room as if Gondarev might lash out at him.

"It's not his doing, Oskar. He's done all we've asked of him. He's been loyal enough. But you . . ."

Gondarev suddenly spun away, heading for the door. He moved heavily, but Louis made no move to stop him. All that Oskar accomplished, when he pulled the door open, was to reveal the Imperial Guards who waited in the hall.

They caught him by his arms and walked him back into the room.

"What? What is this?" he cried.

A moment later Slowslop entered. "Have a seat, Oskar," said the Supreme Commander. The guards pressed Gondarev down into the chair that faced the Sensorama.

"Commander, I—I demand to know the source of these accusations."

"The source? Why, words from your own lips incriminate you." He took the transcript from Louis and held it out in front of Gondarev's eyes. "Do you deny having this conversation?"

As Gondarev glanced at the paper, his entire body sagged. He sat limp in the chair. His head fell forward.

"I thought not. Well, your honesty is appreciated, even at this late juncture. Secure him well."

This last command was made to the guards, who fixed the straps onto Gondarev's arms. Finally realizing what was in store for him, Gondarev began to struggle.

"Dr. Reif, your assistance please," said Slowslop. "Is there any way to calm him, as you would any other recalcitrant prisoner?"

Reif came forward slowly. There was a small black case on the desk. From it he produced a hypodermic needle and syringe.

"No," Gondarev said. And he began to howl.

"I'll need his arm," Reif said, and Slowslop nodded. The guards released one of Gondarev's arms and pulled back the sleeve, holding the limb steady while Reif made the injection. They strapped him in again, but it was less critical now, for he had ceased struggling. He sat with his head resting in the padded clamps, staring forward into the faceted globe that stared back into the room like the compound eye of a fearsome metal insect. His mouth hung open.

"Now, Dr. Reif, if you please . . . I believe we have a selection of test memories for implantation."

Reif nodded, drawing over another case. He clicked it open. Inside were a number of capsules containing specimens of ore, some artificially deposited in geometric crystal patterns, others rough lumps of refined stone.

"None, sir . . . none proven effective yet, as I have tried to explain."

"I understand the Sensorama still leaves something to be desired; but even a crude result will be appropriate for this patient."

"Sir, he . . . whatever he's done, it . . . he doesn't deserve . . ."

"I'll be the judge of what he deserves." Slowslop looked over the case of ore capsules, and then shook his head. He took one from his pocket. "Try this one, if you will. It was prepared at Lord Orlovsky's explicit instruction." He leaned over to put his mouth near Gondarev's ear.

"Oskar? Can you hear me? On this crystal, if I am correctly informed, some of our specialists have recorded the entirety of Lord Orlovsky's *Mentations and Excursions*. You'll be honored to learn that we're giving you the first trial. What better way to reform you, I wonder, than to imprint these valuable and fascinating ruminations at the deepest levels of your psyche? And if you are less than a model citizen at the end of your reeducation, I will be very much surprised and disappointed."

Gondarev emitted an agonized moan.

Slowslop handed the capsule to Reif. "Go ahead, Doctor."

Reif went to the rear of the Sensorama and inserted the capsule. Louis knew events were now out of his hands. He had done what needed to be done; every day that Gondarev sent his transmissions to the Republic posed a greater danger to the Empire and its populace. Who knew what damage had already been done? Gondarev had been privy to many of the Empire's secrets—the Sensorama only one small part of the greater plan.

The Sensorama device began to whine and glow, the gleaming sphere turning, the surrounding mirrors rotating and swiveling. He had watched enough men in this condition to know what came next, but he still was not immune to it. It frightened him, for always he imagined himself in their place. If some enemy of his within the Empire ever found a way to incriminate him, however falsely, the same fate might be his.

Gondarev's body began to vibrate, as if strong electrical currents were being discharged into his flesh. As the prismatic sphere spun faster, throwing its focused light straight into the prisoner's eyes, his shudders gradually ceased. Louis smelled urine; a wet stain darkened Oskar's lap, but the man himself was oblivious. Drool spilled over his lower lip. He was rigid, eyes fixed on the luminous whirling target. Already, the personality Louis had known was being erased.

Louis started to back away, as he often did at this point. He had never been able to witness an entire procedure. But he froze with his hand on the doorknob, realizing that everything was different now.

He was in charge of the Sensorama Project. He had not realized what that meant until this moment. He could no longer leave, no longer disclaim responsibility for what went on in this room. He must stay to the end.

It was his duty.

Slowslop turned to see him standing by the door. Louis had already released the knob. Now he stepped forward, nodding, ready to take charge.

The Supreme Commander was smiling, beaming, delighted. But why? Was he pleased with Louis's demonstration of loyalty?

Or was it simply the destruction of Gondarev that made him smile?

■ ■ ■

That same evening, Louis stepped out of the elevator and into the West End Hotel lobby. Normally the rich, comfortable furnishings of the old hotel calmed him, but tonight his mind was full of images of Gondarev transformed: his eyes vacant, lips trembling and slick with drool. It had been difficult to see Oskar's mind slowly degraded, the proud officer reduced in a matter of hours to a condition Louis heretofore would have considered unimaginable. Now he no longer needed to imagine; the main difficulty lay in trying to forget.

Still, duty had compelled him to turn Oskar in, and there was no doubt the move would improve and consolidate his position. In fact, he stood now as Slowslop's right-hand man, with no other officer even close enough to vie for that position. Oskar was gone.

Gone.

He did not understand at first why he was so troubled. He had led dozens of men to the Sensorama.

The difference was that he had known none of them. It was possible to imagine that their utter collapse before the xenium rays was the result of some internal weakness, something that would have been an obvious character flaw if he had only known them.

Now he knew otherwise. He had observed Gondarev for years. The fact that as a double agent he had insinuated himself so high in Army Intelligence only increased Louis's respect for his abilities, his cunning. No, Oskar was not a man who should have melted under the first rays of the greenish glare.

It meant that anyone was vulnerable. He could not stop thinking of Gondarev's eyes, how they had seemed to sink away into his face, how his face itself had seemed to recede from the room, tangled in the skein of shadows cast by the Sensorama.

He pushed through the doors and onto the street, hoping a short walk in the fresh air would clear his head. Instead he saw Orlovsky towering above West End Square; Orlovsky, in whose name all of this was accomplished. Would Gondarev's fate have been necessary had Orlovsky not come to power? Things had sometimes been uneasy between the old nation and the Republic, but at least there had been peace for several generations. With the Revolution, with the coming of the Empire, all that had changed. Paulo's whims were unpredictable. It was no wonder Onegin had felt it necessary to plant a man as close as possible to the aging lord.

Aging . . . and failing. His manias frightened Louis. He suffered lapses of memory, episodes of strange behavior that could not adequately be described by the word "senility." In the grip of such weaknesses, it was quite possible he could trigger a war—or something worse. They were building weapons in the mountains to the west, in the underground labs; weapons powered by the meteoritic ore. Xenium fueled the trains; it drove the Empire itself now, and its properties were still incompletely understood, as unpredictable as the Emperor himself. It was a dangerous combination.

Only Slowslop, cold and implacable, seemed unperturbed by Orlovsky's madness.

Louis waited for a word from Theodore Slowslop. Waited for the call to overthrow Orlovsky and establish a new order.

He waited, and wondered if he would answer. Would he follow Slowslop? Were the Supreme Commander's motives any clearer than Orlovsky's?

Louis walked, trying to find some clarity in the crisp night air. Suddenly he realized that the world seemed to be shimmering with colors that should have been confined to Room 306.

He glanced up at the third floor of the hotel and saw a pair of windows glaring with the spectra of the Sensorama. The shades should have been drawn—that was bad enough. But the machine itself should not have been in operation, not without supervision.

At that moment, someone moved across the glass. Each room in the hotel had a tiny decorative balcony, which he hardly would have trusted with the weight of a flowerpot. But someone was standing on the balcony of Room 306, silhouetted against the Sensorama's glow, spying on the room.

He let out a shout, and the voyeur's head turned slowly. Louis stood petrified, recognizing a face he had not seen in nearly two years.

It was the boy—the one from the Restricted Zone, from the hospital.

The shout died in his throat. He pulled his gun, aimed without a second's thought, and fired.

The window flew into shards. The boy turned away slowly. Louis fired again, this time hearing cries from within the hotel. He was certain he had hit his target, for the boy had seemed to fall forward, into the room.

A bellboy and several Imperial Guards rushed out onto the steps of the hotel. "Watch that window!" Louis ordered them, running past into the lobby. There was no time to wait for an elevator; he leaped a cordon and rushed into the stairwell, and threw himself up the stairs to the third-floor landing.

The corridor was chaotic. Guardsmen had poured into the hall, and several were now pounding on the door of Room 306. They stopped when they saw Louis, but he merely nodded for them to continue. An instant later they smashed the door in.

Six guards rushed into the room with Louis at their heels.

The shattered window allowed gusts of cold air into the room; the carpet gleamed with broken glass. Other than that, it was exactly as it had been all afternoon. The Sensorama whirred to a halt, its inner lights dimming, but there was no sign of an operator. The chair in front of it was empty. A guard came out of the bathroom, shaking his head.

"There was a boy," Louis said hesitantly. The men gave him a puzzled look.

He went to the window and leaned out, risking his weight on the rail of the balcony. Other guards moved on the grass below, probing the hedges with flashlights.

"Who . . . who was the first one here?" he asked, and a young man stepped forward. Louis remembered his name as Kunz.

"I've been stationed at the door all night, sir."

"And no one came out?"

"Not since Dr. Reif, sir, no. That was about half an hour ago, after they took the, uh, captain away, sir."

"Reif," he repeated. He looked up at the ceiling. Room 406 was Reif's. "You three men, come with me. I want you to check the halls, check every room, and continue to search the environs. I'm sure I hit him. He couldn't have gone far. There should be a blood trail at the very least."

He hurried up to the fourth floor. A strange stillness prevailed, as if it were in another world from the rest of the hotel. Listening for a moment at the door of Reif's room, he thought he heard chamber music, very faint.

He turned to the guard stationed at Reif's door. "Have you heard anything from him tonight?"

The guard shrugged. "He's been quiet all evening, at least since Commander Slowslop was in to see him earlier."

Louis knocked sharply. "Dr. Reif? It's Louis Hausmann. Forgive me for disturbing you, but I have to make sure you are all right. Dr. Reif?"

There was no answer. He supposed Reif could have been in the bathroom, but in that case he would make his apologies later. The door locked from the outside, and he now carried Gondarev's keys. It took him nearly a minute to find the right one.

Inside, the bedclothes were turned down, the pillow plumped, a sheet of paper and pen laid out under the desk lamp. The radio played softly next to the desk. The bathroom door was open; a toothbrush sat on the edge of the sink, with a wormlike strip of beige toothpaste gleaming on the bristles. He went to the window and tried without success to raise the shades. They had been sealed shut; the window itself was bolted from without.

Reif was gone. Along with the boy who might never have been.

"Sir. Look there."

Louis turned. Kunz was pointing at the center of the bed, as if reluctant to approach the tiny lump of matter there. It was a tiny disk of xenium, rounded and porous, as if swiftly melted and cooled. Had Charles been pilfering samples from the Sensorama's power core, gathering shavings which he secretly fused for a private supply? Or did Reif have access to the material from some other source?

There were those who feared to touch the ore, following unfounded reports of illness at the mines; but Louis was not one of them. He plucked it from the sheets, found it only slightly cool to the touch—just cooler than his body's temperature. And while the upper surface was fairly smooth, the obverse of the disk showed a checkered pattern like that of finely woven cloth.

He dropped it in his pocket like a coin or a talisman, stroking it between thumb and forefinger while he wondered what it meant, and where to turn next for answers.

The boy was the most maddening part of the puzzle.

What if Oskar's exposure had something to do with it? What if the boy worked for the Republic? That had been their suspicion when he first appeared, hadn't it? Had a boy come attempting to rescue Gondarev? It was ridiculous. How did Charles Reif figure in this? The pieces didn't fit together.

The one man who might know something was Oskar Gondarev.

"Call the Commander," he told a guard. "Tell him to meet me in Gondarev's room."

Louis trudged hopelessly down to the second-floor officers' quarters, past his own room. Gondarev had been locked in; a guard was stationed outside. Hausmann motioned for the man to let him in, then closed the door behind him.

The only light came from the panel of the radio cabinet. Oskar lay flat on his back on the bed. His eyes were open, staring upward. He made no move as Louis walked toward the bed.

"Oskar. Can you hear me? Do you remember anything?"

One treatment, he thought. After one treatment, he cannot be completely expunged. There must be something left of the man.

"Oskar!" he said again. "Answer me! That is an order!"

Gondarev's eyes slid lethargically toward Louis, fixing on him. Gradually his head followed. He stared without blinking, and then he began to smile. His eyes closed sleepily, then opened again.

"Hausmann," he said thickly. "I saw you there."

"Oskar. Listen. Do you know of a boy?"

"The boy . . . yes. Is he here already? So soon?"

"You know him? Who is he? Is he one of Onegin's?"

"He comes from beyond. The angel of lurid light. If you have seen him, then you . . . you must listen. I see you in the dark, Louis. The boy is not there. *They* are here now. There!" He raised his hand weakly, pointing toward the center of the room. "In the branches, do you see them? Who planted that tree, Louis? Why here? Why does it grow here?"

"Please, Oskar—"

Gondarev's arm swept sideways; his hand clenched Louis's wrist. "Please don't let them find me."

"Who do you mean?"

He drew Louis closer to him, down to the bed, his mouth inches from Hausmann's ear.

"I should not be here. I cannot swim. Bear me up. I beg you, Louis! I will drown! Please!"

Louis put his arms around Oskar, trying to draw him up, but Oskar seemed to grow heavier, as if another force in the room were pulling him down. Suddenly Oskar's eyes rolled up, his muscles went slack, and he flopped back onto the bed. This time he seemed to be unconscious.

Louis whispered his name, then moved back. As he turned, the door swung open and Theodore Slowslop stepped into the room.

"Sir, I—"

He was not sure what he meant to explain, but Slowslop nodded as if he understood. Arriving at the bedside, he pulled back one of Gondarev's eyelids with a thumb, leaning close as if to look inside his skull.

Slowslop began to make a strange noise in the back of his throat, a faint high sound like a repressed shriek.

"Sir?" Louis said after a moment.

Slowslop made no move. Louis stepped around the bed, ducking to catch his eye. "Sir?" The sound grew higher and higher, while at the same time receding, as if a droning insect were dying in Louis's ear. Something about Slowslop's expression, or the lack of it, alarmed Louis. He put out his hand to give the Supreme Commander a slight shake, to bring him back from wherever he had gone.

It was the first time in Louis's memory that he had ever touched Slowslop without express invitation.

For an instant he had the distinct impression that his hand was passing through Slowslop's arm, as if through a glossy black mist. Then he made contact.

The room was suddenly overrun with corrosion, the walls gleaming with a metallic sheen, everything bubbling and blistering, as if the world had been carbonized, reduced to an ashen shell. Before he could register this, the images already had begun to change. Water rose from the carpet, flooding the floor, coming to his ankles, swallowing the bed, closing over Gondarev's face, swirling down his open mouth, rising past Slowslop's wrist. Louis gripped Slowslop's arm more tightly, terrified to let go, terrified to lose himself here. Slowslop still had not moved, even though Gondarev was now lost beneath the surface of the iridescent waters, opaque as mercury though they looked clear as air.

Louis could hear insects, the same high shrilling that emanated
from Slowslop's throat. A horrible chittering song came from the
trees whose black clutching forms suddenly emerged from the walls,
snatching at the sky, dragging long limbs through the water. He
looked around wildly but the world was dark. The only light came
from beneath the water, shimmering from sunken objects whose
shapes were blurred, tiny balls of light that made him think of the
Sensorama's xenium core, the light from the three-dimensional
scanner, the light in the boy's eyes . . .

Far in the distance he could see things that were not trees,
shapes too angular to be natural. He was unwilling to move toward
them. He would not let go of Slowslop for anything in the world.

Out in the dark, light began to play along the edges of the shapes,
painting them in colors of rust and decay. A train . . . he swore he saw
a train half buried in the mud, draped in the strange sharp leaves, and
beyond were the skewed lines of toppled scaffolding. Why could he
see them now, when an instant before, they had lain lost in darkness?

Then he saw the lights, discrete points of luminescence swarming
through the trees, through the branches, catching him in a cold glare
that felt like scrutiny. They rose above the wreckage, limning it in
cool fire. They cast no reflection on the water—if what he saw was
water. He stood utterly still, wishing he could quiet even the beating
of his heart, anything to avoid their attention. The lights rose and
fell above the ruined hulks, tracing glowing paths in the blank and
staring windows, weaving through the branches of the trees.

Slowly, Louis turned his head; movement of any other kind was
almost impossible. The water held him prisoner. He found Slowslop
looking back at him, mouth agape, as if surprised to see him here.
The Supreme Commander's eyes were glowing beneath the smoked
lenses of his spectacles; his luminous irises bore the pattern of the
wallpaper of the West End Hotel, unchanged, uncharred. In the
center of his pupils, a prism full of greenish gold light spun and
flickered and dazzled. It was the Sensorama, spinning there inside
Slowslop's skull, a miniature Room 306 sucking him in. He was
about to suffer Gondarev's fate.

Groping desperately and instinctively for something with which
to save himself, his fingers closed on the small disk of xenium he

had taken from Charles Reif's bed. Simultaneously, his other hand unclenched from Slowslop's arm as if blasted away.

The bright shapes in the trees, like the disembodied eyes of astral watchers, plunged toward him, converging on a single point. He raised a hand to ward them off, covering his eyes, holding up the metal ore—and then he realized that everything had changed again. He was back in Gondarev's room.

The only point of light now was the radio cabinet, its glow as soft and muted as the music it emitted.

"All right," Slowslop said suddenly, looking at Louis as if nothing unusual had occurred. It was inconceivable, wasn't it, that the Supreme Commander could have shared his momentary delusion? Slowslop stepped away from the bed, hands clasped, deep in thought. "He's no use to us now. Nor to Onegin. We'll continue to treat him, of course, just to be certain; but that should be routine. I believe you can handle the device yourself, can you not?"

"But . . . but Professor Reif . . ."

"I have given the order for his death, wherever and whenever he may be found. In the meantime, I'll expect a full report on exactly how he managed to escape. Not that our friend Oskar will be able to follow in Reif's steps."

Gondarev's eyes were closed now. His breath was ragged, uneasy, and he whimpered in his sleep. Louis remembered quicksilver draining down the man's open throat.

Slowslop put out a hand to clasp Louis's shoulder. He flinched at the touch, but this time there was no shock, no sudden shift of scene. He could feel the xenium "coin" digging into his palm, razor edged. He thrust that hand into his pocket and let the token fall.

"It's on your shoulders now, Louis. But I know you're the right one. The only one."

"Thank you, sir," he said, and then he glanced toward Oskar, as if the man might be eavesdropping.

"Don't worry, Louis. He's as good as dead." Slowslop allowed himself a small smile. "Better."

THIRTEEN

THE MONORAIL RIDE FROM EAST END STATION TO
George Tessera's laboratory complex should have been the most
depressing stage of Elena's commute, but for some perverse reason it had always delighted her. The overhead track carried the
small car down an avenue lined with enormous factory storage
tanks and power stations, grubby monstrosities that looked as if
they had come from some squalid, far-distant future, although
she could remember this zone from her early childhood. As a girl,
traveling alongside her father, the huge grim shapes of industry had seemed marvelous and terrible at the same time, and
something unaccountably magical still lingered in them. They
had no purpose she could understand; it was difficult to ascertain if they were still operable or if they had been abandoned for
years.

The water tower was somewhere in the heart of the zone. The
monorail went no farther, and she had neither the inclination nor
the authorization to proceed deeper into the smoky, acid-reeking
industrial jungle. Sometimes she saw gray-suited figures, hooded,
gloved, and masked, in the middle distance, among the squat towers. But they were not commuters on her route. Almost invariably,

unless George accompanied her, she was the monorail's only passenger.

Today, as every day, the car slowed to a stop alongside a suspended platform and Elena disembarked, taking metal stairs down to the cindery earth. The spiral stairs leading up into the water tower lay just ahead, thin blue wafers ascending among the massive black legs of the tower and the surrounding latticework of reinforcing girders. As she climbed to the main floor of the tower, she heard voices on the platform suspended just above—George and another man. She slowed to listen, but they must have heard her coming. She heard her brother say, "Elena?"

She climbed to the next level.

"Louis, what are you doing here?"

Louis looked anxious, weary, his uniform rumpled. George Tessera stood beyond, his face very grave. Her brother seemed small and cold in the huge hollow tower, out of place among the research equipment.

"I've come here for answers," Louis said.

"Your brother seems to believe we know more than Army Intelligence," said George with faint sarcasm.

"I know that you in particular have secrets, Dr. Tessera. I have been in charge of tracking the whereabouts of every member of the Sensorama project. All seven of you—or should I say, all six?"

"I see why you didn't pursue a career in mathematics, Lieutenant."

"Do you want me to tell Slowslop what I suspect about Horselover Frost?"

George stiffened slightly.

"He's the only one of you I've never been able to track down. Odd, considering that he was supposed to be the head of the team. But I have been in the old university archives, examining some of your original reports, and interestingly enough, the few papers and journals of Horselover Frost all seem to be in your handwriting."

"I was his assistant," George snapped. "I did a great deal of paperwork for him."

"Really."

Elena said, "What are you saying, Louis? That you can't find Dr. Frost, and it's somehow George's fault? Maybe he's gone underground and joined the Third Force. Maybe he's defected to the Republic."

"Maybe he never existed," Louis said levelly.

"That's ridiculous. I met him myself."

"You?" Louis paled. "What?"

"I met him years ago, at the Academy."

"But . . ."

George gave her a grateful look. "You can't blame your failure to find him on the rest of us, Lieutenant. Dr. Frost has his own reasons for seclusion. He was always secretive, preferring to work through intermediaries."

"I don't . . ."

Her brother gave her such a stricken look that she nearly pulled him to her. "I . . . I don't know what to think anymore."

"Are you well, Louis?"

He held out his hand and opened his fingers to reveal a small lozenge of what looked like rarefied xenium. "Do you know what this is?"

"Where did you get that?" George Tessera asked.

"Charles Reif has been working in our employ for some time," Louis said.

"So I've heard."

"Last night he disappeared, and I found this in his room. This and . . . and there was a boy at the hotel at the same time. A strange boy I saw once before, nearly two years ago."

"A boy," Elena repeated. Suddenly she felt as if she had tapped into Louis's madness—as if, all along, they had shared it without realizing.

"What else?" George said.

"I had . . . visions. I don't know what else to call them. I saw a place. A swamp, I guess. It was full of wreckage—a train, all sorts of machines. And strange lights."

"Lieutenant, can you be honest with me?" George said, gripping Louis's arm. "Has Reif been working with the Sensorama? An advanced model?"

Louis nodded slowly.

"And you . . . have you spent much time in proximity to that device?"

"A fair amount, yes."

"May I ask, since we are sharing secrets now, may I ask to what use the Sensorama has been put?"

She saw in Louis's face the conflict of duty and terror. He knew he must not speak of these things; and yet, to save himself, he must. Terror, or rather truth, finally won out.

"It—Dr. Reif, that is, under Slowslop's orders . . . at Orlovsky's call . . . they have used . . . attempted to use the thing as a . . . a re-education device."

"Reeducation? Don't you mean brainwashing?"

"Not exactly—I mean, that wasn't their intention. But it has proved difficult to harness the thing. What the Emperor wants is to instill utter devotion in all his subjects. To eradicate reactionary thinking, yes, but also to . . . to make himself a god in the eyes of every citizen. The results have been erratic, at best. It's one thing to erase thoughts; it's another to write in new ones. Slowslop claims to have some method—and I thought you, or some members of your team, might have developed it—a method for actually inserting new memories. He uses crystals of this ore, this xenium. But I am not at all certain they work."

"Where does he find these crystals?"

"I don't know. I assume Slowslop has another group working on that. He delivers them himself."

"May I see it?"

He held out his hand for the xenium disk, and Louis gave it to him.

"Elena," George said, "why don't we take a look?"

The water tower was dominated by the huge xenium-driven analyzer. A laser hung suspended thirty feet above the platform, set in a movable mount. Even as Elena placed the lozenge in the analyzer, directly beneath the laser, she felt it was pointless. George and her brother were looking for empirical explanations to a mystery that remained stubbornly irrational. Xenium's properties remained as mysterious as its origins. Despite her devotion to

George Tessera and his projects, she felt increasingly certain that whatever answers were to be had would not be discovered in laboratories. It was symptomatic of Orlovsky's Empire that every new discovery must be considered in practical terms, put immediately to work—ideally, as some sort of weapon. All the while, the evidence surrounding them implied that true knowledge ran deeper than mere applications, and a stranger reality held sway. It was frustrating now to see George ignore every odd aspect of Louis's story and concentrate on the mere physical attributes of the disk.

While George powered up the laser, Louis asked, "Why did you ask about the Sensorama?"

"The device generates a field, Lieutenant—one we have not had the time or authority to properly investigate. The earliest models, including the original Beam Machine we developed in the Academy, merely seemed to draw forth old and buried memories, occasionally recombining them into images that appeared strange or unfamiliar. We had hopes of understanding the brain, the nature of consciousness itself, with careful application of the device. But then came the Revolution. In developing the next model, the first Sensorama, we realized it might be possible to imprint memories—new memories, that is . . . false images. But the means of doing so was unpredictable. We had hardly finished building the device when Slowslop seized it, and Charles disappeared. If Dr. Reif made claims for its utility, then I am afraid they were false claims."

"It does *something*, Professor. I've seen its effects."

"Oh, I'm certain it does. Especially now that it has a xenium core. Our biggest problem was finding a suitable power source. But xenium is more than merely a source of energy. The objects it powers display unpredictable behavior. I'm afraid that by standing near the Sensorama, working in its proximity, you could be subjected to some of the same effects as the victims."

Louis gave him a look of horror.

"Yes, Lieutenant. You might have made a victim of yourself. Ready, Elena?"

She nodded, then stepped away from the analyzer. George touched a switch, and a beam of cold green xenium light lanced down from the tip of the laser.

There was a burst of light from the disk itself, and then a high tone rang through the water tower, echoing from the high metal walls, making the entire chamber ring sympathetically. The wail continued to rise, filling her mind with shifting pools of resonance. The tower seemed to melt into a realm of pure sound. Her mind filled with images that grew from the tones: scents and textures and emotions, a complex sensory symphony.

But across the mesh floor, Louis was down on his knees, hands over his ears, eyes squeezed shut, mouth wide. He might have been howling, but she could hear nothing but the music. She turned to see how George was reacting, and received another shock.

In George's place, before the analyzer, stood Horselover Frost.

The scientist was unchanged since she had last seen him. He gave her a smile, a nod, and then began to walk toward her. As he moved away from the analyzer, George reappeared, as if Frost had momentarily eclipsed or emerged from her mentor. George stood motionless, unblinking, staring straight into the heart of the xenium ray. But Professor Frost walked right up to Elena.

"You are beginning to understand," he said. "That's why I came to you, Elena, and why I have come again. They have all had glimpses of what is coming—they have all seen beyond, and denied their visions. You are the only one who tries to understand. There is something in you we can reach."

"We?" she said. "Who are you?"

"I am an echo from your future. I ride shock waves that weave above and below the plane of spacetime. You and I can meet only at certain predictable points where your timeplane intersects with the wave. This far from the timepoint of impact, the oscillations are very broad and slow, and we can touch only infrequently. But as we come closer to the center, to the instant of impact, the waves grow shorter and more compressed. It becomes possible to meet with greater frequency. Near the catastrophe itself, there is something very close to perfect continuity, a total collapse of time."

"What catastrophe?" she asked. "What is the source of this shock wave?"

Horselover Frost looked back across the room at George Tessera. "Ask him," he said. "They know. They all know. You may think them criminals for hiding the knowledge, but we cannot judge that. We come only to offer you an opportunity. Since you show the promise, the capacity, to understand."

The ringing had begun to die. To fade away. George Tessera was moving very slowly toward her, as if he had glimpsed Horselover Frost.

"Wait," she said.

". . . soon," said Frost, and as the ringing faded so did he.

Louis stood up slowly, uncovering his ears, and looked into the empty heights of the water tower, as if wondering what he had heard. Amazed, he turned to Elena. "Did you hear that?"

She nodded. "I don't understand it, but I heard it."

George, looking vaguely puzzled, turned back to the instruments. She came up beside him, heard him mumbling to himself.

"Hmm," he said, walking over to the bit of xenium. It had fused again, and was now cooling in the shape of the receptacle.

"Well?" Louis asked.

George shrugged. "It's pure xenium," he said. "Nothing in the least unusual."

■ ■ ■

Ask him, ask him, ask him.

Horselover Frost's words went round and round in her mind, thrumming hypnotically just below the rhythms of the train. *Ask him ask him ask him.* This particular rhythm did anything but lull her.

Was it possible that a disaster could send shock waves radiating in all directions, not only in space but in time, so that echoes of the future catastrophe would be perceptible before the occurrence? Was this a rational explanation for premonitions?

But if so, then why didn't all disasters cast a shadow back through time? Why couldn't she foresee every event of any significance?

Perhaps the disaster involves xenium, she thought. George had always been puzzled that it didn't give off radiation far more intense than they had measured. What if it emitted a form of radiation undetectable to them because it propagated not through space but through time?

With Suburbia Station just ahead, Elena rose and started making her way toward the end of the car. The train slowed, hissing to a halt. As she opened the door, she found a black cordon stretched across the opening. She could have sworn she had boarded at this end. She turned about and went the other way, but when she reached the opposite door the latch was frozen. She leaned on it with all her weight, then pounded several times in case a conductor might hear. No one answered and the door would not budge. She started back to the other door.

Traversing the length of the car seemed to take an age; her body, leaden, dragged her down. The train was moving again, accelerating out of Suburbia Station. She saw the station sliding past the windows, and then they were out in the tunnel, in the dark. Moments later the night landscape, the industrial forest of towers and girders, stretched out before her.

Furious, she went back to the cordoned door and threw it open.

This time the way was clear. No cordon blocked her way. She stepped into the small foyer, peering around to make sure there was no cordon anywhere, nothing she might have overlooked.

Rather than reenter the car which had given her such trouble, she determined to keep walking. Soon they would reach National Observatory Station, where she could disembark and catch the next train back to Suburbia.

The next car had six private compartments. A long aisle ran past the closed doors. She stood at the window outside the first door, faintly aware of murmurings from within one or more of the compartments.

What kind of catastrophe? she wondered again. What could it possibly be?

If George knew the truth, it must relate to something he was working on. And the thrust of George's research, she knew—although she did not as yet have authorization for direct involvement in that project—was development of a weapon.

A xenium bomb.

Was that it?

Would there be a research disaster? Something she herself might be involved in?

Or would the bomb be completed and detonated in war with the Republic, causing the disruptive timewaves?

How far off was this disaster? How much time did she have?

Her only hope was that it might be preventable. The binoculars had shown her a glimpse of the future, but she had managed to alter events when the time came to live them. At least her own behavior was within her control.

The train was slowing again. This time nothing stopped her from disembarking. She found herself alone on the platform of National Observatory Station. She headed through the gate, toward the passage that would take her to the opposite platform. At the far side of the outer lobby was a doorway leading into a waiting room, and a movement there caught her eye.

It was the boy.

He stood just within the doorway, waiting for her. As she caught sight of him, he twirled and slid away out of sight.

Tonight she did not hesitate to follow him. She wanted answers, and nothing the Empire had to offer—nothing in science or industry—would calm her mind. Even George Tessera, her mentor, was suspect now, if only because he had closed himself off from all but the most limited possibilities. Horselover had not appeared to George after all. It was up to Elena to understand.

Crossing through a room full of waiting pews, she reached steps leading down into another access tunnel. The steps, like the tunnel below, were of gleaming whitish tile; but the raw walls above the tile looked as if they had been melted from solid rock. She felt as if she were moving down a throat. There went the boy, gliding up the stairs at the far end. By the time she reached the spot, he was gone.

At the top of the stairs, emerging between gates of black iron, she found herself on the red brick path leading to the doors of the National Observatory. The walk was lined with metal pillars and arches topped by softly glowing lamps, and beyond the arches were trees that seemed to be lit from within. Hybrid gingkos with sharp leaves, strange geometries. The observatory was a towering confection of frosted glass and steel, seeming seem as delicate as sugar and ice, yet housing an enormous telescope. One of the dome's high sliding panels was open tonight, and the snout of the telescope thrust toward the heavens. She had no call to visit the observatory, but the boy had beckoned, and she felt the pressure of uncertainty. She was surprised to find the doors of the observatory open. Inside, primitive cycads thrust up alongside the public path, contributing to the impression that this was a large conservatory; yet the mass of the telescope dominated the place. As she walked forward on the red tile path, she saw a man at the base of the telescope, sitting on a chair inside a small enclosure. He was bent forward with one eye to a viewing lens, making small notations on a pad.

"Excuse me," Elena said.

The man turned quickly, startled. She was no less startled to see him.

"Dr. MacNaughton?" she said.

He didn't recognize her at first. He looked as if he had to come back from far out in the darkness he'd been studying. His face was long and heavily lined; he looked so much older and more worn than she remembered him. It had been years, after all, since before the Revolution. "Is it . . . ?"

"Elena," she said. "Elena Hausmann."

"Yes, Elena!" He stood up and, somewhat awkwardly, put out his hand. She shook, although for a moment she felt they would embrace. Once they had been so close. It was sad, now, to feel so stiff and formal with him.

Distracted, he looked around the small space, then motioned at the chair. "Why don't you have a seat?"

"No, I'm fine. I missed my station, and thought I'd stretch my legs while I waited for the return train to Suburbia."

"Are you sure you won't sit?"

As he reached to pull the chair over, he upset the pad on which he'd been scribbling. It was stuffed full of loose papers, scraps of notes and equations; some of them slid to her feet. She helped him gather the sheets, noticing that his hands were shaking.

"Are you all right, Doctor?"

"Please, Elena . . . it's been a long time, but call me John. George mentioned you were working in his lab. He says you're doing wonderful work. I'm so sorry things went . . . well, didn't work out as we'd all hoped."

She nodded. "And what are you working on?"

"Me? Oh!" His nervousness seemed to increase. "This is just a hobby. I have use of the observatory some nights. My real work is out at the Army Hospital, assisting Constantine. We've been scattered all over, haven't we? Thomas Reich was assisting with mining operations, last I heard. He built some kind of excavator. What he's up to now, I don't know."

She looked down at the sheets in his hand, and saw a small pencil sketch of a tiny teardrop shape surrounded by a faint halo, trailing a long tail. The little ellipse had a line running to it, labeled "*Coma.*"

She pointed at the sketch. "Is it visible now?"

John MacNaughton went white, following her eyes to the page in his hand. His fingers tensed, nearly crumpling the paper. "As . . . as a matter of fact . . ."

She slid into the chair, leaning to the eyepiece.

"Elena . . ." He plucked at her shoulders, hesitant, but she could sense that he wanted to pull her away. What was he hiding?

And then, remembering Horselover's words, she had a wild insight. "*They all know . . .*"

"George told me," she said impulsively.

John gasped; his fingers tightened. Then he sighed and closed both hands on her shoulder.

"I—I'm sorry," he said. "You must think I'm a fool. I didn't know he'd told you."

The viewfinder was cloudy. "Touch here," he said, positioning her finger on a focus knob. She rolled the knob and suddenly the cloud sharpened into a brilliant white spark surrounded by fainter light.

"That . . ."

"That's the comet," he said. "It's beautiful, isn't it?"

"Yes."

"It's hard to imagine that something so beautiful can be so . . . can mean the end of everything. Of course, it's not everything, not on a cosmic scale. It's just us, isn't it? And what are we really? Insignificant. Who cares if there's one civilization less in the universe? Who will remember, in all the vastness of creation, that we ever existed?"

His words were like something from a dream; they scarcely seemed to touch her. And yet this, she knew, was why the boy had brought her here tonight. This was George's secret. Not a bomb, but a comet. A catastrophe.

"When, exactly?" she whispered. "Do we know for certain?"

His voice was grim. "To the day."

"How much time do we have, John? How much time?"

Looking at her, he began to grow even more worried. "George didn't . . ."

"He wouldn't tell me," she lied. "That's why I came to you. I have to know. There are things I must put in order."

"Put in order?" His long face stretched further with amused disbelief. "There can be no order, after this. Nothing will remain. Do you know what it means, Elena? The sky will ignite. The mountains will turn to liquid. Earthquakes could split the planet to its core. And then darkness and cold; after the fire, ice. No one can escape, nothing can survive. There is no bunker deep enough. Even the Ark is a ludicrous gamble. Supposing it's ready in time, where can we possibly go?"

"The Ark," she whispered.

"You . . . you are coming? You must be coming," he said. "Surely George wouldn't have mentioned this unless . . ." He studied her eyes, and then his face fell. "You didn't know, did you?"

She stared at him fixedly, afraid to betray anything more.

"Please don't tell me you . . . you didn't even know about the comet? Elena, please, I couldn't live with myself if I . . . if I thought . . ."

"I knew," she said, as firmly as she could. "My brother is in Intelligence. He is very close to Slowslop."

"Oh, yes, then I suppose he would know. And George didn't tell you."

"No."

He nodded. "The truth is, I wish more people knew. We have pushed for full disclosure to the public. Eventually everyone will know. We'll be held accountable then. And if word of the Ark gets out, if it spreads, there will be trouble. There's limited seating, to say the least, and no time to build a fleet of ships. That was the original plan, but now Slowslop's narrowed everything down to just the prototype. Poor Thomas. He has pushed himself to the limit building even one of the things. If we had time, we might have managed to set up an assembly line, but . . . but time is the one thing we don't have."

"When?" she asked again.

"You're better off not knowing."

"I need to know."

"There's no changing it."

"Then what is the harm in knowing?"

"What is the good?" he said. "Don't ask me again. You already know too much."

She saw determination in his eyes, held back by dread. And in fact she was not so sure she wanted the complete truth. The knowledge would come soon enough, wouldn't it?

Instead she returned to the eyepiece for a final look. The comet streamed toward earth, its tail scarcely more noticeable than a hairline scratch on the lens.

As she stared, something swam across her eye, a blurred shape that wouldn't be blinked away. It settled against the field of stars, rippling and swarming, gaining substance, until she saw the face of the boy staring down at her, blank and yet beseeching. The comet burned in the center of his forehead.

Who are you? she asked him silently, urgently.

What are you trying to tell me?

"You should leave now," John MacNaughton said, pulling her away from the lens. "You can't just stare into it like that. It's not healthy. I—I've done too much of it myself. It's like looking into the eye of death."

And in fact she did not want another look at it. The image of the boy still clung to her eyes, superimposed wherever she looked.

"Catch your train," John said, not unkindly, giving her a gentle push toward the doors. And Elena went.

FOURTEEN

SLOWSLOP KNOCKED ONCE AND LET HIMSELF INTO Paulo's office without waiting for a response. The old man was at his desk, scribbling away, and did not bother to raise his head.

"What is it?"

"My lord. With all due respect, I do not believe you are taking the wisest course in this matter."

"This is none of your concern, Theodore. None at all."

"My lord, that may be true in a very broad sense, but as a specific matter, Miss Hausmann is an old acquaintance, and I believe it would be most unwise—"

Paulo slapped his pen down. He would have thrust himself to his feet, but his trembling hands could hardly find purchase on the edge of the desk. "Are you saying I am a fool?"

"Far from it, my lord. But in this instance, you lack a certain perspective. Your judgment is clouded by passion."

"Yes! For once! And a grand thing it is. To hell with judgment! I have paced myself for too long, planning every move by inches. It's time for a leap, Theodore. She is the only thing in my life I have not been able to predict. Why must I wither to a fleshless, juiceless old mummy, without once having tasted anything but the life of the mind? She is my passion. I lost her once before, but I will not lose her now. If I do, then all is meaningless. I might as well lose it all."

"I only meant, my lord, that you risk a breach of security in telling her anything. At least in doing so this soon."

"I want her with me. Even if it means eliminating someone else. That is all. That is final."

"But—"

"That is final, Theodore. Now leave me before she arrives. I will not tolerate your presence this evening. Unless *you* are the one who wishes to be left behind."

Slowslop bowed as was his custom, and backed out of the room. He went immediately to his own quarters, locked his door, and then went into his inner room.

He had amassed quite a collection of xenium crystals, arranged in partitioned wooden trays. Some were encysted or encapsulated, others sat in the open air. Some were rough nodules of ore with impurities that affected the material's properties in useful ways, while others were pure and gleaming spheres and cubes and fragile lattices. Slowslop plucked out one piece shaped like a lightning bolt or jagged *S* and set it on the desk before him. Beside it went the crystal labeled *"Boy."*

Slowslop removed his spectacles, folded them, and placed them on the desk. Then he sat very still for perhaps an hour, his mind occupied with a hollow rushing sound, as if he were himself a train plunging through a tunnel in perfect darkness. When it seemed that he could accelerate no faster, that he was in fact no longer moving at all, he reached out and took hold of the two xenium crystals.

Suddenly he was moving through the walls of the West End Hotel. It was disorienting for a moment; he had not traveled thus in a very long time. He took pains to separate himself from the wallboard and other conglomerations of inert mass that filled the building, so heavy that they had acquired something like self-consciousness. But his identity was stronger than all the random accretions of matter, and old habits quickly took over. With great deliberation and increasing agility, he transferred himself from wall to floor and then through the ceiling of the room below. It would have been a taxing leap to cross the relatively diffuse atmosphere of the corridor, so he instead confined himself to the solids. Touching first the brittle glue that bound the wallpaper to the wall, then the hollows and wires and mortar between the boards, he gradually made his way into Orlovsky's dining room, groping blindly up into the table and chairs, dismayed to find them empty. For a minute he nearly snapped back to his accustomed form.

They must be nearby. He sniffed for some vibration of Orlovsky, and caught instead a whiff of Elena Hausmann.

With the perception came instantaneous transition. He was there, in her hands. She gazed down upon him, but did not recognize him as Slowslop. By reaching out lightly he could feel her lips moving, as if whispering his name. By a deft recalculation, he translated movements into sound, just in time to hear her say distinctly, "Oh, Paulo, you've dedicated it to me after all?"

Slowslop could not hear Orlovsky's response. He was too engrossed with the sensation of being a book in Elena's hands. She was turning his pages, lifting him gently and setting him down upon himself again and again. The pressure of her eyes was subtler and even more thrilling than the touch of her fingers. His only displeasure came from knowing exactly which book he must be.

He slid downward, along her hands, her arms, over her body and legs, until he merged with the floor. There he waited like her shadow, clinging to her warmth but unable to touch her, unable to merge with her whole mind. He could read nothing but echoes, now mixed with Paulo's dry, distant grumblings. Slowslop grew very thin and enormous, then, coating the interior of the room, curving down along the light fixture, reaching into the filaments of hot wire which rang with every word spoken below.

Paulo said, "Of course, my dear, it was written for you. Only for you. I suppose it is my apology for earlier harshness. Perhaps I—I retaliated too cruelly those many years ago. In fact, I'm sure I did. But you must understand, my dear, I felt cruelly used. I felt there had been such a—a sympathy between us, and that you had made your feelings clear to me in every way."

"My—my feelings?"

"And so, spurned, I could not control myself. My passion, for once, got the better of me. I could not help but . . . but take out my anger, and

I suppose I contrived to revenge myself in the way I thought would do you the most harm. I knew your hopes for a career. I knew and yet—yet I loved you so much I couldn't bear to lose you."

"Paulo, my lord, please, I'd rather not stir up such things. It was long ago and—"

"Stir them up? But they have never settled, Elena. I am full of torment over what I did. My feelings for you have continued to deepen over the years. I still want you with me."

"I . . . I don't . . ."

Slowslop strained toward her, and the fragile filament burst. In the suddenly darkened room below, he sensed the old man's desperate rush forward. Paulo's vague form was attempting to engulf Elena.

"It's all right, my dear!" Everything in the room now rang with Paulo's voice; Slowslop's mind was filled with the horrible buzzing. "I'm here to protect you. I can take you away from this place. If you will only be my bride, I will save you from a fate that few suspect. You can be among the chosen, my darling—for I choose you."

They struggled. More than that Slowslop could not ascertain with any specificity. Her voice was choked, indistinct. Paulo said, "You are the unicorn, Elena. My unicorn. You are the reason for all I have done. I built this Empire for you, my sweet child. Now come! Open your mouth! Share it with me!"

She tore away somehow; and then Slowslop felt a part of himself torn open. Light poured through the wound. Elena rushed out into the hall, toward the elevator.

In a rush of darkness, Slowslop retracted. A cyclonic gathering of thought, black with emotion, dimmed his private cell. One hand relaxed almost imperceptibly and the other tightened, this one clenching the scanner's storage cell. After much practice, he had learned to project and animate the captured matrix; the essence had eluded him, but he still had the form.

Leaping out again, more concentrated now, he found Elena in the elevator, ascending. It was almost too late to stop her, but he laid a finger on the wires beneath the control panel and the car slowed to a halt. Another touch and the doors slid open.

Slowslop let himself congeal.

Elena's eyes widened with recognition, although it was not Slowslop she saw hovering in the corridor.

So, he thought. *She knows him.*

He had suspected as much.

He withdrew slowly down the corridor, waiting to see if Elena would follow. As hoped, she stepped from the car. He pulled back faster and she began to hurry after. He spun around and plunged straight through his door, sure that she was following.

Slowslop dropped the crystals and pushed himself away from the desk, moving as quickly as he could, although every motion seemed to drag through the thickened air. Reaching the door, he caught himself and slumped against it, exhausted; but there was no time to waste. He staggered into the outer room, nearly throwing himself forward. Everything seemed painfully bright.

He opened the door before he had properly recovered. He did not want to give her the opportunity to doubt what she had seen.

"Elena," he said, without slurring her name.

"Theodore?" He could see the light of trust dawning in her eyes.

His head dropped forward, but he dragged it upright; his eyelids sank, and as he hauled them open he realized that he had forgotten his spectacles. He clapped his hands over his eyes, whirling away. "Just a moment," he said, peering between his fingers. He went back to the inner room and grabbed the glasses from the desk, wondering what she had seen.

When he came back, she was still standing in the hall. He motioned her in, feeling stronger now, almost himself again.

"Please come in," he said, motioning her into the room, closing the door behind her. "What brings you here? Ah, I remember. You and Paulo dined together this evening."

"I—I really don't know why I'm here," she said with veiled expectancy, as if hoping he would be able to explain.

"You . . . you look shaken," he said. "Can I get you anything? Please sit."

"Thank you. I'll be all right. It's just . . . it's . . ."

The sight of Elena in distress due to Paulo's madness drove him to madness of his own. The old man had gone too far. Slowslop's disappointment was vast—and reserved mainly for himself.

"It's Paulo, isn't it?" he said quietly, taking her hand.

Elena looked on the verge of tears, but she fought them back. There was some of her old anger there, the look he remembered from that day many years ago, in the greenhouse of her family's home. But something cooler, a mature and calculated anger, now prevailed.

She nodded. "Yes. Again."

He led her to a chair and drew one up for himself. "I should have warned you."

"Why, Theodore? How could you? It's none of your concern."

"But I know him. I saw this coming. It has grown and festered and I should have found some other way to release it."

"Don't be ridiculous. It's not your fault."

"What did he tell you, Elena? What did he ask?"

Her face reddened. "He said I was his unicorn. That the symbol of the Empire, all of it—it was me. The unicorn. It's preposterous, really."

Slowslop nodded. "And did he tell you what it means to him? To be his unicorn?"

"I . . . I'm not sure I follow."

Slowslop found Orlovsky's greatest secret very easy to betray. "He saved himself for you, Elena. The unicorn comes only to the virgin, and he has kept himself . . . 'intact' is not the word I seek, exactly. 'Pure'?"

Elena's hand went to her mouth. In her eyes, horror mixed with amusement.

"Can you . . . are you serious?"

"He is a foolish old man. He would jeopardize everything for you, and yet he is worth not one of your tears."

"Don't worry about me," she said. "I won't shed any this time, not over him. Unless . . . ." Suddenly she looked stricken, pale. "No, he wouldn't do it again. He—he wouldn't."

"In his way, Elena, I'm afraid he is very predictable."

She rose suddenly. "Oh, no. No, Theodore, not again. What can I do? I have been working so hard with George. I feel we're so close, and . . ."

Slowslop moved close to Elena, never touching her. "I promise I will do what I can to ensure your safety."

"He can't take it away from me again. Not now."

"If he can be reasoned with, Elena, I will reason with him."

She blinked away tears. Making a muffled apology, she put her hand on the doorknob.

"I will do what I can. Please don't worry."

But she was gone. The door swung shut but never quite closed until Slowslop helped it into place.

He made no attempt to follow her. He sank back into his chair, staring at the door, letting his mind expand outward through the hotel, for once unconcerned with what might happen if anyone sprang in on him right now—not that it would be possible to surprise someone who was aware of every movement in the West End Hotel.

But then, through half-open lids, he saw that someone had come upon him without warning after all.

It was the boy, standing just inside the door, blinking at him.

"You," Slowslop said, uncertain if it were a trace image, something emitted by himself, or if the escaped essence of the actual boy were out raising havoc in the Empire.

He rose to his full height and took a step forward, but the boy did not waver.

"Well?" he said. "Are you going to speak?"

The boy blinked.

"Am I supposed to think you are inevitable?"

Blink. No change in expression. Nothing. The scanner had done some injury, weakened the boy significantly, he was glad to see. The messenger seemed unable to deliver any message.

"Begone, then," Slowslop said, casting up his hand and turning away. But he could sense the boy behind him, and he could see his reflection in the curved metal hood of the desk lamp, in the glass that covered a framed photograph of the Imperial Museum. After a moment the boy pressed forward out of these images, materializing against the wall Slowslop stood facing.

Blink. Blink.

"There is nothing you can tell me that I don't know already."

Blink.

And then it occurred to him why the boy was hounding him, why he hung around wordlessly.

He had forgotten. Forgotten what he was and why he was here. Forgotten the nature of his errand.

So he clung to Slowslop, hoping for clues. The boy must have sensed the scanner crystal in the next room; must have known that the rest of him was in there. But he was unstable, unable to bridge the gap; Slowslop blocked the way and straddled the abyss. Slowslop made unity impossible.

Slowslop began to chuckle.

"So that's your story, isn't it?" Slowslop was greatly amused. "Well, you won't find wholeness here, my friend—my child. Only fragments. Bits and pieces of the Empire, of the planet, all the finely scattered particles. You're only the first of many. And I can scatter you farther, keep that in mind. You won't know who to haunt if you're not careful."

But he was talking to emptiness now. Talking to himself.

The boy was gone.

He was fatigued. He must replenish himself. The night's efforts had taken a toll, and there was still much to be done. Always so much to be done.

FIFTEEN

ELENA DISEMBARKED AT DOWNTOWN STATION AND found a telephone. It had been so long since she had used the protocol that for a moment she thought she had forgotten it. But her fingers remembered.

She dialed, listened for three rings, then hung up and waited.

How much time was left?

Uncertainty touched on every aspect of her life.

How much time remained until the comet's arrival?

How much time did she have before Orlovsky exacted the next round of his revenge?

She picked up the phone and dialed a second number. This time she let it ring once.

There was little she could do to prepare for annihilation. If there was indeed an Ark, then her chances of being aboard it now seemed slim. Unless she conceded to Paulo's wishes, he would make sure she died with the rest of humanity.

But in the brief time she had before losing her position, she must do something. She must remember her duty to the Third Force. If nothing else, she still had that. It had been her consolation, her satisfaction, in the years when she had nothing but the drab library job. To know that she was working against Orlovsky, as a courier, in whatever capacity she could, had always meant a great deal to her. And now she must again restore that meaning to her life.

A third number, followed by four rings.

She knew her duty. Knew as well that if she were to fulfill any part of it, she must act now, before Paulo lashed out at her. She doubted Theodore could do much to stop him. He had not managed to shield her before.

Finally she called the intended number.

"Yes," she said when it picked up, "this is the Imperial Library. Is Mr. Moholy available? Would you please let him know that the volume he reserved has just been returned and is available for lending. Several others have reserved it as well, so he should contact us immediately."

No one had spoken by the time she returned the phone to the cradle, but she knew her message would reach him. He knew where to find her. She hoped he came soon. She did not relish waiting Downtown all night.

And who knew what position she would be in tomorrow?

■ ■ ■

The Nova Express did not officially exist, even though several times a day you could hear it humming through the north-south tunnel that ran deep below the commuter platforms of West End Station. The gates to the underground platforms were always locked, and the train never slowed as it passed through. It took on no passengers. Fully laden, it began its journey at the refinery in the Restricted Zone, among the mountains to the north of West End, and carried its freight to the ordnance factory, which was part of the Army depot to the south.

But this morning, as it headed back to the mines, the Nova Express would make a rare stop in West End Station and take one passenger aboard.

Elena waited impatiently at the locked gate while Louis fumbled for the key. It was one he had never used; it had taken him an hour to locate it among Gondarev's possessions.

"Please, Louis, they're doing me a tremendous favor stopping for me here. I really can't be late."

"I know, I know, I'm hurrying."

She had phoned in Gondarev's prearranged signals, which Krystoff had given her. This had ensured the engineer would stop and wait at West End for exactly five minutes.

She had been unable to think of any better way to get down to the platform than to enlist her brother's aid, little as she liked to drag him into this. She had improvised a suitable lie, but it hardly explained her obvious desperation. She could hear the train waiting below.

"Please, Louis!"

Finally the key slid in with a grating noise, and turned. Louis threw off the chains and stood back, grinning. "Next time you'll board at the depot, as you're supposed to. I suppose I should search you before you enter."

"Don't be ridiculous. Oh . . ." She tried to say it casually. "The key. So I can get back out."

He glanced down, looking faintly puzzled, but knew there was no time to question her. He handed it over. She kissed him, then turned and ran down the stairs, down the corridor of pink marble tile, and under a wide arch into the one railway station she had never entered in her life. It was all stone arches, diffuse lighting, cavernous ceilings, so quiet that it was hard to believe all of West End Station sat above her. The only jarring sound came from behind, as Louis wrapped the chains around the gate and locked it up again.

The Nova Express did not clank or hiss or hum; it gave off a sound like wind howling over a plain. The ore-powered engine emitted a rhythmic thrum that seemed akin to silence. She searched the engine for the face of the engineer, but saw nothing—no viewing slit, no human eyes. The locomotive was almost featureless, low and sleek, streamlined like a missile. She ran alongside, looking for a passenger car. The train was built to carry ore, machine parts, and other cargo, but it generally carried at least one passenger car as well, for ferrying military personnel. Tonight it carried only two cars. The first one was unlocked.

Just as she clambered aboard, the train began to surge forward.

She found herself in a car of closed compartments, but she felt sure there were no other passengers aboard. She went along the aisle, trying doors, finding all of them locked, until she came to the sixth. She opened the door and went in.

A shiny silver suitcase rested on one of the seats. Her heart nearly stopped when she spied it. Someone must have left it here, she thought. Another passenger.

But as she stepped closer, she wondered it if might have been left for her. Was this part of Gondarev's plan? According to Krystoff, the former officer had arranged for a chain of events that would culminate in his defection—his return to the enemy Republic. If the suitcase were meant for Gondarev, then she might need it herself.

She sat down next to it, flicked the latch, and opened the case slowly.

The interior was thickly padded with gray foam. Embedded in the foam was a mysterious oval object like a long narrow egg with pointed tips. It was made of polished gray metal with silver ribbing; small translucent windows like portholes opened into its core. The pulsing glow inside the thing, orange and blue and golden green, was unmistakable.

She shut the case quickly, fearing it was something that should not yet exist. George would have told her, wouldn't he? He was a member of the bomb development team.

She had expected something massive, something capable of destroying the Republic. Surely this couldn't be it.

She would have to leave it to the Third Force to analyze. Its eventual use was not her concern.

After all, with the greater cosmic cataclysm just ahead, what did she have to lose? There was a chance of toppling the Empire before the end arrived. Perhaps then, with the populace mobilized and Orlovsky gone, they would find a way to build an army of Arks and carry millions to safety.

These, she told herself, were her motivations.

Tonight had nothing to do with revenge.

She closed the suitcase and watched the dark landscape, but all she could see was her own reflection gliding over the countryside, melting into something else, someone else. Her face . . . the face of the boy . . . Horselover's face . . . all seemed to merge. She jerked awake, discovering that the Nova Express had plunged into a tunnel. Stone walls, growing brighter. The train began to slow. They came out into a huge round subterranean enclosure. Light flooded down from the rippling dome of gray stone.

She was waiting at the door by the time the train came to a full stop. She leaped down into the roundhouse, hurrying toward the engine. Ahead were several elevators lining one arc of the vast circle.

No sooner had she passed the engine and stepped off the platform than the segment of track on which it rested began to wheel about, spinning the train effortlessly. Half a dozen other engines waited to roll out of the station; the one that had carried her rotated until it was completely reversed, then glided backward, parking itself alongside the other trains.

She watched it with dread, clutching the silver suitcase, feeling exposed and vulnerable. She had no idea which elevator she was supposed to take. Gondarev—or at any rate, Krystoff—had said nothing about an elevator.

Finally a man stepped out of the locomotive. For a moment she nearly turned and ran; then she scrambled to remember her story, fearing an interrogation. But her final emotion was relief, for the train operator was a friend—an old friend. She had not seen him since her days in the university, when he had worked alongside all the others on the Beam Machine.

"Hello, Elena," said Thomas Reich, appearing genuinely delighted to see her, as if they were meeting at a party. A brilliant engineer, he had always been the jolliest of them all, young and athletic, fond of working with his hands.

He started to put out his hand, then laughed at himself and embraced her.

"You're part of this?" she asked.

"I sometimes lose track of which hat I'm wearing," he said. "How have you been, Elena?"

The question threatened to pitch her into turmoil, and he must have sensed it.

"Don't answer," he said quickly. "How are any of us, after what we've endured? And considering what lies ahead . . . well, still, it's good to see you."

"Is this what it seems to be?" she asked, tapping the silver case.

He nodded. "I'm afraid so. I'm not exactly pleased to see it in your hands, either."

"It fell to me," she said. "I just don't know if I'm doing the right thing anymore."

He put his hand on her arm and started walking her toward the nearest elevator. "None of us does. We only hope we don't do as much harm as others who might be in our positions."

"I'm not sure what's expected of me."

"Don't worry. I am. It was worked out in advance by Gondarev—except you won't be running home to Onegin at the end of it."

The elevator proved to be not an elevator at all, but merely an automatic door into a short corridor, ending in another pair of doors. Passing through these, she found herself on a high walkway that followed the walls of a large rectangular room. In the center of the room was a raised platform, set with rails and large enough to carry a train car. A pair of huge metal doors at the end of the room opened into the stone heart of the mountain. A tunnel lost in darkness. The train cars must come through here to be loaded with ore, then brought back out into the roundhouse. But the place was quiet now.

Thomas led her along the walkway and into a room full of research equipment, some of which she recognized from her work with George Tessera. Monitors showed views of the huge main chamber, the roundhouse, and sections of the mines.

Thomas typed commands into a keyboard beneath one of these monitors, and on the largest screen appeared a picture of old tracks, half buried in dust, that ran right up to a blank rock wall. A few dim lights illuminated the scene, but it did not look like it was much visited. Thomas played with the control systems, and before Elena's eyes the rock wall slid or melted away. She could not tell if it had been a solid door or an illusory screen of some kind. The tunnel thus revealed was dark, but something massive sat within it.

"We hid the load in a blind tunnel far from the main excavation site," Thomas said as he continued to enter instructions. Slowly, the bulky shape inside the tunnel moved forward onto the tracks. It was a transport wagon, something between an ore hopper and a railroad car. It was difficult to be sure of its size, due to the image's lack of scale.

"When you off-load it," he said, "the track wheels will retract and rubber tires will come down. You won't have as far to haul it as Oskar would have."

"How did you end up helping him?" she asked.

"We've been in touch with Onegin for some time. He has been willing to listen to our warnings about the comet, out of concern for his country. His Command Tower contains a warning and detection system; he has been making his own plans to escape the impact. It's our poor luck that the xenium ore has been found only in the Empire."

"Then if Gondarev had smuggled it out . . . would it have gone into making weapons?"

"Some of it, yes. Onegin planned a preemptive strike against the Empire. But only so that he could get control of the mines and turn them to full-scale production of a fuel source for a ship capable of carrying us away from Earth before the comet's impact. If Orlovsky had put all his effort into manufacturing Arks, we might have some hopes of saving many people. With the Republic and the Empire working together, a huge rescue effort might have been possible. But that opportunity is almost certainly lost. We'll be lucky if we finish one Ark in time."

"But now you're helping *me*. Why?"

"I don't believe Onegin can make any difference, Elena. But maybe a well-planned strike, something coming from within the Empire, can open the gates for him. At the very least, the rest of us would be free to make a last desperate effort, without being hampered by Orlovsky's madness."

The car had been rattling along the tracks, moving into broader and brighter sections of tunnel. It came to rest on a massive elevator that lifted it up through a wide shaft. When it rolled forward once again, she thought she could sense the approaching vibration of its passage.

"Come along," he said, motioning her toward a door in the far corner of the control room. They stepped onto a walkway in the main chamber. She was in time to see the cargo wagon coming down the main track. Within seconds the car had come to a halt on the movable platform.

Thomas took her down a side flight of steps to the main floor. The cart was perhaps one third the size of a regular cargo car. Thomas continued to manipulate the operation from a control bank on the main floor. The platform was lowered to the floor and slid to the far wall, where another pair of doors opened into the roundhouse. One of the Nova Express locomotives waited outside. Thomas maneuvered the cargo load to the rear of the train.

"It doesn't look like much," Thomas said, "but it's refined ore, carried back from the ordnance factory. Slowslop has been diverting a portion of all refined ore for his own purposes; and Gondarev diverted a further portion of that. There is enough pure xenium there to bring the Empire to its knees, but it's only a fraction of what would be needed to fuel humanity's escape. Now, the rendezvous point is between West End and the Restricted Zone, just out of the mountains. Whether you want to go back on this train or not is up to you."

"I can't be caught here," she said. "It would be best for me to get back to Suburbia."

"Fine. We'll stop in West End to let you off again."

"I don't know why my presence was even necessary. It all seems automated."

Thomas shook his head. "I wouldn't do this for anyone else, Elena. Gondarev I knew, and his cause. Onegin was our best hope, but . . . he is helpless to assist us unless we can open the gates for him. I know you, and I'm sympathetic to the Third Force. You have some understanding, at least, of the powers in play here. And the great risks."

"I wish I understood more."

He gave her a searching look. "Let me show you something."

A door beneath the stairs led into another room directly below the control station. It was dark except for utility lights and a faint, familiar luminosity that seeped from a covered mound, two meters in height, in the center of the room. Thomas switched on the overhead lights and pulled away the covering cloth, revealing a cubical pile of polished xenium ingots. The ingots were stacked in columns, separated by sheets of a light silver alloy—the same stuff her suitcase was made of. The panels hung from an overhead track and pulley assembly, which apparently allowed the silver sheets to be manipulated by remote.

"The pile has a mass just below critical," he said. "These ingots are super-refined. Nothing we transport comes close to this density, this purity. We couldn't have survived this long otherwise. As an extra precaution, those separators, which are made of a xenium alloy, help prevent a chain reaction. The shields aren't really necessary until we exceed critical mass. So let me do just that."

From a pallet on the floor against one wall, Thomas lifted another ingot and carried it over to the pile. He set the single ingot gingerly atop one of the stacked columns, then returned to Elena's side.

"Now I'll remove the shields."

Thomas picked up a hand-size control box and began to flip toggles. One panel after another withdrew slowly from the pile. As the last panel cleared the pile, Thomas said, "Now watch the clock."

A large clock hung on the wall to one side of the pile. The time was 3:51.

Elena felt a sudden wave of nausea, as if the ground had surged away and come up again beneath her feet. At the same time, the minute hand of the clock sprang backward five minutes, then rushed forward to 3:55. A sourceless heat bathed her; she felt as if she were blazing with golden fire, but she could see nothing. Nothing but the minute hand, gathering force and speed, swinging back to 3:40 then ahead to 4:04. It continued to alternate like a pendulum, covering more time with every stroke. She gripped Thomas's arm, feeling as if the movement were taking forever. The room began to flicker, and she kept thinking she caught glimpses of herself entering, shadows of herself and Thomas scattering across the floor, translucent ghosts watching the clock. The minute hand seemed to stop again, resting directly on the 12, and then it blurred—disappeared.

Thomas also vanished. She was unsure of her own location, but

Thomas flickered into existence again, somewhere ahead of her. She saw the remote device hanging in midair, frozen in its fall, Thomas seeming to hover with both feet off the ground, several yards away. He seemed to be running for a moment, but then he appeared perfectly still.

One of the silver panels, she saw, had snagged on the edge of an ingot column. It was crumpling, refusing to slide back down between them, no longer inhibiting the reaction.

In the next flash of perception, Thomas was at the pile, caught in midleap with one foot extended to kick at the ingots.

And then he was falling to the floor in continuous time, while several of the columns toppled and slid against one another, eroding an entire corner of the cubical pile.

Thomas lay gasping where he had landed. She rushed to his side. "Are you all right?"

"Fine," he said. "That—I've never let it go that long. I don't know what might have happened if . . ." He caught his breath. "We should scatter them more, just to be safe. I know it sounds superstitious . . ."

She helped him shove a few of the ingots farther from the pile. Then Thomas gasped.

"What is it?"

His eyes were on the clock. It now read 4:47.

"The rendezvous," he said. "We're late!"

Leaving the xenium pile in a tumble, they rushed back out through the open gates into the roundhouse. Thomas hurried to the locomotive and hauled himself up, then signaled for her to join him. He helped her into the high car and busied himself at the controls. As he started up the engine, xenium light began to glow from a round grilled portal, filling the car with its radiance. The light triggered a sense of bewilderment. She was back in the room with the xenium pile, helping separate the ingots; she was watching the alloy shield crumple as it came down into the pile. She felt as if she were a disconnected series of Elenas, each slightly overlapping the other but without making contact.

The train surged forward, leaving echoes of Elena in its wake. Thomas gripped her wrist, as if sensing her disorientation. She came back to the moment, but she still felt as if she had left parts of herself behind, or scattered them ahead of her.

It seemed to take an age for the turntable to point them into the exit tunnel, but at last they were rushing through the dark passage. The cabin was not equipped with a forward window, only a monitor that carried an image of the track directly ahead. On this screen she watched their headlamp streaming along the tunnel walls. The beam suddenly spread out into darkness. Above were faint specters of stars, but the sky was less than perfectly black. To the east she saw the first brushstrokes of gold against a violet backdrop. It was a miracle they had not met the first shift of workers coming into the roundhouse. She wondered what would happen if another train were already coming along from the Army depot. Their schedule had been destroyed by the ill-advised pile experiment.

Now that they were in motion, Thomas seemed to relax again. There was nothing they could do but race for their destination, somewhere out on the monotonous steppes.

"What you saw back there," he said, "is only the merest sign of the xenium's power. To harness it has been a mixed blessing. Slowslop keeps pushing for its inclusion in every possible device; it makes an ideal self-contained power source. The tiniest piece provides what might as well be an infinite supply of energy. What I fear is that as xenium becomes pervasive, we approach a technological crisis point—something akin to critical mass, but on a scale as wide as the Empire. It's as if the experiment you just witnessed were being conducted on all of us, but with nothing to arrest or contain the reaction. There's so much xenium in everything these days—in this train, in our cameras, our batteries . . . what is the ultimate effect? I have experienced time distortions subtler and stranger than the one we deliberately created. What is the stuff doing to us?"

"And to make a bomb, you need only reduce the scale of your demonstration down to an atomic level."

"Exactly. Those big ingots were separated by inches—an immense distance in subatomic space. Now imagine the mingling of atoms; imagine compressing concentrated xenium to a critical density, if only for an instant. What sort of energy would be released?"

"But how would you achieve that sort of compression?"

"With a suitable explosive. The only thing we've found that seems likely to work is another xenium device."

His eyes went to the suitcase in her hand.

Elena felt herself go cold. "This?"

Thomas nodded. "The trigger."

"But who built this? And why?"

"Slowslop, of course. And for exactly the purpose we've been discussing. He has had us working on a bomb all along. Every other device springs from that basic research."

She looked down at the suitcase with horror.

"In itself, terrible as it may be, that is nothing. It's only a detonator." His eyebrows lifted and he stabbed a finger at the screen. "There they are."

Several small black specks waited beside the track. As the train approached, slowing, Elena saw a large truck surrounded by several waiting figures in dark outfits. Thomas brought the Nova engine to a full halt, then opened the door and climbed out.

Elena put her head into an icy predawn wind. The eastern horizon was starting to burn. The sight of the orange sky, with every star now washed out by the sun, set her on edge. This was all happening too late. As she jumped down to the frosted earth, one of the figures rushed toward her.

It was Krystoff, and he was raging. "You're late!" he cried. "Look at us—the sun is nearly up!"

"It couldn't be helped," she said. He started to speak, then growled and turned away, signaling the others to bring the truck around. The driver, Marnham, maneuvered onto the track at the end of the train. Two men worked to latch the loaded car onto the truck, while another unfastened the couplers that held it to the train. The car let down a series of hard rubber tires while the metal wheels retracted. Marnham pulled his load gradually off the track, onto the hard-baked earth.

"I'd best get on now," Thomas said. "You're coming back to West End, aren't you?"

Krystoff looked as if he wished to speak to her, but there was no time. She hesitated.

"Make up your mind," Krystoff snapped.

"I already have," she said, but at that instant someone let out a cry. The sun had just crested the horizon. Elena squinted into the light, wondering why it looked speckled with black. The spots grew larger, coming nearer; she could hear the angry buzz of engines.

Everyone began to shout at once. There must have been other craft circling silently above, an advance fleet, for suddenly shots were cratering the earth around them, cracking rocks and throwing dirt. Krystoff grabbed Elena's hand and hauled her toward the truck. Ada Gauss put out a hand to help Elena into the bed, but no sooner had she grabbed Elena than her fingers loosened. She sagged and toppled headfirst into the dust.

Krystoff scrambled in, and then they were moving. Krystoff tried shouting orders at Marnham but he couldn't be heard. The heavy load was slowing them, and they were cruelly exposed by the glaring sun, which now showed a sky full of aircraft.

Elena glanced back at the track, surprised and relieved to see the Nova Express already vanishing toward the south. Few of the aircraft seemed interested in following it, which was all the worse for the Third Force.

Krystoff climbed from the bed of the truck, making his way through the open passenger window and into the cab. She watched him through the rear glass, feeling as if he were a million miles away. She waited for death from above.

Several planes had picked them out, silent gliding shapes so beautiful that she found it hard to fear them. She crouched down, knowing there was no way to outrun them, not carrying such a load. If she decoupled the railcar, the truck would make better speed; escape might just be possible. It made no sense to abandon the xenium now, after all this work, but it made less sense for all of them to die. The xenium could be replaced, but not Krystoff Moholy. After Diaghilev's arrest, Krystoff had been the only one to take full control of the Third Force. He had overseen its day-to-day operations for so long now that his loss would be a blow from which it might never recover. They had all been fortunate that Krystoff was ready to step in when the old man vanished. There was no one comparable to take Krystoff's place.

Certainly not Elena. She was a positive liability to the Third Force now. Otherwise, how could they have ambushed the party so easily?

She made her way carefully to the back of the truck. Checking the cab, she was horrified to see Marnham lolling sideways, the top of his head laid open, skull and scalp hanging by threads of flesh. Krystoff struggled into the driver's seat, taking the wheel; the truck had already slowed so much that escape seemed impossible. The earth here was rutted by erosion gullies; the surprise attack must have sent them far afield from their planned escape route.

Elena stepped down on the truck's rear bumper and reached for the coupler. The latch was complicated. Once she had figured out the mechanism, she still had to hammer it loose with her heel. At the third kick, the coupler swung open, the truck gave a lurch, and she fell.

She came down hard in the cold bottom of a gully. The suitcase hit the ground beside her. She lay still, trying to catch her breath. The ravine held a fair amount of shadow, but she didn't count on it hiding her for very long. She blinked up at the sky, waiting for the first of the elegant aircraft to spot her. She saw the xenium car poised at the edge of the gully, as if the slightest pressure might send it toppling down on her.

That thought brought her to her feet. She grabbed the suitcase, dismayed to find it falling open when she lifted it. The detonator nearly dropped out. She set the case down and tried to force it shut, but the latch was twisted and useless. She took out the device, cradling it in her arms, and started looking for handholds up the side of the ravine.

A figure appeared next to the railcar, looking down.

"Professor Frost," she whispered.

He bent, lowering his hand to help her up. "It has begun," he said. "Come up now, quickly."

"Begun?" she said. "But the comet—"

"Not the comet. The cataclysm. It begins here." She scrambled up beside him; he caught her under the arm and helped her to her feet. He was anything but a ghost, she realized.

The sound of engines grew louder as the aircraft circled around to investigate. She wanted to crawl beneath the railcar; it was her only shelter. But Horselover Frost stood in the open with one eye cocked at the heavens. She began to feel she might be safe with him.

"What do you mean?"

"It begins here. Now. With you."

At that moment, a shadow crossed over them. Elena looked up at the swooping plane, so close the pilot's eyes gleamed in the rising sun and the sparkles made pinpoints of glare in her own eyes. As he passed, a large canister tumbled from the belly of the plane and plunged twenty feet to the earth without exploding.

She watched it, waiting for the blast. It had been triggered; it *would* explode.

Calmly, holding her gaze with his own, Horselover Frost reached over to the detonator and did something to it she couldn't quite see. Then he put his hands on her shoulders and shoved her down, pushing her underneath the railcar. She knew his purpose, without his speaking it. The device would act as detonator for the xenium overhead. Somewhere in all that density of exploding mass, the chain reaction would begin, and she would be at the heart of it, her own matter mingling with the xenium inferno.

There was a flare of green and gold, inexplicable colors. Somewhere in the distance she heard her brother Louis calling her name. She thought she could see him bending over her, in a room of the West End Hotel. Beyond him was a whirling sphere of xenium light. And then it exploded—and she was flung into the blaze.

SIXTEEN

16 December
Year 11 of the Imperial Age

Lieutenant Hausmann,

The Sensorama is not a weapon of destruction.

Some twenty years ago, as you know, we began experiments on the Beam Machine at the Academy of Science. The Beam Machine was a type of hallucination-inducing machine that extracted images lying dormant in the subconscious. It was intended as a therapeutic appliance for the treatment of psychological disorders. At the time, we thought it would prove effective in the treatment of such conditions as amnesia.

With the Revolution, the establishment of Orlovsky's Empire, and the closing of the Academy, the Beam Machine project was brought to a halt.

It was Charles Reif's idea to resume the research approximately ten years ago. He gathered our colleagues at the Imperial Museum and started doing experiments. We rechristened the machine "Sensorama" and regularly conducted experiments there at the museum. It was around then that you were first dispatched to the museum by Army Intelligence. Realizing that our activities were now being monitored, we came to a decision. The new Empire's policy of prosperity through military strength would inevitably result in war. If the Empire engaged the Socialist Republic in an all-out war, human civilization would come to an end. As long as Orlovsky remained in power, there could be no future for us.

Using the Sensorama we embarked on research into hypnosis. We attempted to induce the memory of specific items of information through the action of electromagnetic waves. Hypnosis per se is not an unusual technique. Moreover, there is no need to use the Sensorama when comparable results can be achieved with the human voice. However, by using the Sensorama a signal could be transmitted directly to the brain. Decisive results could be achieved without alerting a third party to the content of the hypnotic suggestion.

In the Version II Sensorama we introduced the message "Nonviolent insurrection. Topple the Empire!" Each subject was to be primed with a hypnotic "key" that would unlock this latent suggestion.

At the same time we developed a plan for the launching of a huge airship. The airship was the key that would unlock the hypnotic message, sending an unspecified number of testees into action. We would achieve, without threat of failure, a nonviolent revolution.

The problem was how large an army of testees we could build up. At that point we hit upon a bold plan. We created our putative mentor, Horselover, and used him to convey messages—meant to be intercepted by the Empire's watchdogs—warning of the military applications of the Sensorama as a brainwashing machine. There is no scientist named Horselover. The plan was carried out at my instructions.

The arrest of Charles Reif was a development that we had anticipated. It proved impossible, employing the technologies at our disposal, to manipulate at will the mnemonic powers of human subjects. With great subtlety Charles acted out his role as the collaborator who redesigned the Version II Sensorama to serve as the Empire's brainwashing machine.

The results of xenium radiation experiments conducted on drugged subjects are largely dependent on the psychic condition and subconscious content of the individual's mind. The convicts suffered a temporary psychic shock, but they did not lose their memories nor did they suffer damage to the nervous system. Each quietly waited for the message to be unlocked by our key.

Unfortunately, we were forced to abandon this plan. It was not fear of the consequences; a circumstance arose that made the plan meaningless. John MacNaughton, formerly of the Academy, is a trained astronomer. Through the intercession of an old friend, he has, for the past year, been observing a cluster of comets. We are faced with the worst possible situation. According to John's calculations, roughly one year from now the nucleus of this comet cluster will collide with Earth. The end draws near. There is no escape.

Using the persona of Horselover I warned the President of the Socialist Republic. What the Republic did with this information is no concern of ours.

However, we do feel an obligation to be honest with the citizens of the Empire. It is for this reason that we have decided to tell you all. We have no illusions about the consequences of appealing directly to Orlovsky. We lodge all our hopes in you. It is unlikely that you will ever see us again.

Respectfully and expectantly yours,
George Tessera

SEVENTEEN

"HAUSMANN! WAKE UP! YOU'VE GOT ANOTHER unicorn!"

Louis sat bolt upright at the sound of Kunz's voice, the hammering on his door. The room was dark, but that meant nothing, even though the curtains were slightly open. He found his watch on the nightstand and checked the luminous xenium-coated hands. It was nearly 3:30, and since he could not believe he had slept fifteen hours, he must have slept only three.

"Are you there?"

"Give me a minute," Louis muttered, groping in the dark for his uniform. He switched on a hooded desk lamp, found his jacket and pants draped over the chair, unwashed and unpressed. Such details went unremarked these days in the general disarray. The hotel's laundry service was erratic, devoted entirely to Lord Orlovsky, promising nothing to lesser members of Army staff. Even Special Agent Hausmann, privy to all the secrets of Army Intelligence, made do with stained ties and dirty linen. These days, he made his own bed as well.

How we are fallen, he thought as he buttoned his collar, staring at the photograph above the desk. Once we devoted ourselves to war with the Republic. Now that it lies in cinders, we rot from within.

The photograph showed the sinister Command Tower of the Republic, once a reminder of everything the Empire had opposed, now a symbol of cosmic indifference. Orlovsky's plans for all-out war against Onegin had ultimately come to nothing, for in one night of meteor showers the Republic had been reduced to a glowing wasteland.

Ash sifted down upon the Empire, stirred by the cold black wind that blew forever from the blasted regions beyond the northern mountains. In the West End Hotel, the furnaces clanked and coughed, and the lips of officers and guardsmen were parched and bleeding, made worse each time they were forced out into the frozen streets. This was a winter like no other in memory. Hail dropped like black lumps of coal; there was no snow, only the fall of pulverized rock and the constant dimming of the light. It was as if the sun itself—which should have ballooned into a fat, dim red dwarf over billions of years—were instead expiring quietly in a matter of months.

Somehow Kunz managed to look freshly starched and well groomed. Louis supposed it was a poor reflection on himself that he had not managed to cultivate the black market connections necessary to maintain a professional appearance. Such things seemed supremely unimportant in the year since Elena's death. Besides, Kunz spent much of his time in what remained of the public eye, while Louis's duties had come to revolve almost exclusively around Room 306. And if any visitors to the Sensorama cared in the least about the appearance of its operator, they had abandoned all such concerns by the time they left the room.

Louis accompanied Kunz to the third floor. A guard in a bellhop uniform was stationed outside 306; he courteously opened the door as they approached.

The woman inside was already strapped into the chair. Her head reclined against the headrests, from which the padding had begun to tear and peel. Her eyes were half closed, her cheeks smeared with tears, her lipstick smudged. Louis checked the pulse in her neck and found it weak.

"We sedated her for you," Kunz said.

Some of her bruises might have been the result of her abduction, but there was no way to ask. He would never know anything at all about her, he realized. Not once the procedure had begun. Louis raised an eyelid, found her pupils dilated. Green eyes. Red hair, of course, although cropped crudely short. A face thinned by recent hunger, freshly scabbed and scarred. Once she might have been pretty, even beautiful; it was impossible to tell. Also irrelevant. Orlovsky was no longer fastidious about such things. She had red hair. That was enough.

"It goes without saying he wants her as soon as possible. It's been a long time since the last one."

"Of course."

"I mean, the few we've picked up in the meantime weren't exactly unicorn material. Not even *he* was that desperate."

Kunz should not have expected an answer but he waited for one anyway. Finally he clapped Louis on the shoulder and went away. Louis turned to the desk. Ore vials were arranged along the wall, under the obligatory photograph of the Command Tower. One was labeled *Excursions*, another *Mentations*, a third, *Unicorn*. Louis selected the latter and fit it into the receptacle at the far end of the Sensorama.

Well, we've made some progress, he thought as he set the machine humming to life. It was now possible to project the condensed works of Lord Paulo Orlovsky directly into the mind of any victim. Once this whole process was utterly haphazard, amounting to nothing more than the scrambling of existing memories, along with a few that seemed to create themselves or arise at random from subconscious detritus. Now that things were more firmly in hand, running more closely to Orlovsky's trainlike time schedule, it was just possible to envision the fulfillment of Orlovsky's plan—namely the reeducation of every Imperial citizen.

Of course, by the time all the kinks were worked out, there would be no citizens left. No Empire, in fact. In the choking dark of an ashen winter, the population had been halved and then halved again. The streets were empty; nothing grew but mushrooms; canned food was more precious than gold.

The West End Hotel was not the only spot in the Empire where cannibalism was practiced.

According to George Tessera, in the letter Louis had passed on to Slowslop after weeks of deliberation, an end more certain than starvation awaited all of them.

A comet . . .

He watched the lights whirling on the woman's face. Despite the tranquilizers, her eyes began to widen, the pupils constricting against the glow. How ironic that the insidious rays of the Sensorama should display the only spark of beauty in this room, if not the entire Empire. The temptation to seat himself before the machine was at times almost irresistible, for he felt convinced that in the moments before madness set in, there must be something to make up for it, some glimpse of transcendence, a world beyond this one. Perhaps that was what drove the Sensorama's victims mad, a longed-for world they could never possess, never revisit in a sane state of mind. But what Louis feared was that even such a blissful vision might be a lie. More likely, the Sensorama's victims spent their eternities in places like the one he had seen on the night of Gondarev's first interrogation. That place, which had seemed so frightening, evil, and unreal at the time, now seemed nothing more than a premonition of the present. They were three steps away from that drowned, corroded world. How or why Slowslop had managed to drag him there he could not imagine.

He stroked the girl's hair gently. She began to shiver. "Forgive me," he whispered.

He touched a switch on the side of the machine and the Sensorama shifted into a slightly faster gear. The girl's jaw clenched, the muscles of her neck going as rigid as wire cables. Her fingers hooked around the arm of the chair and began to tremble as Orlovsky's blithering treatise on the unicorn was dumped into her brain, a congealed mass of cold inanities. How many others had he subjected to the treatment? How many other sad redheaded women? He had lost count, for no matter what individuality they seemed to possess when they were brought into Room 306, by the time they left it they were merely the next in an identical series of soulless dolls.

THE THIRD FORCE

Orlovsky's unicorns . . .

But this time something went wrong.

The woman was no longer looking into the spinning xenium core; her eyes had rolled up until she was staring into her skull. She spasmed, stiffening in her restraints, and would have pulled the whole chair over if it hadn't been bolted to the frame of the Sensorama. Louis reached for Charles Reif's old medical kit, kept always at hand on the desk, a hypodermic needle waiting inside. He plunged the needle into her arm and she slumped instantly. The whirling golden lights slashed his eyes sidelong, threatening to pitch him into his own seizure, but there was no time to shut off the machine. The woman was gasping, a horrible ratcheting sound deep in her throat, as if something had derailed in there among the organic machinery. She seemed to be choking. He uncuffed the arm restraints. She would have slid to the floor if he hadn't caught her under the arms.

Gently he laid her down and put his fingers to her neck, his head to her chest.

No pulse. No heartbeat.

Was it the Sensorama or his injection that had killed her? He pulled her head back, fingers under her jaw, and put his lips over hers. How could they have been so cold already? He forced air into her lungs, watched her chest rise, felt the breath expelled back at him. Then he put the heel of his hands on her breast and began to push, push, push, although hope already had left him.

He gave another breath, and finally listened for a heartbeat, anything.

She lay so quiet. Cold and quiet.

The Sensorama spun on and on, casting its cracked light over the dead girl's green eyes. They looked exactly the same shade as the glowing xenium tube.

Dead . . .

And then she reached up and seized him by the arm, holding him there, fixing him with her eyes. "*Louis . . .*"

He bent closer. Her face was changing, melting, flowing into something else—someone familiar.

"Elena!"

Louis tried to pull away, but she drew him closer. "Louis . . . I'm coming . . ."

"You—you can't be. You're dead. You're both dead!"

She pulled herself upright, clawing at him, and now there was little of the other woman visible. Elena was with him; she had come through the light that bathed the room.

The light, he thought. That explained it. He had absorbed so much of the xenium radiation that he had become another victim. He was hallucinating.

"I—did not—die," she whispered. "I—am—traveling."

"No," he said, tearing away from her, going to the window to reassure himself that the world was still veiled in ash as it had been. *When I turn back,* he told himself, *this illusion will end. I will be alone with a dead woman.* Or perhaps the illusion had started earlier than that, and the woman's death had itself been a terrible false nightmare. He realized that he must shut off the Sensorama. Only then could he begin to separate the glinting emerald strands of illusion that had grown tangled among the drab gray fabric of reality.

When he turned to face the machine, she was standing there, waiting for him. Still his sister. Completely Elena now.

"You're not real," he said under his breath, to give himself courage. He shut his eyes and walked to the machine and felt for the switch that turned it off. As it powered down, whining into silence, he stood with his eyes closed. She was a product of the rays, he told himself. Now the machine was quiet. Now she was gone.

"Louis," she said. "When am I?"

He turned to face his madness.

"You are dead," he said.

Elena shook her head. "No. Unless this is some dream of an afterlife, I am . . . I am alive. Not fully here, I think. But somewhere ahead, I am whole again. Ahead, behind . . . they don't make sense to me right now."

The specter was being reasonable; therefore he must fight it with reason. "There was an explosion, Elena. Out in the desert. You were—aiding the Third Force. You were a spy and a traitor and . . .

and you died for it. The explosion destroyed everything within a radius of miles; it made a crater. We had radio accounts of the attack, and then they ended, but there is no doubt you were caught in the center of it."

"Yes," she said, her eyes glinting, coming forward to take him by the arms, "but I am moving forward now . . . unless the pendulum swings backward, too. I simply cannot remember. There is interference; the waves have created a moiré pattern in time. My explosion was so tiny, though, in comparison to the next."

"The next," he found himself repeating, slipping into her madness. He found it was impossible to completely deny such a perfect illusion; he could not tell his sister that she did not exist. "You mean . . . the comet?"

"Yes. It will cause major time distortion. I—I can feel it from here. It's a nearly solid mass of xenium, I think. All space seems to warp in around it. The incredible density . . . and its voice. It has a voice, like a chorus, like many voices. It is *alive*, Louis. That is the wonderful thing. For a little while, I was able to hear it. I was there, rushing through the void . . ."

She swung her eyes toward the Sensorama, then strode to it and stared.

"There is so much pain imprisoned here," she said, reaching out as if to stroke the cold chassis of the monstrous machine.

At that moment, someone rapped sharply on the door.

"Louis!" came Kunz's voice. "Is she ready?"

Louis leaped to the door, latching it from within, his heart hammering. "Not quite," he said.

"Paulo is impatient. The table's set, you know."

"Well, I—"

"Was that her talking? It sounds like she's coming along fine."

"She's not ready," he said.

"No? She'd better be ready soon. And I'm going off duty now. Can you take her down yourself?"

"Yes," he promised, listening until he could hear Kunz talking to someone else farther down the hall. Then he looked back at Elena, hardly believing that she still remained.

"Elena . . ."

"What do they want?" she asked.

"Orlovsky has involved me in a nightmare."

Her strange eyes narrowed. He tried to see the face of the other woman within hers, but failed. The other one had died and Elena had somehow taken her form.

"After your betrayal, he went insane. I mean—worse than that, because he still functions. The guardsmen search the Empire for women to . . . to . . ."

"What, Louis?"

"He erases their identities and rebuilds them around his notion of . . . of the unicorn."

"The unicorn?" she whispered. "But Theodore said that . . . that I was his unicorn."

Louis lowered his head. "He remakes them, Elena, in your image. Women who resemble you."

"My God, Louis. And you . . . ?"

"It is my punishment for having given you the key to the Nova Express platform. I now help make these women. The alternative . . ."

She clasped his hand. "I know the alternative."

"And now he expects you," Louis said. "All the others . . . first they dine, and then . . ." He shook his head. "I never see them again, Elena, but there are rumors of a disposal team."

She looked at the floor, and through it, as if she were able to penetrate it with her eyes and pick out Paulo Orlovsky in his bunker far below. Her expression was grim, but she raised her eyes to Louis and smiled.

"You are supposed to deliver me," she said, "and so you shall."

"Elena?"

"Tonight he will meet the *true* unicorn."

■ ■ ■

Louis rapped softly on the door to the dining room, and after a moment a servant opened it. The long table, as always, was set for two. As they entered, Elena with her arm through Louis's elbow, Lord Orlovsky rose from one end of the table and came to meet them.

"Lord, I am happy to say that Elena has accepted your invitation to dine."

Louis studied Paulo's face as he presented his sister, but it was as if nothing registered there. The old man smiled and mumbled as he always did, bowing and kissing her extended hand. He was expecting Elena, after all; why should he be surprised to see her? Every one of them, in his eyes, was Elena. The real one was indistinguishable from the fakes.

Orlovsky took Elena's hand and led her toward the table. Louis, dismissed, watched his sister, still far from believing that she was real. Who or what had he really delivered into Orlovsky's hands?

Then she glanced back at him and winked, her eyes flaring with a golden green light whose source he thought he knew. If this was a dream, then he must obey dream logic.

As he stepped into the hall and closed the door, Theodore Slowslop appeared before him. In the same instant, Kunz materialized at his elbow, taking him by the arm.

"Sir! You startled me."

Slowslop said quietly, "I regret to inform you, Lieutenant Hausmann, that you are under arrest for treason."

With one hand, Kunz removed Hausmann's pistol from his holster. "Sorry, Louis."

"On—on what grounds?"

Slowslop pulled a folded sheet of paper from his pocket. Louis had carried it around long enough to recognize George Tessera's letter. For weeks he had wondered what to do with the information in it; finally he had decided that Slowslop ought to see it.

Apparently he had misjudged the Supreme Commander.

"Upstairs," Slowslop said.

They took the elevator to the third floor. Walked to Room 306. Inside, while Slowslop waited with folded arms, Kunz took Louis's watch and emptied his pockets.

"Now leave us," Slowslop said. "I will want a guard outside the door at all times."

When they were alone, Slowslop adjusted his spectacles in case his eyes might be exposed. Then he spoke with great care, as if he had planned his words long in advance. "I am disappointed in you, Louis."

"But I have been completely loyal! To you, to Lord Orlovsky, to the Empire. I merely passed the letter on; I didn't say I put any stock in it. This talk of comets and the end of the world—surely it's madness."

Slowslop seemed not to be listening. "I knew Elena was a member of the Third Force, but I thought you were wiser than that."

"Why did you let her work with us if you knew that?"

"She was a valuable conduit for misinformation. I hoped it would be possible, through her, to trace other members of the organization, much as you may blow smoke into a gopher hole to trace the network of tunnels and discover other openings . . . leaks. I convinced myself, however, that your allegiance to the Empire was pure, uncompromised even by affection for Elena. It pains me, therefore, to find both of you guilty of treason."

"I—I have sacrificed my entire life for the Empire! Even when it meant turning my back on my family!" For a moment, tears of frustration blinded him. He felt like a child again, terrified of disappointing his tall and mysterious idol.

"You know, I have kept you by me like a son all these years. I have thought of you as my own. I never expected this of you."

"Please, Mr. Slowslop."

Slowslop put out a hand, and Louis clasped it. Slowslop drew him to his feet and led him several paces across the room. To the Sensorama.

"Sit, Louis. It is your time now."

"No . . ."

"Please. No fuss. You were always a man of pride. I hope you will not require tranquilizers."

Louis stared at the chair, at the dreadful faceted hemisphere. This was not really happening, not to him. Not after all this time. Not at the hands of his own Supreme Commander. Not on the very night his sister had returned and he had believed there might be some hope left in the world.

"Sit, Louis."

He had obeyed that voice for so long, despite any personal mis-givings, that when it spoke he hardly knew how to disobey.

"Do not be insulted if I take this precaution," Slowslop said, fas-tening the restraints. "In spite of yourself, you may struggle and attempt to tear away. You know how it happens."

Theodore sounded almost tender now, as if he regretted what he did.

"Please," Louis said. "You don't have to do this."

Slowslop leaned closer. "How long have you been in touch with the scientists? What else have they told you?"

"Nothing, I swear."

"You visited George Tessera shortly before your sister's betrayal. Did it begin then? Have you been meeting with Horselover all along?"

"No! And the letter proves Frost doesn't exist!"

"Ah, but who wrote this letter? And for what purpose?"

"I believed it was Tessera's letter, and if I'm wrong . . ."

"Now, did I say you were wrong? George Tessera plays evil games; he knows how the mind works, and how to pervert it. The reality of our situation is very different from what the scientists tell you. He writes of a great comet coming, of the end of the earth, of an Ark that can carry us all to freedom—but those are lies, Louis. He hopes you are a fearful, superstitious little child, afraid of apocalypse and Armageddon, especially when they're couched in terms of science and nature. By filling you with fear, he convinces you that you are doing the right thing in opposing the Empire."

"I don't—"

"It says right here that the scientists have planned their own insurrection all along. Using the Sensorama to plant subconscious messages in patients. Do you believe there is any hope of success? Do you believe a comet is coming? Do you believe there is an Ark that can carry you away?"

"I don't know what to believe! That's why I gave the letter to you."

"He appeals to your sense of duty. He urges you to warn the world. But even giving credence to his improbable scenario, what is the point of warnings? What is the purpose of warning the world, when there isn't room for more than a handful aboard the ship? If an Ark existed, everyone would want a place aboard it."

"Then . . . is the comet coming, or isn't it?"

Slowslop gave Louis a sad, beautiful smile. "I'm sorry, Louis."

"An Ark *has* been built. And you—you knew all along."

"I'm sorry. There are so few seats. And the supply situation! He should not have sent you this letter."

"Please! I'll take my chances here on Earth. I'll die with the rest of them, only don't—please don't—"

But Slowslop drifted away, around the side of the Sensorama, and the crystal sphere began to spin. And as it did he lost that thought. And the next thought. And the next.

■ ■ ■

Louis came to consciousness slowly, his head feeling hollowed out, blinking up at the ceiling of his room—once Gondarev's room. He was in his bed, fully dressed atop the unmade sheets.

Memories returned slowly. His eyes burned; greenish stains seemed to swell across the ceiling and then subside. The light . . . fragments of strange visions . . . he had seen the ruined world again, in the twirling beam of the Sensorama, but it had not been as bad as he feared. Slowslop had been kinder than expected; after one session, he still retained something of his mind. But perhaps that was wishful thinking—there were flaws in his perception.

He found himself standing at the window without any memory of having risen from the bed or crossed the room. Watching his face in the black glass.

A face swam out of the night, drifting toward him. For a moment he thought it was the boy again, a face made of green light, but when he spun around he discovered Kunz standing there staring at him, hesitant.

"Louis, are you all right?"

"I—I don't know." He steadied himself on the edge of the desk. "What's happened?"

"Slowslop asked me to look in on you. He said to tell you he was mistaken about you. He will talk to you later, but I gather that

under interrogation, you only confirmed your loyalty. I don't
think you were under the beam long enough to be damaged, Louis,
but still, we should have you examined."

"I feel all right," Louis said, but he was not at all sure that was
the truth. In any case, there was no physician in the West End
Hotel. Orlovsky loathed doctors and traditional medicine.

"Well, get some rest, then. He'll look in on you later, all right?
I'm sorry about this, Louis, but I suppose you should be grateful. You've now been cleared of all possible suspicion. I'm afraid
that by the end of this, we might all be spending time in Three-
oh-six."

Louis searched Kunz's face, but the other man seemed ashamed,
afraid to meet his eyes. He retreated hastily from the room.

After a moment, Louis put on his uniform jacket. He found
his heavy winter overcoat in the closet and put that on as well.
His possessions had been returned, everything but his pistol.
Maybe they were afraid he would kill himself, as Gondarev had
done.

He opened the door and went into the hall. The corridor was
deserted. He took the stairs to the lobby, where the bellboy
watched without expression as Louis pushed his way into the cold
morning or night or whatever it might have been.

The ash swirled in eddies along the streets; the cement was icy
and slippery. He made his way cautiously to West End Square, seeing not a single pedestrian or car the entire time.

Although West End Station was empty, the trains continued to
run on time. He boarded a waiting Beta, showing his officer's pass
to the conductor, who nodded and looked past him as if waiting for
the next passenger. But Louis felt quite certain he was the only
person aboard the train.

He opened the door of the first private cabin he came to. The
train pulled out of the station the instant he took his seat, as if it
had been waiting for him.

Louis closed his eyes and tried to recall what he had seen in the
Sensorama's beam. Snatches of voices . . . glimpses of a dark body
hurtling through the night . . . Elena. Was that only a dream?
Surely she had not returned. He had been a victim of the rays for

longer than he realized; everything was altered in their golden light. There were no definite answers, no absolute reality he could be sure of.

At the end of the line, East End, he found himself in another empty station. He realized that his only motive was to put himself as far from the Sensorama as he possibly could, so that he could be sure of escaping even its subtlest effects. He needed time to sort what he knew from what he merely *believed* he knew.

Passing the monorail station, he recalled the day he had visited George Tessera and Elena at the water tower. Tessera had vanished months ago. All the scientists had eluded him, one by one. First Charles Reif, then Constantine Wallace and John MacNaughton. Thomas Reich had disappeared immediately after the raid on the mines and the explosion in the desert. When the Nova Express was intercepted en route to the Army depot, the Imperial troops found it empty. Then Wilhelm Draun had vanished. Tessera was the last to go. The six could not have defected to the Republic, for there was no Republic left. If they were continuing their projects in secret somewhere, all the resources of Army Intelligence had been unable to discover where. Louis might have thought them all dead, assassinated by agents within the Empire itself, had it not been for the letter from George Tessera which had catalyzed his own fall from grace.

No, he would not revisit the water tower. There were no answers to be found there, he felt certain. Whatever he sought lay somewhere in himself. He needed only time and solitude to draw it out. He felt some silent need, and he would satisfy it once he understood its nature.

Several minutes' walk from the station he found an inn whose lights glowed with a warm old-fashioned incandescence. The innkeepers had spurned the latest xenium bulbs, and he was grateful to have no reminders of the Sensorama. His room was small and neat and full of antiques, stirring memories of the days before the Revolution. He sat in an armchair near the dark window and thumbed through several old books that had somehow escaped confiscation, looking over faded pictures of the nation as it had been in his father's day. Sepia prints of the early railroad showed crude steam engines on ponderous tracks that scarcely joined West End with Downtown. It had taken days to cross the nation from end to end, with much of the journey conducted in coaches. The detour around the Great Abyss had involved a full two days' journey until the rail bridge was built.

As he looked at the books, Louis realized that he had once pored over these same volumes in his father's library. He found it strange that every one of them, closely examined, evoked vague echoes from deep in his memory.

On the second day, he left the books untouched and merely sat staring at the swirling blackness of the sky. He slept and woke and slept again, without ever moving. All the while, his thoughts roamed in a dark land, scavenging for shards of understanding. He did not try to follow the process. It was enough to keep his mind blank, to let things sort themselves out. Feelings and emotions rose and passed away; he watched them as a neutral observer. On the third day, he reached a decision. He had not consciously realized what he was contemplating until the plan appeared fully formed in his mind. He understood that he had no alternative if his life—or death—were to have any meaning at all. He must act now.

That same evening, Louis boarded a Sigma that carried him toward West End. At Downtown Station, the train stopped for an inordinately long wait.

Eventually a conductor put his head into Louis's compartment. "Excuse me, sir, but this train is being taken out of service. I'm afraid it will be impossible to reach West End by rail tonight."

"What's the problem?"

"I'm not at liberty to say, sir."

Louis made his way onto the empty platform. Moments later, the Sigma shut down completely, whining into silence with a noise that reminded him of something else he couldn't quite name. He paced along the platform, wondering how long the delay would last. How could he keep up his resolve? He had been determined to complete his task tonight, no matter what the cost. But now, even if he could find a car, the roads had been allowed to lapse into disrepair. He might find the route impassable.

A movement at the far end of the platform caught his eye. There was a small station office alongside the tracks. Someone stood just within the doorway, watching him.

A small figure in gray, wearing short pants and dark stockings. A boy.

By the time Louis reached the door—and he ran—the boy was gone, the office vacant. It looked as if it had been recently occupied. A cup of coffee sat steaming on a desk; photographs of trains were tacked on the wall above.

Louis wandered to the far end of the room, where a row of long-handled levers jutted from the floor like weird metal stalks.

Looking at the levers, he found himself remembering the books in the inn. Downtown Station had grown up around the earliest railway in the Empire. Although almost nothing remained of that original station, for a time the old train line had been maintained and preferred over the new one laid down by Otto Hausmann. It was still kept operable in case of emergencies. He felt certain that Slowslop would not have allowed the track to decline during what amounted to a state of constant emergency.

He reached out and put a hand on one of the levers.

"Sir, you'll have to come out of there."

A station guard stood in the doorway. Louis reached into his inner pocket and drew out his Army identification. The guard snapped to attention.

"I need to get to West End," he said. "I have a message for Lord Orlovsky which must be delivered tonight. Can you reroute that Sigma onto the old line?"

"The old line? Certainly, sir! Allow me."

Louis stepped aside. The guard grasped several of the long levers, squeezing the handgrips and hauling them back with a ratcheting sound. Then he went to a microphone on the desk and spoke urgently into it: "Engineer! An officer will be boarding immediately. Wait until he boards, then bring the train onto the original line. He has urgent business in West End."

The guard straightened. "It is done, sir."

Louis hurried back to the train as it came whining to life. The train veered left before leaving the station, plunging down a section of old tunnel. In the dark, he thought he saw a flare of xenium light. Ghosts of the Sensorama still haunted his eyes, even this long after his session in the rays. Suddenly the train slid out into the night.

He doused the lights in his cabin and took a seat at the window. Somewhere in the distance the new line ran parallel to the old. He could see the dunes rise and fall across an astonishing distance, as if the ash were lighter tonight. For a moment he thought he glimpsed stars above, but that was certainly a delusion. Ahead of the train, far out across the plain, he saw something glowing. Red and enormous, like an immense lump of coal, it throbbed in the darkness as if someone were rhythmically fanning it.

A meteorite? he wondered. Had it ruined the rails?

In the darkness, and at such distance, there was no hint of the track itself. Only the luminous rock, pulsating as it cooled.

Slowly it passed. Slowly it fell behind. And then the darkness continued unbroken until the few faint lights of West End appeared in the distance. Formerly the skyline had been the glory of the Empire; now it was remarkable to see a lit window in the once proud houses. He thought of his own home, where he had spent his childhood, and how he had allowed all that to crumble away in the Revolution; how he had denounced his dead father and his mother, who had not lived more than a few months after Orlovsky's speech of ascension. Had he killed her? he wondered. Had he broken her heart?

Elena thought so.

And what had become of her? He should have been there to rescue her from Paulo. He should have done what he was planning tonight; he should have acted ages ago. Then none of those poor women would have suffered. He felt as if he had been in a trance for years; only now was he truly awake. Only now had he discovered his free will, and he was ready to put it into action. No longer would he follow the whims of Orlovsky, the schemes of Slowslop. Tonight, at last, he was his own man.

Just outside of West End Station, the old line merged with the new. No one watched him disembark. No one saw him cross the square. He lurked near the caged garage of the West End Hotel, checking the hands of his watch, until the expected time arrived.

The heavy cage retracted and a covered truck groaned up the ramp from the hotel basement. As the truck drove out, Louis slipped inside and hurried down the ramp into the dark cavernous interior. There was no guard at the loading dock. He passed through to a short corridor, stopping just short of the kitchen, where he could hear someone whistling desultorily, pots and pans clanging. He peered around the doorway, saw a solitary figure hosing an enormous platter at an even more enormous sink. After ascertaining that the dishwasher was not Orlovsky, he slipped into the stairwell.

Louis's keys were still in his pocket. He let himself into the lowest corridor. Orlovsky's subterranean bunker, although it would have been a boon to Onegin at the time of the Republic's aerial bombardment, ultimately would not keep Paulo from harm.

Louis entered a dark room. He recalled the layout well enough, but still he went blindly, groping ahead until he touched the polished wooden surface of the dining table. He made his way to the end and then took a few more steps until he touched a doorknob. The door opened into Orlovsky's study, lit by one shaded lamp. He went to the door on the far side and listened there for a moment, until he realized he heard someone humming.

He eased the door open and looked into Orlovsky's office.

For a moment he could not tell the source of the noise he heard. Paulo's desk was covered with papers, but Paulo was not there. Beyond the desk, the door into Orlovsky's private bathroom was ajar. Shadows moved there, blocking out portions of light. He could hear someone moving around inside; and, faintly, running water.

He crept across the office and put his hand on the door. Slowly, he pushed it open.

Lord Paulo Orlovsky stood at the sink washing ink from his hands and staring into the mirror. He was so engrossed in his reflection that he did not see his assassin until Louis's arm was already around his throat.

Paulo fought, but he was weaker than a child. Louis merely

leaned back, lifting him easily off the ground. It was like hefting a bag of dry sticks. Orlovsky's neck snapped with a sharp crack.

"Your Revolution ends here," Louis whispered as he lowered the limp body to the tiles.

He backed out of the bathroom, leaving the door ajar. Orlovsky's legs stretched across the doorway.

Stepping into the hall, he found himself suddenly bereft of purpose. He had hardly expected to survive the crime; he had not planned beyond it.

Minutes later, Louis let himself into his old room. They would hardly think to look for him here. And if they did, he was prepared for that.

In fact, no preparation was required. None at all. No subterfuge. That would totally baffle his pursuers.

He hung his overcoat in the closet, draped his jacket across the chair back, and lay down on the bed fully dressed.

Then he closed his eyes and waited, listening to the hushed sounds of the old hotel. Soon, very soon, the silence would be broken.

In the meantime he slept, and his dreams were green and golden.

EIGHTEEN

SLOWSLOP UNFASTENED LOUIS HAUSMANN'S ARMS from the chair and took him, limp, across his shoulder. The session should have been sufficient, but only time would tell. While Paulo's unicorn treatments disgusted him, they were also quite instructive; he had learned a great deal about what the Sensorama could and could not do. There would be no certainty of the program's efficacy, of course, until Hausmann actually accomplished the deed. Slowslop doubted he would have long to wait for that confirmation.

Kunz and another agent regarded him with mild shock when he strode out of Room 306, bearing Louis thrown over his shoulder like a sleeping child.

"Sir, if you need help—"

"I'm returning him to his room. If you would unlock the door . . ."

Kunz hurried ahead of him, holding the elevator, pressing the button to carry them to the officers' floor, and then rushing to open Hausmann's room. Slowslop laid Louis on his bed, fully dressed except for his jacket, which he draped across the desk chair to accord with the images he had imprinted.

"Is . . . how is he?" Kunz asked.

"I fear I misjudged Lieutenant Hausmann," Slowslop answered with studied poignancy.

"You mean . . ."

"I suspected him of involvement with the Third Force and other counterrevolutionary elements. But now I am quite certain I was wrong. He is a man of integrity, our Louis."

Kunz looked both relieved and worried. "I'm glad to hear that, sir."

"Indeed. Let him sleep for now, Kunz. But keep watch, and when you hear him stir, let him know my misgivings. I will look in on him tomorrow."

"Do—do you think he'll be all right?"

"I expect so. It was a relatively short session, and his integrity is such that . . . I have the highest hopes."

"Very good, sir."

Slowslop left Kunz outside the door and then made his way down to the subbasement, toward Orlovsky's suites, wondering how it would all fall out. He must wait three nights to be certain. What was three nights, considering the years that had gone before? Slowslop was nothing if not patient. The vastness of his patience was something those around him could never have comprehended.

Aboard the Ark, however, they might begin to understand.

Slowslop had gathered a prizeworthy collection, amassing the finest intellects of this world. Anything less than the finest minds would have been unable to refine the xenium ore and harness it to the tasks he had set them. He had relied on six geniuses to master the ore, to build the Ark, to engineer their own doom under his constant instruction; and they had not failed him. Brilliant, every one of them, and their souls would sustain him on a long flight through the void.

Only one thing, one flavor, would be missing on the journey.

Elena was lost to the world, and he had no replacement for her.

He had looked forward to tasting her, more than any of them. The minds of the scientists were deep and complex and would take eternities to fathom, but still . . . they were *dry*. They lacked some essential quality Slowslop craved.

But Elena . . . Elena!

He had never expected her to take such an active role in the resistance. She had been an ideal catch for the Third Force, with her festering hatred of Orlovsky, but he had never expected her to engage in violence. If he had foreseen such a result, he would have approached her differently. He had meant to keep her distant from Orlovsky, so the old man would have no chance to harm her; Slowslop had wanted to keep her tethered to the Empire, but away from risk of injury, until he was ready to present her with a seat aboard the Ark.

Limited space indeed.

He could hardly have told Orlovsky that the *Emperor's* seat itself was reserved for Elena. For he had no intention of letting the mindless old fool—his soul a bottomless sinkhole of psychosis and perversion—aboard his ship.

Elena's absence from his plans had almost stolen the heart from them. He needed one more mind for the flight, but wherever he looked he saw nothing but mediocrity. He hated attempting to scramble for a replacement at the last minute, after years of careful study and cultivation. Could he do without a full complement? With his rations reduced by one-seventh, could he physically survive the flight?

It remained to be seen.

If nothing else, Orlovsky's absence was now guaranteed. He pitied Louis Hausmann slightly, if pity was the word for what he felt. (Such human concepts had always managed to elude him.) "Pitied" Louis for being the one man ideally suited to the task Slowslop had set him. He imagined how Louis, loyal Louis, must have agonized since receiving the "Tessera" letter. Slowslop had watched him with interest in the weeks since the missive's delivery, wondering what slow processes were under way in the man's mind, waiting for Louis to act. If Louis had not eventually presented the letter to Slowslop, then Slowslop would have arranged to find the letter on his person, and things would have looked even worse for the poor lieutenant.

It was a cruel joke (if "cruel" was the word for it) to have mixed fact and fiction in the letter, so that Louis would never be sure of the truth. But he had believed the biggest lie of all, which was that George Tessera had authored the letter.

THE THIRD FORCE

George Tessera, at this late date, was in no condition to write letters.

Arriving at the door to Orlovsky's dining room, he knocked lightly. Paulo was involved with another of his unicorns, his false Elenas. He would be furious at the interruption, but Slowslop was not bothered by the prospect. Orlovsky's conduct was offensive not because of the physical harm he visited on the defenseless women, but because of the disgrace to Elena's memory. At least Slowslop remembered her as she actually was. He could see her simultaneously in all the stages of her too-short life: as a child, as a teenager, as a young woman, as an adult. He would never permit anything to corrupt his memory of her. But Paulo, in his perverted human way, cared little for truth. All he desired was self-gratification; it hardly mattered to him if the object of his desire were an illusion.

Life was wasted on such vermin, Slowslop thought. He would have extinguished him long ago if he had not required Paulo for his own ascension.

Now that Orlovsky was finally dispensable, now that the Ark was ready at last, he was glad to have put the old man's death into motion.

He knocked on the door and opened it, expecting cries of dismay from his lord.

But the table was empty, dishes cleared away, the candles burned low in their holders.

It was later than he realized. The session with Louis had taken quite a while.

He pushed on into the study, expecting to find the room choking with cigar smoke, brandy snifters set out on the table beside an open copy of Orlovsky's treatise *On the Unicorn*. That was the usual tableau. But tonight the room was undisturbed, as if they had not paused here even for a minute.

The next door opened into the office, and he did not expect to find them here, although Orlovsky might have treated the rapt, mindless girl to an explanation of every photograph on the wall behind his desk. The bathroom door was ajar; Slowslop caught sight of himself in the mirror and paused a moment, wondering again at the face he found himself wearing.

There was one more door in Orlovsky's suite of rooms, and Slowslop was particularly reluctant to open it. He had never interrupted Orlovsky in his own bedchamber. But the time for discretion was past.

He hesitated a moment. Then, without knocking, he opened the door and stepped inside.

Slowslop recoiled at the sound of labored breathing in the darkness, repelled by the thought of intruding on what passed for reproductive functions—however symbolic they might have been in Paulo's case.

Sensing his intrusion, the topmost figure in the bed twisted around to look at him. In the light from the office, he knew himself to be a silhouette: but just beyond the limits of the shadow he cast, he saw a vision wholly unexpected.

"Elena!" The word was torn from him. Never had he felt anything like this—not even in the moment, ages past, when he first realized the extent of his abandonment on this forsaken planet and dimly grasped what sort of machinations would be necessary to gain his liberation. That had been a horror based upon successive layers of denial, stemming from a betrayal he should have been able to predict. This was a situation for which he was completely unprepared. And with it came such torrents of hope that he could hardly staunch them. She had not died. She would ride in the Ark. He would save her for last. His plans were complete.

Complete in every way, he saw, as she slipped sideways in a panicked attempt to elude him. For there on the bed, with his clothes in disarray, his eyes wide, his mouth gaping, lay Lord Paulo Orlovsky. His life fluttered somewhere near the ceiling, a faint dark ebullience that dissipated even as Slowslop noticed it. Elena still clutched the pillow with which she had suffocated him.

He came toward her cautiously, one hand out, meaning to reassure her. "Elena, take care . . . it is I, Theodore."

"You," she said, looking at him oddly. There was something strange about her, although he could not measure it.

"All's well," he said quietly. "Stay calm. This can be easily managed. I will protect you now."

"He's dead," she whispered.

"You did well, Elena. His madness would have destroyed everything eventually."

"No. His madness never would have destroyed us. Not utterly; not like the comet . . ."

"You know," he said. "That is excellent." He felt a great urgency to keep her close by him. He must get to the Ark immediately. Meanwhile, another part of him was calculating how to resolve this situation by taking advantage of existing arrangements.

He thought he saw a way.

"You must understand already the need for secrecy and haste. I suppose the Third Force trained you for that, Elena, but you would do well to remember that they no longer exist—no more than the Empire exists. There is only us now, and we must make the best of this. We must save ourselves. Do you understand me?"

"I begin to," she said, staring at him—into him—more keenly than anyone ever had. He felt that she did understand; that she had penetrated his multilayered disguise and now, alone of all humans, beheld his true nature. What she saw seemed to fascinate her; he did not sense horror or revulsion, only curiosity. But perhaps that was only wishful thinking on his part. She was indeed remarkable.

"Remain here for the moment," he said. "I will soon return. It will be necessary to remove you in secrecy from the hotel, but first I must make other arrangements. I will be glad to do this for you, Elena. It is an honor to serve."

She rose, no longer unsure of herself. "Thank you, Theodore."

She watched as he lifted Paulo from the bed. The old man weighed nothing. He reentered the office, closing the bedroom door behind him, and carried the body into the bathroom. There he laid Orlovsky on the floor tiles, at a rather specific angle, so that his legs were just visible in the doorway to anyone entering the office.

The position would correspond exactly with the one in Louis's memory, leaving Hausmann convinced of his part in the murder. Although Louis's assassination attempt had been preempted, he could still take the blame for it. Any confusion over the matter of three missing days would no doubt be attributed to his recent session before the Sensorama. Besides, who but a lunatic would have had any reason to murder the Emperor? By definition Louis must be considered insane.

As he crouched in the bathroom, putting the final touches on Orlovsky's position, he heard someone enter the office, and then an exclamation.

Slowslop straightened, turning to find several guards in the outer doorway, staring at him in disbelief. It was Orlovsky's disposal team. One of them took a step into the room, looking frightened of Slowslop but even more fearful of the corpse. Allegiance was such a fragile concept. When the guard drew close enough to see Orlovsky's face, he stumbled back, signaling for the other men.

"Murderer!" the man cried. "He—he killed the Emperor!"

Slowslop raised his clawed hands to show they were empty, but it became a gesture of surrender. The guards had their weapons out, ready to fire, as if they had been waiting and hoping for such a moment. He saw now clearly in their eyes how they had always feared and hated him, always wished for the moment when they might have an excuse to vent the emotions they scarcely understood. Most humans sensed his true strangeness instantly, instinctively, but their intuitive awareness was so deeply buried beneath layers of rational thought that they easily dismissed it from their conscious minds with minimal assistance from Slowslop. Nonetheless, the animal knowledge remained. He was ever the alien, ever the stranger. Now all their confusion and blind hostility surfaced.

A moment ago he had been their Supreme Commander; now he was their prisoner.

One of the men started toward the bedroom door. Slowslop suddenly blurted out, "I acted alone!"

The other two looked at him as if he were insane. The third pushed the bedroom door open and slipped inside. Slowslop tensed, waiting for the discovery. After a moment the man came out, shaking his head.

"Just another dead girl," he said. "Orlovsky must have finished with her first."

"Dead? But . . . but she can't be. She . . . she was . . ."

"What? Don't tell me you did her, too?"

Slowslop strode quickly to the bedroom. They were too startled to kill him before he reached the threshold. His hand found the light switch and the room sprang into view.

The woman lay facedown on the bed, tangled in sheets, half unclothed. They were the same clothes Elena had been wearing, but the woman's hair was ragged, short-cropped; reddish, but not the ashen red of Elena's hair.

One of the guards slipped in past him and put his hand on the woman's shoulder, and pushed. As she sprawled onto her back, Slowslop gasped.

In all the eons of his existence, he had never seen her before.

■ ■ ■

First they employed the routine methods of interrogation, but even working their way through ever harsher methods of physical torture did not give them the satisfaction they so evidently wanted.

Slowslop denied his involvement in the assassination. He accused Louis Hausmann, but that was patently ridiculous. Hausmann was barely conscious even now. He had been under constant guard, at Slowslop's own instruction. At the approximate time of the murder he had been observed in a comatose state. Guardsman Kunz was particularly mocking of Slowslop's feeble attempt to implicate Louis, who had been Orlovsky's most loyal officer in the years since the Revolution.

Finally, he authored the murder they wanted to hear, casting himself in the role of lone assassin. There was no point in trying to lay blame on a woman who had been dead for over a year.

It was his last significant gesture—to protect Elena Hausmann, wherever and whatever she might be. To absolve her of suspicion in case she had survived. He felt he owed her that much. He knew he would miss her.

For himself, he accepted that personal survival was now impossible.

Eventually, as he knew they must, they brought him to Room 306.

Slowslop, although he had done much to promote and develop the Sensorama's capabilities, had nonetheless avoided ever placing himself directly in the gadget's path. The potent rays were new to the human mental field, and their effects therefore unpredictable. But he knew exactly what the effect of concentrated xenium radiation on himself would be. He had witnessed it before, on others of his kind, in the endless cosmic war that had preceded his terrestrial incarceration.

It could be a vengeful substance, xenium. It knew all he had done to it. He had not so much harnessed the stuff as *enslaved* it. And, as suited an element that was little more than raw condensed consciousness, it had a very long memory indeed.

In the early years of the Empire, a small cluster of meteorites had fallen in the northern mountains. Slowslop was suspicious. They were too well aimed, too localized, not to have been deliberate. Such a shower of stones should have triggered massive climatic upheaval, more like the events which had followed the Republic's bombardment. Having ordered an investigation, he was not terribly surprised when the ancient deposit was unearthed in the region near the meteoritic strike zone. One had been a finger pointing to the other, an obvious indicator for those who cared to look. Slowslop had suspected at that time that these were merely forerunners of a larger force. The only question in his mind was whether he could capture the power of the xenium to engineer his own escape before the destruction of the planet was certain.

It had been a very close race. He had nearly won.

It was not without pride that he allowed himself to be strapped into the Sensorama. Pride in the technologies whose rise he had overseen, the unparalleled explosion of growth in a stagnant society. Had he had more time, or more direct access to the future, he might have accomplished unparalleled feats. Created empires of his own.

He could hardly bear to watch the guardsmen fumbling with the Sensorama. They had only the faintest idea of what they were doing. They thought to erase his mind, or extract further secrets, but they might as well have attempted to perform brain surgery with hammer and anvil. The only agent with any training or proficiency on the device was Louis Hausmann. He almost begged them to bring Louis to him.

Then, as if by accident, someone switched the thing on.

They fell back, silenced as the stray sweep of xenium rays

caught and snagged on the raw edges of their noisy, undeveloped psyches. They watched the machine for a moment, stupid apes hypnotized by the colors and the rhythmic whir.

Then, noticing the preliminary changes in Slowslop, they began to focus their attention on him.

The first beams were agony. He shut his eyes and turned away, but someone wrenched his head around and tore off his smoked spectacles, smashing the lenses under a bootheel. There was no turning away after that. He plummeted into the whirling facets of the outer crystal hemisphere, toward the incandescent xenium core. Emerald fires burned in there, cities of golden light, vast empires of molten ruby and amber fire that beckoned but offered no refuge. Slowslop's eyes began to blaze. There were cries in the room, of surprise and animal terror; and the men were right to fear, for they were about to see his power for the first and last time. These privileged few, if they could bear the sight, would know Slowslop stripped to his essence, reduced to his elements.

Xenium waves wove and rippled, casting nets of light into his depths. The skeins of fire entangled with his atoms, infusing him with pain, and then rhythmically unwove again.

Bound to the rays, Slowslop, too, unraveled.

He could no longer hear the screams, but he could feel the men, could feel his essence burning through them, singeing the walls of the room. It was scarcely a warm breath compared to the fires that were bent on Earth's destruction, but none of the men survived it. The floor smoldered; the ceiling burst into flame. Hot motes of light, like small bright mobile suns, fountained from what was left of him. The Sensorama pulsed and hummed and bored its way deeper into his core, neglecting nothing, the golden voice of the light growing high and fierce and triumphant.

Slowslop exploded into energy, but none of it escaped. The separate spheres of radiance collapsed upon one another, and then there was a brighter explosion, one that seemed to tarnish the walls. When it subsided at last, nothing remained of the entity known as Slowslop.

Nothing but a small lump of xenium, faintly warm to the touch.

And no one to touch it.

■ ■ ■

Louis came to consciousness slowly, his head feeling hollowed out, blinking up at the ceiling of his room—once Gondarev's room. He was in his bed, fully dressed atop the unmade sheets.

Memories returned slowly. His eyes burned; greenish stains seemed to swell across the ceiling and then subside. The light . . . fragments of strange visions . . . he had seen the ruined world again, in the twirling beam of the Sensorama, but it had not been as bad as he feared. Slowslop had been kinder than expected; after one session, he still retained something of his mind. But perhaps that was wishful thinking—there were flaws in his perception.

He found himself standing at the window without any memory of having risen from the bed or crossed the room. Watching his face in the black glass.

A face swam out of the night, drifting toward him. For a moment he thought it was the boy again, a face made of green light, but when he spun around he discovered Kunz standing there staring at him, hesitant.

"Louis . . . I have terrible news. Orlovsky is dead!"

Something is wrong . . .

"Louis, do you hear me?"

"Dead? No . . ."

"It's hard to believe, but even more unbelievable—Slowslop confessed! No one knows what will happen now. But you—you're all right?"

Louis looked down at his hands, remembering how he had broken Lord Orlovsky's neck. Why had they not questioned or suspected him? Why suspect Slowslop? And why would he have confessed to the murder?

"Stay here for now. After what you've been through, you should conserve your strength. The situation is changing quickly, but I'll let you know if you should have cause for worry. I'm going up again to see what's happening."

"Up?"

"They have him in Room Three-oh-six. For interrogation. Some of the men—they're going too far, I think. But there's no one to stop them now."

"I should say something."

"No, Louis. Rest. Wait. I'll be back."

As soon as Kunz was gone, Louis sank down on the bed. A decision had to be made. He would leave the hotel, catch a train to East End. He needed time to think, time to himself in a distant place. He needed to reach a decision. He could feel a plan forming inside him.

He had a sudden glimpse of himself in a quiet inn, paging through old books and waiting for inspiration. It came with foreknowledge of a plan, blunt and effective, to assassinate Orlovsky.

But he had already done that! He himself had killed Orlovsky. He had already been to that inn! Why did events of the past seem like visions of the future?

I killed him, he told himself. *I killed him—or will kill him.*

It was madness . . .

He opened the door and went into the hall. The whine of the Sensorama penetrated the ceiling and walls; the whole building resonated with the sound. As he made his way toward the stairs, the noise began to rise in pitch. Then the screaming began.

Louis threw himself down the stairs, diving into the depths of the hotel. He had never known men were capable of such sounds, and he did not want to know what might have elicited them.

The cries were followed by an explosion of inexplicable softness. Louis curled into a fetal ball with his arms over his head, pressed into a corner of the stairwell. It felt as if a warm hand were pushing down on him—more, reaching *into* him. For a moment, he was flooded by memories of childhood: His first glimpse of the tall stranger with hidden eyes who accompanied his father home one afternoon, in the presence of Lord Orlovsky. *"Louis, this is Mr. Slowslop. Theo, this is my son."* Young Louis had gone from fear to admiration, asking his mother for shiny suits like the ones Mr. Theodore wore.

As these memories revisited Louis, he felt certain that Slowslop stood over him and touched him on the crown, as if in benediction.

Louis raised his head. It was not Slowslop who stood in the blackened chamber. It was the boy.

The boy withdrew his hand from Louis's head and melted back

through a door that looked like tarnished silver. Louis rose and pushed the door open. The boy waited down the hall, at the door of Slowslop's room. His expression never changed, but Louis knew he was meant to follow.

The door was locked. Louis drew back, prepared to hurl himself against it, but then he heard a click from the other side. When he tried the knob again, it turned without resistance and the door swung open.

Slowslop's outer room was no surprise. Louis had conferred with the Supreme Commander on many occasions. But he had never entered the inner room, and it was this door that now stood open.

Louis stepped in hesitantly. The room was almost bare, furnished in a plain style that betrayed nothing of Slowslop's personality. The boy waited in a corner, watching Louis with his usual blank expression.

"What?" Louis said. "What do you want from me?"

The boy raised his arm, pointing at a wardrobe.

Louis wondered if he dared. The rest of the hotel was silent; even the rumble of elevators was halted. He had never heard the place so still, at any hour.

Inside the wardrobe hung several of Slowslop's glistening suits. Below them were two bright silver xenium-alloy suitcases. He set the cases on the bed.

One contained the scanner Slowslop had entrusted to him years ago. The sight of it made him shudder. He turned to the second case.

Inside, embedded in gray shockproof foam, were eight sealed flasks. Seven contained crystals of purified xenium. The eighth was empty.

Despite his blank expression, Louis divined that the boy expected something more. He pried out the capsules, finding each one labeled on its end, although the labels were a puzzle in themselves.

The first was labeled *Draun*.

The second, *Tessera*.

Wallace, MacNaughton, Reich, Reif, and . . .

Boy.

The boy extended his hands beseechingly to Louis. His face had not changed.

Louis struggled with the cap a moment, but he wasn't sure how to unseal the thing. Finally he dropped the flask onto the floor and crushed it under his heel.

The capsule shattered with a squirt of glass; the wires twisted, the lump of ore tumbled out. As the boy moved forward, Louis stepped back. The boy knelt before the lump, put out his hand, and touched the crystal.

The ore evaporated under his touch. Simultaneously, the boy seemed to solidify. When the crystal had completely vanished, the boy smiled up at Louis. Smiled.

The boy picked up the scanner, switched it on, and placed it in Louis's hands.

A transparent blue grid appeared on the small screen. It wrapped itself into a three-dimensional form, a framework of wire depicting some sort of airplane, long and sleek, with stubby wings.

The Ark, he thought. This has to be the Ark.

Before he could get a clear look at the thing, it began to recede. Around it, a larger grid appeared. This one was a map, a maze of paths he didn't recognize until he saw a large circular structure from which a long stretch of rail extended. He instantly recognized the roundhouse in the mines, inside the Restricted Zone. The labyrinth represented the mining tunnels.

When he looked up again, wondering if he would be permitted to ask questions, the boy was gone.

Louis fit the vials back into their foam bedding and started to shut the case. Remembering the empty one, he plucked it out to read the label.

In his precise script, Slowslop had written:
Elena

NINETEEN

"ELENA . . ."

Dazzled by the glaring greenish light from the Beam Machine, Elena struggled to wake, hauling herself up from visions that were already receding. She clung desperately to the memories, but retained little more than scraps and a feeling . . . a feeling she knew would haunt her to the end of her days.

"Elena, my child, wake now. We must be quick."

Her eyes were open but still unseeing. A jumble of images seemed to spiral together in the twirling rays. She saw most clearly her hands around Paulo Orlovsky's throat, as if her thoughts of vengeance had fulfilled themselves in an hypnotic dream. The image of the old man struggling weakly underneath her was sharp and terrible; less clear was the memory of what he had done—or tried to do—to her. In the dream he was withered and frail, even more horrible than he had looked that afternoon when Slowslop presented his proposal of marriage. How strange . . .

The rest of the dream had an epic feel, as if it had lasted hours and hours, although she had only just activated the Beam Machine here in the basement of the Academy. She remembered mundane details of her life in an evil regime, so real that she knew she could have traced back through every instant of a dozen or more dreamed years. But already that dream was fleeing, leaving her once more with the despair and panic that had ensued from Orlovsky's overtures—his proposal, through Theo, of marriage.

"Elena, please."

A hand on her arm, and suddenly her eyes cleared.

"Professor Frost," she whispered to the white-haired man who bent over her.

"Yes, dear. You know my name, though you haven't met me yet."

"I know you," she said, but wondered, *From where?*

From a dream? He seemed part of the laboratory; she knew he was an old associate of George Tessera's, and yet . . . yet she did not know him.

She tried to climb up from the chair, but he lightly held her down. "No, no, don't get up. You'll be leaving again, flung back into the future. But I wanted to talk to you here, now, before it all begins. This far from the cataclysm, we can have a bit more time together. The shock waves are much less compressed."

"What . . ."

"This is where we meet, Elena. It is also where we say goodbye." He had set the Beam Machine at a low gear; the sphere of lenses continued to spin, but without the same intensity. She was barely able to look at it without feeling her mind might be pulled inside out.

"A comet is coming. At this moment it is many years in your future, but in another few moments you will find yourself nearly at the point of its arrival. If you are to escape, you must act quickly. We have sent a ship to rescue those we can. I'm afraid other forces, our ancient enemies, have done their best to obscure the message and mislead and confuse you. But a beacon, in what you know as the Republic, has been sending a signal into space. If it still stands, we will meet you at the tower."

She started to speak, but he put a finger to his lips.

"Don't ask questions now. You will understand again when you spring back—memories are part of the time that gives rise to them, and it would be impossible for you to make sense of this now. But you will know what to do when you return."

Silenced, she tried to sit still and listen, though she could not understand why she trusted him.

"Far beyond the visible edge of your solar system is another star," he said. "A dark twin to your sun. It has no planets of its own, no dark Earths, but occasionally it passes near a cloud of much smaller bodies that are inhabited and sends some of them tumbling toward your bright sun in the form of comets. This particular comet is also a ship and a world and an intelligence unto itself. Although for you its arrival means utter destruction, the comet considers itself on a rescue mission. Only by destroying your world can it liberate others of its kind imprisoned here. The energy generated by the collision, and the arrival of a concentrated mass of elemental consciousness, will enable those trapped forms to escape."

"Why are you telling me this?" she asked. "Why me?"

"Because no one else can hear me. To George Tessera, I am only a vague idea that took shape in the past. He thinks he invented me. Now, remember the ship. Go to the tower. There won't be much time."

He stepped back to the controls of the Beam Machine.

Elena tried to follow him with her head, but the charged sphere was spinning faster now, and she could no longer look away. "I don't . . ."

Words fell away. She soared into darkness, and beyond it was a sky full of fire. A roar was followed by silence streaked with glaring specks of heat.

She lay in dust, bits of rock biting into her cheek, her palms, her knees. She rose slowly, stiff and shaken, brushing dirt and splinters of stone from her flesh.

The sky above was a roil of black smoke. As she watched, something came blazing down through it, a line of fire that slashed through the soot and vanished somewhere over the horizon. She heard the sound of its impact, a dull missile thudding into the earth, and then she felt it underfoot. A dark blossom of dust began to bloom at the edge of the world.

Around her, the land had been scraped clear of features. No trees, no weeds, nothing but rock and ash. She knelt to examine the spot where she had woken, and found among the pulverized dust a variety of metallic nuggets that were odd and glassy, as if they had been melted and cooled. She picked one up and studied it in the faint light available. It reminded her of something she had seen in the museum as a child. A fragment of meteorite.

Suddenly she remembered everything.

The explosion—the xenium detonator. Orlovsky's death at her hands. A frightening timeless dream of shuttling through darkness at tremendous speed, then slowing and waking and looking around at odd corners of the world, only to find herself ripped out of them and hurled again through the void to some other momentary resting place.

Where—and when—was she now?

Under the murky canopy, there were no stars by which to navigate; nor was she certain that it was even night. With no other recourse, she began to walk.

She must have been at the bottom of a vast depression, a huge bowl or crater, for she felt that she was climbing. She must have woken at the very center and bottom of the crater, for whichever way she struck off, the ground began to rise.

It might have been hours or days before she reached the rim of the crater. Her sense of time was at best unreliable. Eventually she saw mountain peaks off to her right. As she climbed, the peaks rose higher above the edge of the bowl, until she thought she recognized them as the northern range. The Restricted Zone.

Following the crater's rim, she finally mounted a severed line of railroad tracks leading away toward the peaks. How long had the Nova Express been out of commission? she wondered. How long had she been away? Did the Empire still stand?

There was nothing to draw her toward West End, not now. Horselover Frost had told her to seek the Republic. The tower of which he had spoken could only be Onegin's immense Control Tower. She followed the tracks toward the mountains. The Republic also lay that way.

Fragments of memory and vision rose and fell from consciousness. Sometimes it was impossible to unravel the strands. It was as if on that long-ago day in her youth, before the Revolution, she had sat down at the Beam Machine, switched it on, and awakened to find herself lying in the fused cinders of a great explosion.

Everything in between might have been an illusion, delirium, an effect of the Beam Machine. Even now she might be sitting in the Academy basement with her eyes wide open, unable to wake, unable to reach out and shut the gadget off. At any moment George Tessera—or the mysterious Horselover Frost—might come in to find her lost in a trance, her mind permanently shattered. All of this, no matter how real it seemed to Elena, might have been nothing more than a lucid dream.

As in a dream, then, it hardly surprised her to hear an engine rumbling along in the smoky dark alongside the track. She stopped, balancing on a rail, and looked back to see headlights emerging from the dusk, followed by a long car that might once have been silver, now tarnished and covered with soot. The sorry, soiled red flag of the Empire hung from the hood. Behind the smeared windshield she could barely make out the driver's features as the car rumbled to a halt.

She stepped down to the car, opened the passenger door, and climbed in beside him.

"Hello, Louis."

He gaped at her. "Is it really you this time?"

"It's really me," she said.

As the car moved on alongside the tracks, he seemed uncertain what to say. Gradually he began to speak.

"I never knew where you went from the hotel. I've been wandering. In a daze most of the time. And then I suddenly felt—no, I knew—that it was time to move on. I've known for a while where I must go, but I resisted it. And now something's brought us together."

"The Third Force," she said.

"No, the underground's shattered. There's nothing left for them to fight against anyway."

"I mean the *real* Third Force. The one we both served without knowing it."

He didn't answer. He kept glancing up at the sky. Occasionally a long trail of light flared above the mist, illuminating vast swirling landscapes of smoke and tumult. "It's coming, isn't it?"

"I think so."

"I hope we're in time. They seem to think we can make it."

"They?"

He looked down at the seat between them. A silver suitcase rested there, like the one in which she had carried the detonator.

He glanced at her sidelong and gave her a strange smile. "Sometimes they talk to me," he said.

■ ■ ■

The Nova Express tracks leading into the mountain were blocked by fallen rock, but the main gate to the mining complex hung wide open. The bunkers were evacuated. They saw no guards, no soldiers, no workers, no one at all.

Louis knew the area from prior tours with Slowslop, but he was distracted. He seemed to be looking for something in particular. It took them hours of wandering the subterranean complex before they found their way to the roundhouse and then to the control room she had visited with Thomas Reich. They went through the control center, down the stairs beneath the large moving platform, and out through the metal doors into the maze of tunnels. Elena was soon lost among the branching passages of rock.

"They must have moved it," Louis murmured eventually, as if to himself. "Or else I missed a turn. I don't know where we are."

They stood at an intersection of passages. The tunnels were utterly deserted, and lightless except for the mining lanterms they carried. As Louis cast his light down one of the branches, a pair of eyes flashed in the distance.

Elena gasped when she saw the boy standing there watching them, waiting. They were deep in the mines, and the rock had a strange greenish hue that meant it was rich in xenium. If she closed her eyes she could feel the stuff watching them just as the boy watched, with no expression she could read.

Louis had fallen still, but when the boy turned and vanished, he grabbed her by the wrist and they began to run.

Deeper they went, and Elena swore that the walls began to shine. She felt as if she were plunging through space again. She could remember something of her voyage—the voice of the comet, the ponderous, inexorable sense of its approach, a slow understanding of its purpose, something she could not quite reconcile with words. The quality of anticipation was pervasive; the entire Earth felt hushed, waiting for its doom.

Suddenly, just ahead, the walls began to shimmer with light. As the boy passed, glowing spheres of pale fire bubbled from the rock in his wake, and swirled and clustered in the tunnel. Louis drew back, nearly turning to run; she could feel his fear, but she could not understand it. The things did not frighten her at all. It was her turn to grab and hold on to Louis.

The spheres of light continued to rise, vanishing through the ceiling of the tunnel, floating up through the earth until the way was clear again. Only now would Louis follow. They hurried on until the boy was in sight again.

The boy had stopped running, and was climbing the wall, pulling himself into a small crevice. By the time they reached the spot, nothing remained but a pair of eyes, golden green, looking out of the rock. The soft, living spheres stared out at Elena, and she thought of the first time she had seen the boy. Was this their last meeting, or their first? Was he traveling in time, like Horselover Frost?

The eyes glanced at Louis, then looked hard to one side, indicating their path.

"Come," Louis said, confident again.

They went deeper, deeper, but at least there were no more branching corridors to confuse them. Finally, they saw something glimmering at the edge of the flashlights' beams. Coming closer she saw a huge machine filling the tunnel. The mine shaft seemed to end in solid rock immediately beyond. Judging from the enormous whorled drills mounted at the front of the thing, at the end of an armature that looked like monstrous clockwork, this was Thomas Reich's excavator, developed for gnawing its way through the heart of the meteorite. But this deep into the earth, she saw none of the telltale gleam of the greenish stone. The miners had apparently moved out of the seam of extraterrestrial ore.

Louis clambered up onto the excavator and gestured for her to follow. She tossed the silver case up to him. By the time she joined him, he had opened a hatch in the roof of the machine and was climbing in. She followed, sealing the hatch behind her, then descended into the cabin on a short metal ladder. The interior of the excavator was all polished xenium alloy, gleaming with the lights of an instrument panel. There was a seat for one operator, and nowhere for a passenger to sit. She clung to one of the metal ribs that ran along the interior of the craft.

Louis was already seated at the control panel, looking over the switches and levers wonderingly. In the center of the instrument panel was a cylindrical lid, which he pushed open to reveal a small receptacle, now empty. He opened the suitcase and took out a vial containing a faintly luminous crystal of xenium.

"I've dreamed of this place," he said distantly. "Or else they told me."

He slotted the vial into the receptacle and instantly the crystal started to glow. The excavator began to whine and hum with a hypnotic rhythm. She nearly stumbled as the craft glided forward, its enormous forward drills spinning around one another like immense gears as the huge bore sank into the stone. The small portal above the instrument panel went dark with jumbled debris, and it became impossible to judge their progress. She felt as if they were traveling swiftly, but it seemed incredible that anything could cut through rock at such a pace.

The bores gave off a shrill whine as the excavator pushed through into emptiness. The drills shut down, and then the instrument panel itself began to change. Many of the switches retracted as other controls emerged to take their place. The view-port was replaced with a glowing monitor. Now the excavator moved into reverse, shedding its drilling apparatus. She could hear all around her the whirring of hidden servos.

"My God," Louis whispered. "What is this place?"

She joined him at the monitor, looking out into a vast cavern that might have begun as a natural formation but now showed clear marks of artificial sculpting. A broad, perfectly flat floor stretched as far as she could see, beneath a high firmament of glowing xenium bulbs. Here and there were the skeletons of machines—ruined or still unfinished. The excavator, now vastly altered, lifted from the ground and began to glide across the field as if it knew its destination better than they. Fragments of titanic aircraft loomed ahead, then flickered away at the edges of the screen. There were things like the skeletons of mammoths made of metal, and ponderous statues that looked vaguely human, reminding her chillingly of the gigantic Orlovsky who stood in West End Square. As they gathered speed, she grew ever more certain that occasionally, in the shadows of the incomplete immensities, she glimpsed smaller human skeletons, tiny scattered flecks of bone.

She thought she saw a wall far ahead—perhaps the end of the cavern—but it curved *away* from them, a convexity that dominated the space ahead. It was like an underground mountain, a self-contained world; she could hardly grasp the scale of the thing as their ship began to rise across its face.

They rose until the lights of the lower caverns vanished below, and still the lamps of their ship showed nothing but the curving bulk of the huge cylindrical thing. Finally, the gleaming shell of it fell away, and their craft's beams lanced across emptiness. She had a last glimpse of enormous curving girders, still unclothed with metal, caging a vast darkness. Whatever this massive thing was, it, too, lay unfinished, abandoned.

They continued to ascend through darkness at a dizzying rate. Elena clung to the back of Louis's seat, her head down, her eyes squeezed shut. Then Louis let out a breath, and she felt the light against her eyes. It was still dim, but brighter by degrees than the cavern.

They were rocketing over the countryside now. The view-screen seemed sensitive to the slightest variations in heat of the landscape, and although the atmosphere roiled with smoke, she could see every contour of the withered earth below. Here and there, dots of xenium green throbbed in the night, embedded in the earth like eerie embers. Forests lay toppled and charred like kindling. Lakes had abandoned their old beds for deeper impact craters. Judging by their speed, they were over the Republic now. It was the first time since her childhood, long before the Revolution, that she had crossed the border. She felt certain that even if she had known the land's features intimately, she wouldn't have been able to recognize a single landmark now, the terrain was so altered.

But one familiar marker now appeared on the horizon, one

every Imperial citizen knew, a nightmarish citadel of scaly silver-black metalwork.

Their ship went silent, gliding toward the spire at incredible speed. It was coming on too fast to take in with the eye; so quickly that they were sure to destroy it and be destroyed in the process. She had a glimpse of huge mirrors spinning and a tremendous faceted crystalline hemisphere sending pulses of the familiar green and gold light up through the smoke. The tower was well known to her from Imperial propaganda, but she had never seen the mechanism that whirled steadily at its peak. It looked like an immense version of the device she had seen in the West End Hotel, a mammoth cousin of the Beam Machine.

She wondered who, in the depths of space, might be gazing down into that beam.

Their ship slowed to a landing inside the Command Tower. She did not realize they had touched down until Louis rose from his seat and put his hand on the ore vial he had slotted into the control panel.

"Thanks, Thomas," he said, as if to himself. He motioned for Elena to get the hatch.

Outside, a freezing wind, laden with icy hail, swept across the deck. They were too near the edge for Elena's comfort. A stray beam of light from the mirrors above stabbed down through the murk and glanced off the surface of a lake far below. The water was black and full of coagulated ash.

Louis caught her elbow, pointing upward. She saw a small ramp encircling the luminous dome high above, a catwalk leading beneath the mirrors. On that ramp, looking down at them, was a man. He sat watching them, his legs dangling over the edge, leaning against a rail. Louis called out, but the man made no move except to swing his legs back and forth.

As they made their way to the center of the tower, Elena looked back at their transport. A far cry from the burrowing excavator, it was a sleek winged craft now. As she watched, it was already lifting off the pad again and soaring out into the darkness, instantly lost from sight. The wind blew stinging ashes into her eyes. She turned to follow Louis.

At the core of the tower, a door opened into a hushed passageway that curved away in either direction. Directly ahead were the doors of an elevator.

They ascended in silence. Louis was shivering. Elena realized that she had been oblivious to physical discomfort, but especially to cold, since waking in the crater. She felt odd in general, but it seemed especially strange that the bitter cold did not trouble her. With warmth to spare, she put an arm around her brother, instantly feeling him grow calm and cease to shiver. He seemed reluctant to draw apart from her when the doors opened and they stepped out onto the high circular ramp.

There was nothing between them and the spinning dome. The mirrors twirled and the xenium light wove its message for the heavens. Even as they set foot on the ramp, however, the dome began to darken and the light ceased to dance. An immense platform opened in sections, sliding over the dome, closing out the sky. She remembered it from pictures of the tower—a landing pad to dwarf those on the lower decks.

Had Onegin known or dreamed, when he built his tower, of its eventual purpose? He possessed no aircraft or dirigibles great enough to require such a dock. Perhaps he had followed the dictates of a dream. Clearly he had possessed a quantity of ore for some time; maybe the xenium had spoken to him.

The man on the ramp did not turn at their approach. He slumped against the rails, his hands limp in his lap, his legs still dangling. By the time they reached him, Elena felt quite certain he was dead.

Louis touched him, then lowered him slowly down onto the catwalk. The eyes were open in the withered face, staring up at the underside of the dock, eyebrows rimed with frost. Moments ago, his distinctive round spectacles would have glimmered with all the mysterious hues of the xenium beacon; but now they were dark, the eyes behind them clouded. He reminded Elena of an aged Slowslop.

"Onegin," Louis whispered.

Then she felt the shadow come over her.

It was not the upper deck, but something above even that.

Something coming in from the night. Without a word between them, they headed for a flight of metal stairs that followed the curve of the ramp, winding up to the topmost deck. She felt they were climbing into outer space. The rails were frozen; a terrifying wind reached through the bars, working steadily to loosen their hands and pry their fingers from the rails and send them flying.

It was worse when they surfaced through the deck, for here there was nothing—no handhold, no rail, no barriers at all. Nothing but the ship coming down from above, quiet as a balloon, vast as a world.

She could see only a fraction of the craft, but it appeared to be made of the same silvery scale as Onegin's tower. And, like the titanic structure they had seen in the depths of the mountains, it looked unfinished. Rods and beams protruded from every part of it, but these seemed to have a symmetry, a purpose. They glowed and hummed like antennae, promising communication. Light spilled from the interior of the ship. As it continued to descend, Louis put an arm around her. A massive, jutting rod touched lightly on the landing field not ten yards from where they stood, and a dark portal appeared in its tip. It barely brushed the deck, continuing to bob as if the ship were a balloon, nearly weightless, barely tethered, anxious to escape.

Louis urged her forward, the alloy suitcase swinging in his grip. As she stepped through the opening, Elena felt no fear. She had already traveled farther than this ship could possibly take her.

Suddenly she was surrounded by old friends. Here were George Tessera and Wilhelm Draun, Constantine Wallace and John MacNaughton. Charles Reif was here, too. She looked for Horselover Frost, but knew she would not find him. He was headed in the other direction; their paths would never cross again.

The other scientists looked as expectant as she. Behind them, the portal closed on a world of ash, but they scarcely glanced back. Another portal was opening just ahead, and her mind now was occupied with trying to anticipate what awaited them.

That sense of anticipation convinced her she was no longer dreaming. This was no delusion concocted in Slowslop's labs. Illusions were limited, their authors eventually exposed. But reality never could be completely known. It always beckoned with further, deeper mysteries. This sense of continual discovery was all she truly required of existence—all the proof she needed.

She had seen the future, she thought, as she stepped through the portal.

But she had never seen this.

TWENTY

DIAGHILEV WOKE SLOWLY, PAINFULLY UNCRAMPING his limbs, massaging his cold arthritic joints as he waited in dread of sensation's return to his numb extremities. When the needles finally withdrew from his flesh and he could breathe without gasping, he opened his eyes and instinctively sought the station clock, which had been his last sight before sleeping.

Twelve o'clock, it said now. Midnight, clearly, since there was no sign of the sun. He felt as if he had slept for more than an hour, but inaccurate timekeeping was unheard of in the stations of the Grand Central Line.

He rose, gingerly straightening swollen knees, and hobbled a few steps toward the exit. The trees were bare, which struck him as odd, since he could have sworn that an hour ago they had clutched a full load of autumn leaves. There was no sign of leaves on the sooty walkway, however. It seemed strange as well that the path was so dark and neglected. The station itself appeared fallen into disrepair, an inconceivable blasphemy in the Empire of Orlovsky and Slowslop. He had noticed none of this when he hiked up from the platform. He had been so grateful to escape the hybrid train's mad plummet that this bit of solid ground had looked like heaven to him. Now, refreshed by a scrap of sleep, his critical faculties had returned.

He hesitated at the threshold of the station, wondering if he should head out into Suburbia or find a more comfortable spot within the station. Before he could make up his mind, he grew aware of a strange luminosity to the night, and a soft roaring sound as of a distant torch that someone had flung through the air. He took a few steps out of the station's shadow and looked up, amazed by the density of the gloom. Thick as it was, it could not hide the ever brightening glow somewhere above. Individual particles of soot were thrown into sharp relief, suspended silhouettes of microscopic matter embedded on his eye like the grains of a photographic scene.

He realized, then, what he was seeing. This picture caught and printed on his mind's eye, burned into the screen at the back of his brain, was the one he had expected to see for . . . for how long? He had never imagined it happening like this, in a cloaking haze so dense that the comet barely managed to pierce Earth's mourning veil.

He felt a prophet's triumph at the truth of his warning, and a poet's dismay at the inadequacy of words to describe the actual event.

It took fifteen seconds for the comet, having pierced the atmosphere, to strike the planet. In that infinitely prolonged span of time, a final shadow streaked across the Empire from end to end: a sleek winged shape, a metal angel promising liberation—but too late. As it flew, feeble cries went up from the ash-choked mouths of those few faithful souls who still lived to behold it: "The Ark! The Ark! The Ark!"

Every dream of insurrection died in that instant.